Praise for

Every Now and Then

"Longtime and new fans of Kagen will delight!"
—Pam Jenoff, *New York Times* bestselling
author of *The Lost Girls of Paris*

"Kagen's trademark blend of childhood curiosity and hidden mysteries shines in this richly imagined coming-of-age adventure."
—Beth Hoffman, *New York Times* bestselling
author of *Saving CeeCee Honeycutt*

"A poignant, beautifully told story about family, friendship and foul-play . . . I can't recommend it enough!"
—Jane Healey, bestselling author of *The Beantown Girls*

"A rollicking good read!"
—Ellen Marie Wiseman, bestselling
author of *What She Left Behind*

"Nostalgic, haunting and edge-of-your-seat suspenseful, *Every Now and Then* is another triumph from Lesley Kagen."
—Wendy Webb, #1 Amazon Charts bestselling
author of *Daughters of the Lake*

"If you are a Kagen fan, you'll recognize this winning combination right away. If not, get on the bandwagon! *Every Now and Then* is for everyone who loves a good story."
—Jill Miner, Saturn Booksellers

"Using true-to-life regional language, Kagen offers us a delightful, entertaining book with very serious undertones. This timely book will certainly expand Kagen's ever-increasing fan base. I certainly recommend this book!"
—Nancy Simpson-Brice, Book Vault

"A complete winner . . . Biz, Frankie, and Viv are sure to steal any reader's heart."
—Pamela Klinger-Horn, Excelsior Bay Books

Every Now and Then

Also available by Lesley Kagen

Whistling in the Dark
Land of a Hundred Wonders
Tomorrow River
Good Graces
Mare's Nest
The Resurrection of Tess Blessing
The Undertaking of Tess
The Mutual Admiration Society

Every Now and Then

A Novel

LESLEY KAGEN

alcove
press

Published in the United States by Alcove Press, an imprint of The Quick Brown Fox & Company LLC.

Alcove Press and its logo are trademarks of The Quick Brown Fox & Company LLC.

Library of Congress Catalog-in-Publication data available upon request.

ISBN (paperback): 978-1-64385-354-3
ISBN (ebook): 978-1-64385-355-0

Cover design by Shira Atakpu

Printed in the United States.

www.alcovepress.com

Alcove Press
34 West 27th St., 10th Floor
New York, NY 10001

First Edition: October 2020

10 9 8 7 6 5 4 3 2 1

For Casey and Riley, Charlie and Hadley.
Forever and always.

Prologue

~

The girls didn't blame me at the time and all these years later they still don't, but I've never quite forgiven myself for instigating what happened during the summer the three of us were eleven. And I never forget.

Of course, not everyone in town has as many years under their belts as I do. Whenever the summer of '60 comes up in conversation, someone not old enough to know better is bound to pipe in, "Time to let bygones be bygones. Water under the bridge. What's done is done." But there's going to come a time when they, too, will understand that the border between now and then is much more like a cobweb than a brick wall and when the past comes to haunt it doesn't ask our permission to do so.

Memory is a shallow grave and it doesn't take much to resurrect the feel of his hands squeezing the life out of me, the sound of Frankie's leg snapping in two, and Viv's scream. A warm breeze ruffling oak boughs on a moonless night or the late train rumbling down the tracks or a dog barking two streets over can be all it takes to bring back the long-ago summer evil paid a visit to our small town and took our young lives as we knew them as a souvenir.

Chapter One

God only knows why my best friends and I loved getting the hell scared of out of us every Saturday afternoon at the Rivoli Theatre or the Starlight Drive-In after the sun went down, but we spent most of our childhood covered in goose bumps and jumping halfway out of our skins.

The radiated ants from *Them!* sounded an awful lot like cicadas. And after we saw *The Fly,* the three of us strained to hear one calling, "Help me . . . please, help me." *The Invasion of the Body Snatchers,* whose main character was a doctor—like my father—who discovered his neighbors were being systematically replaced by soulless alien duplicates grown in pods scattered around his small town—like ours—had the girls and I spying into our neighbors' windows for weeks to ascertain whether any of them had been similarly afflicted. But it was *The Tingler* that almost did us in. Unbeknownst to us, the owner of the theatre had fastened a vibrating device called the *Percepto!* beneath the seats, and when he activated it at just the right time, it felt like that alien parasite had crawled off the silver screen and into our little spines and we ran out of the emergency door screaming and swatting at each other's backs.

But while every day back then might've felt like an anything-can-happen day, to the best of my recollection, which, if I do so say myself, remains remarkably sharp for a gal on the dusky side of her sixties, our lives were pretty ho-hum. Except for the arrival of a reclusive widow who most of the kids in town believed to be a practitioner of the dark arts, juvenile delinquents who admired one another's muscles in Founder's Woods, and the occasional escapee of Broadhurst Mental Institution, nothing much out of the ordinary occurred in Summit, Wisconsin—a town deemed so unremarkable at the time that a popular travel brochure left the "Points of Interest" section blank—until the record-breaking heat showed up.

Box fans began flying out of Mike Hansen's hardware store so fast he'd begun talking about retirement up North. Husbands returned home with five o'clock shadows to drink bottled beer that wouldn't hold a chill while their wives prepared cold cuts instead of the usual meat and potatoes. For kids seeking relief from the heat, there was the creek and a community pool, backyard sprinklers, and ice cream at newly air-conditioned Whitcomb's Drugstore, but only if you were lucky enough to nab one of the seats at the fountain counter before some other sweaty pint-size Lutheran or Catholic did.

Of course, I know now that heat wave was a harbinger of the horror to come, but we had no hint of it when that summer started up. Other than getting released from St. Thomas Aquinas School a week earlier than usual because the soaring temperature had made the nuns and the classrooms uninhabitable, the first day of our three months of freedom began the same way all the rest of them had.

Frances "Frankie" Maniachi, Vivian "Viv" Cleary, and I—Elizabeth "Biz" Buchanan—spent the morning playing foursquare and jumping double Dutch over at Grand Park. When the church bells clanged twelve, the two of them waded into the creek to catch bloodsuckers and continue their bickering, and I rode home only semi-hoping that upon my return I wouldn't find that one of them had drowned the other.

* * *

There were quicker ways back to Honeywell Street, but I took the long way that afternoon. I wanted to pass by the cemetery where my mother had been laid to rest.

I never got the chance to know her, but my father remained devoted to her. He never took off his wedding ring, and he kept a picture of her in the pocket watch that he checked often, as if he was lost in time and was using her face as a compass. With my tawny, straight hair, light blue eyes, and the slight gap between my front teeth, I was the spitting image of her, and a day didn't go by that I wished I weren't.

When Aunt Jane May found me crying into my pillow late one night, I'd broken down and confessed, "I bet every single time he looks at me he wishes I died instead."

"Hogwash," she'd said with a dismissive shake of her head.

"Then how come he barely talks to me?"

Her eyes grew shiny, but she scolded back the tears. She wasn't against showing emotion, but she could be penurious with it. "Your father is the strong, silent type, is all. And if you repeat this I'll deny sayin' it, but I suspect he feels real bad about not being able to save Gus's life and depriving you of a mother." She slapped her thighs and got up off the side of my bed. "Ya want to know more—come to me. Now say your prayers and go to sleep."

So she's the one who'd told me that my parents met at the University of Chicago in the spring of 1947. Newly anointed

Doctor of Medicine Lionel Dwight Buchanan and freshly minted teacher Augusta Elizabeth Mathews fell in love at first sight. Almost as if the two of them knew they'd live happily, but not ever after, they tied the knot just half a year later. And nine months to the day after they returned from their honeymoon, my father picked up his very pregnant wife's older sister at the train station.

Jane May Mathews, a registered nurse by profession, had traveled from the family home in Louisiana to help care for the newlyweds' bouncing bundle of joy for a few weeks, but when an infection claimed her younger sister's life shortly after she gave birth to me, her visit turned out to be a permanent one. My mother's funeral took place the same day I was baptized.

Aunt Jane May ruled our roost from that day on, and during the summer months when Frankie and Viv spent most of their time at our house, they fell under her jurisdiction as well. The kitchen was her command center and that's where I found her after my ride back from Grand Park that afternoon. Like a sea captain christening a ship before sailing off on a grand adventure to an unknown land, baking peach pies was my aunt's way of smashing a champagne bottle across the bow of summer, and I was expected to be her first mate.

"You're late," she said when I came through the squeaky, back screen door of the house. "Wash your hands." After I did so and got situated on my kitchen stool, she launched into one of her lectures. "You girls are old enough now to keep in mind that the hideout isn't just a place to cook up your wild schemes. It's a memorial to your mother built with your father's blood, sweat, and tears and it's about time you treated it as such." This had come out of the blue and when I didn't respond quickly enough for her liking, she added, even more prickly, "At the very least, the *first* night you spend up the tree this summer should be treated like an auspicious occasion."

The Grand Opening celebration at the car wash outside of town popped into my head, but I was pretty sure that's not what she meant. She would've called that "showy" or "ostentatious." Something religiously themed would be more up her alley.

"Are you saying that you want the girls and me to hold some kind of service for my mother tonight?" I asked. "Light candles and say prayers?"

"Lord, no," she scoffed. "Gus wouldn't like that." She stilled her hands and gazed out the window above the kitchen sink with that faraway look she got sometimes when we talked about her sister. Like she was remembering her, or listening, for she was a great believer in life after death and communication beyond the grave. "What I want—no, what I *expect*—is for you three to keep this evening respectful, but full of promise. Less like a vigil . . . more like a baptism."

This was a nice idea, one I believed the girls and I would've had no problem putting into practice, if she had brought it up before Frankie and Viv began to spiral out of control. Don't get me wrong. The two of them had been born stubborn, so it wasn't like I hadn't been ripping a bone of contention out of their mouths before they beat each other to death with it for most of my life. But we were eleven years old, nearing twelve, that summer and coursing hormones and the soaring heat had turned their squabbling into heavyweight bouts that I was expected to get in the middle of, and I'd just about had it.

"But . . . how am I supposed to get the two of them to treat tonight auspicious when they won't listen to a thing I say?" I whined. "You know how they are and it's gotten worse. They won't stop pickin' at each other and they can't agree on nothin'. Not what games to play, what movies to see, what books to read . . ." I threw my floury hands into the air. "I swear to God you're gonna have to stick me in the mental institution if they keep this up."

My aunt did not own a pair of kid gloves and loathed self-pity, but peach pie had been her sister's favorite, and I suspected the smell of one already wafting out of the oven that afternoon reminded her of how the two of them had similarly tussled when they were girls our age. Because instead of admonishing me, she said, "You know what you girls need to do? You need to take turns coming up with adventures tonight. That's what your mama and I did at the start of every summer. And you can't just say what you want to do, you got to list it down on paper so you can keep track of what you're takin' on. Seeing your ideas in black and white will cut down on spats. Speaking of which"—she lowered her already deep voice that anchored the alto section in the church choir—"you tell Frances and Vivian that I don't care how hot their blood is runnin'. They can spend the rest of the summer acting like she-cats, but I highly suggest they treat tonight with the dignity it deserves. If I suspect otherwise"—she raised her hand above her head and brought it down sharply on the pie dough three times. "Get my drift?"

Hard not to, and after I returned to Grand Park and broke up a screaming match between Frankie and Viv, I passed on Aunt Jane May's "suggestion."

Frankie didn't give me any lip, but Viv spit a loogie and said, "She told ya she's gonna paint our rears red if she finds out we didn't treat tonight like a suspicious occasion?"

And then Frankie had to shove her and say, *"Auspicious,* numnuts," and there was more tit-for-tatting until it came time to head home and devour the supper Aunt Jane May had set out on the screened porch so we wouldn't miss hearing the first call of "Olly olly oxen free."

As always, the game of kick the can with the neighbor kids lasted until the streetlights popped on, and after the girls and I shouted our battle cry, "All for one and one for all," we raced back down Honeywell Street to commence what we'd been dreaming about all day. The first night we'd spend together in our summer home away from home, our inner sanctum and repository of secrets of all kinds. Our hideout.

Chapter Two

∾

All the houses on Honeywell Street were worthy of admiration, of course, but they were nothing more than ladies-in-waiting to the crowned jewel of the neighborhood—the Buchanan homestead.

Our cobblestone driveway was lined with purple lilac bushes that filled early summer evenings with their heady perfume. A smattering of sugar maples, gasp-worthy oaks, and birches with trunks that peeled like sunburns dotted the front lawn, and the flower beds were always planted with whatever was blooming at the time.

The house was three stories of stone smothered in ivy up to its waist. The front porch was wide and a white swing hung from its rafters. The windows were paned and shuttered, and atop the shingled roof sat a wooden cupola that'd been built in the early 1800s by the founder of Summit—Percival James Buchanan.

Because my great-grandfather was a coffin maker, respect for the dead and expert carpentry skills had been passed down in our family for generations, so Doc—what my father insisted everyone call him, including me—had that bred into him. He couldn't help but go above and beyond my mother's deathbed wish to build for the daughter she'd never know a hideout like the one she and her sister had when they were growing up. He was a man of few words, my father, so he never told me as much, but I believed he picked the towering backyard oak to set it in—it's uppermost branches seemed to tickle the underbelly of heaven—and painted it a bulls-eye red so my mother could see it from the Great Beyond and know that he'd kept his word.

Commiserate with the amount of pain he was in, Doc ended up building me the Taj Mahal of hideouts. A high roof and canvas shades above the two windows kept the girls and me dry when a storm blew in. Aunt Jane May had sewn feather-stuffed sleeping mats, and when we weren't using them, they were kept in a corner next to a bookshelf brimming with comic books, mysteries, and a couple of dog-eared ladies' magazine. Assorted board games were stacked alongside hula hoops, a jump rope, flashlights, and anything else the girls and I came across that we didn't think we could live without. On the walls, eight-by-ten pictures of movie monsters that we'd begged off the owner of the Rivoli Theatre were made all the more spooky when the train lantern we'd found beside the railroad tracks threw shadows on their faces—if they had ones.

Of course, Frankie, Viv, and I didn't believe in monsters anymore, but on the off chance one of them *did* materialize in the hideout, we were prepared. We weren't too worried about the creature from the Black Lagoon sloshing out of Grand Creek and tracking us down, because with those flappy feet of his, we figured he'd have a hard time climbing the ten wooden steps that led up to the hideout. Zombies would be a cinch to evade because they moved like mosey was their fastest gear. A crucifix nailed to one of the walls served as both a plea to the Almighty to keep us safe and a deterrent to Count Dracula. There was also a cardboard "Keep Out" sign, but it wasn't used to ward off unearthly monsters. When I couldn't take another minute of Frankie's and Viv's behavior, I'd tell them to take a hike, hang the sign outside the door, and they wouldn't be welcomed back until they had their tails between their legs.

Thankfully, it didn't seem like I'd have to resort to such a drastic measure that first overnight, though, because it looked like the two of them had taken Aunt Jane May's warning to mind their manners to heart.

The three of us downed only our fair shares of the root beer and peach pie she'd set in the tin bucket that was affixed to the tree. We took polite turns reading Nancy Drew's *The Sign of the Twisted Candles*. They weren't sore losers when I told them, "Colonel Mustard killed Miss Scarlett in the library with the candlestick." And when I reminded them that we were supposed to write down what we wanted to do that summer, there was no arguing about who'd be the scribe. Viv had begun dotting every "i" with a heart, Frankie was overly committed to her slant, but I planned to be a writer when I grew up and believed that good penmanship was important and had the Palmer medals to prove it.

Even though I very much liked the idea of us honoring my mother's memory, I didn't count on that happening in the way Aunt Jane May wanted it to. I was an inordinately hopeful child, some might say pathetically so, but expecting the other "Tree Musketeers"—we began calling ourselves that after we began spending our summers in the boughs of the backyard oak—to remain somber and respectful for an entire evening? That was a fool's mission. If I could just keep the peace, I thought, I could congratulate myself on a job well done, and with that end in mind, I smoothed a piece of paper down on the hideout floor, picked up my favorite no. 2, and suggested a summer adventure I was sure all three of us would have no problem agreeing on.

"Number one," I announced, "visit Broadhurst and try to sneak into the Chamber of Horrors." We'd ridden our bikes to the mental institution on the edge of town the previous summer and wouldn't dream of giving it up. "I heard they might be bringin' Wally Hopper in." I looked up at Viv swaying her narrow hips to "Cathy's Clown" coming out of our aquamarine transistor radio. "You know anything about that?"

Viv cupped her ear and yelled, "What?"

I turned the radio down, but she bent over and cranked it back up.

"The kid killer," I shouted. "Did you hear anything about him getting moved to Broadhurst?"

Her mother, Fiona Cleary, owned the only beauty parlor in town and the gals talked so loudly under those dryers that Viv heard all the latest rumors floating around, or acted like she did. It was sometimes hard to tell Viv's fact from her fiction, but in the looks department she was exactly as advertised. She reminded me of a matchstick, lean like that, with dark, red hair that her mother kept in a pixie cut, which was in keeping with her personality. She couldn't sit still for long, slept with her green eyes half open, had the temperament of a leprechaun whose gold had been stolen, and lied effortlessly, convincingly, and with pleasure. She was also a master at coming up with risky plans, and whenever the three of us found ourselves in hot water, she was our mouthpiece.

Viv stuck her fists on her hips and asked me, "Where'd ya hear that about Hopper?"

Realizing my mistake too late, I mumbled, "After Mass yesterday," and tried to change the subject. "I really like that blouse you've got on. It brings out the color of your—"

"Who was spreadin' that rumor?" Viv said. "Which gal?"

I didn't want to tell her, but along with keeping our promises and other sacred oaths, complete and timely honesty with one another was one of the Tree Musketeers' most important rules, so there was no getting out of admitting that I'd heard that juicy tidbit come out of the mouth of the gal Viv saw as her gossip rival. "Evelyn Mulrooney said it."

"Oh, for crissakes, you dumb chump." Viv hawked a loogie through one of the windows. "How many times do I gotta tell ya that even if that so-and-so acts like she knows everything that's goin' on in this town, she doesn't know shit from Shinola!"

I glanced behind me to see if Frankie would come to my defense, but she was concentrating on creating one of those paper fortune tellers and in her own little world, in more ways than one.

Unlike Viv and me, Frankie wasn't born in Summit and she wasn't all white. Her Caucasian father was never spoken about, but whoever he was, he was one smart cookie and she took after him. She and her mother, Dellatoria "Dell" Martin, had moved to town from Milwaukee nine years ago after Dell had been hired by my other next-door neighbor, Salvatore Maniachi, to keep house and help care for his crippled twin sister, Sophia. Of course, the Maniachis knew that Dell and Frankie were a package deal, and they welcomed the lovely three-year-old into their home and their hearts. But not everybody in Summit would be as generous. A "colored" maid was one thing, but a "mulatto" child living on our side of the tracks? That was verboten back then. So when the town busybodies got around to asking who the little girl with the year-round tan, beige eyes, and wavy dark hair belonged to, Salvatore Maniachi told them Frankie was an orphaned relative. I wasn't so sure the small but dedicated group of Germans in town who believed the whiter someone's skin was the better fell for that lie, but Frankie was such a close match to the Maniachis' Mediterranean coloring that everyone else in town seemed to. Far as we knew, anyway, nobody except those who'd take that secret to the grave knew for sure that the beauty and brains of our threesome was passing herself off as a "bambina," and if anyone ever *did* find out—there'd be hell to pay.

I nudged Frankie's bare foot with mine. "Did Jimbo say anything to you about Hopper?"

The same way Viv stayed on top of gossip at her mother's beauty parlor and I learned about the healing arts from my aunt and my father, Dell's cousin, Jimbo, who'd moved to town the same time she and Frankie had, would give us behind-the-scene information about the goings-on at the mental hospital. Mostly Jimbo, who was an orderly up there, shared stories about the criminally insane patients who were confined at Broadhurst because we begged him to and he was a pushover where we were concerned. Like the killer known as the "Blackjack Scalper," who'd stabbed a couple of gals in Kenosha twenty-one times and fashioned wigs out of the hair he'd cut off by the roots. But he told us gory details about other Wisconsin killers, too. Like Ed Gein, the "Butcher of Plainfield," who'd murdered all those poor gals near our state capitol, upholstered his furniture with their skin, and fashioned bed posts out of their skulls. And soon after Wally Hopper got charged for ending the lives of the young

Gimble sisters in Milwaukee, Jimbo had us on the edge of our seats yet again.

"After Hopper got caught, he told the police that he'd murdered those little girls, but it wasn't his fault," Jimbo told us on the sagging porch of his Mud Town house, the spot where he did his best telling after the sun went down. "He said that someone made him do it."

In the tradition of all world-class storytellers—I learned my trade at the feet of a master—Jimbo knew how to build tension. He paused so long that I had to ask, "Who'd Hopper say made him do it?"

He took the last swallow of his long-neck beer and rolled the brown bottle across his brown forehead. "That man believes Michael the Archangel commanded him to strangle those little sisters."

Now, Jimbo's stories could usually raise the hair on the back of our little necks, but that night the girls and I rode our bikes back over the railroad tracks like we were getting chased by the minions of hell *and* heaven. We slept in a puppy pile for the next week, telling one another whenever the hideout creaked in the wind or a coon knocked down a garbage can, "Quit bein' such a titty baby. Nobody's gonna murder us and blame it on a saint. That kind of stuff doesn't happen in Summit, right?"

After Frankie shook her head to my question about whether Jimbo had shared any extra information about Hopper getting moved to Broadhurst, Viv couldn't leave well enough alone. "You sure he didn't tell you something about that kid killer?" she taunted Frankie. "You sure you're not holdin' something back?"

I tried to cover up the edginess in her voice by chirping at Frankie, "Your turn! What do you wanna do this summer?"

Frankie wouldn't holler over the radio like I'd been. Raising her voice wasn't her style, unless Viv pushed her too far. But when she tilted her head toward the glossy pictures of the movie monsters taped on the wall, I knew what she meant, and I said, "Number two—see scary movies."

"Monsters are fine," Viv said, like she was above that sort of thing now. "But I need as many pointers as I can get if we're gonna find out who Aunt Jane May is trotting hotly with. Write down spying on her and seein' more romance movies, Biz."

Soon after Viv's breasts began to bud (a recent development) and she'd grown a few red hairs down there, she went full-out boy crazy. She dragged Frankie and me to a couple of those mushy movies and had begun to see love everywhere. She was sure Aunt Jane May was sneaking out of the house at night to meet a "tall, dark, and handsome mystery man" and she'd been bugging Frankie and me to follow her for weeks. Of course, we'd told her, "No dice," and tried numerous times to explain that even if she was right and Aunt Jane May *did* have a suitor, we couldn't risk getting caught spying on her, but would Viv listen? No, she would not. Once that girl latched onto something, it was like trying to remove lint from a black velvet dress.

While I'll admit to being hopeful, I wasn't stupid. I knew I'd reached a fork in the road and that neither path would deliver me to my intended destination. If I didn't write down on the list *Spy on Aunt Jane May* and *See romance movies*, Viv would throw a fit. If I *did* write her requests down, Frankie would get hot around the collar because romance of any kind, but especially watching smooching on the big screen, made her want to vomit into her Cracker Jack box, as Viv well knew.

When the two of them butted heads like this, I'd learned over the years that nothing I'd say would convince them to back down, so I did the only other thing I could think of to keep things on an even keel. I faked a yawn, lowered the train lantern, and told them, "Holy cow, I'm beat, aren't you? Let's figure out the rest of the list in the morning. I made up a story in honor of tonight. You ready?"

One of the few things they could agree on was how much they loved falling asleep to one of my stories, so when all I heard was the bullfrogs croaking in the sliver of Grand Creek that ran behind the hideout, the Harris's dog barking two streets over, and the late train rumbling down the tracks, I thought the excitement of the day had finally gotten to them and they'd drifted off.

Relieved and grateful that we'd made it through the sleepover without any major upheaval, I rolled over and was about to do what Aunt Jane May had asked of me, when Frankie's voice came out of the darkness with a demand.

"Get up, Biz," she said. "I want to add something to the list."

And all I wanted to do was commemorate my mother by breathing in the lingering scent of the pink and white peonies she'd planted along the backyard fence to welcome me into the world and think about how my father's saw and pounding hammer must've covered up the sound of his tears when he built the hideout at her behest.

But ignoring Frankie wasn't an option. She'd toe me in the back until she reached my spine if I didn't slide the paper out from under my pillow and say, "Make it quick."

Like the howl of a werewolf, the high-pitched buzz of a flying saucer, or the sound of beating bat wings warned us of impending doom in the third row at the Rivoli every Saturday, when I looked up and saw her lovely mouth twisted into a malicious grin that night, I knew Frankie was about to do something I really wished she wouldn't, and how right I was.

"Put down that I dare Viv to talk to Audrey Cavanaugh," she said.

It takes your brain a few seconds to register an injury and that's about how long it took before Viv gasped like it was her last, and I said, "Aww, Frankie. What'd you have to go and do that for?"

Summit prided itself on what most of the Germans in town called *Gemutlichkeit* and the rest of us called friendliness, but when Audrey Cavanaugh moved into the old Jasper house down the block from us, she wouldn't play along. She didn't show up at Mass or the Harvest Festival or the lighting of the Christmas tree in the town square, nor did she RSVP any of the invites to the coffee klatches the Ladies Auxiliary held around town every afternoon.

Predictably, our new neighbor giving the town the cold shoulder set the gals gossiping, but just about nothing could get children's tongues wagging faster than a mysterious stranger showing up a few days before Halloween. Quicker than you could say, "Double, double, toil and trouble," word got out among us that Audrey Cavanaugh was a witch, so you better watch out. If you got caught in her talons, she'd chop you into little pieces and toss you into the stew she needed to partake of once a month to sustain her supernatural powers, the scope of which varied depending upon the descriptive powers of the kid doing the telling.

Name-calling, shoving, and Indian burns were par for the course, but daring Viv to talk to the Summit Witch? It was the cruelest thing I'd ever seen Frankie do. And the most confusing.

Because even though she kept her feelings well hidden, I knew that she loved Viv more than she did me. I'd catch her looking at her sometimes in a different kind of way. And by the light of the moon, I'd seen her press her cheek against sleeping Viv and breathe in her exhales and tenderly stroke her hair. And I was pretty sure she purposely agitated Viv into arm wrestling just so she could hold her hand.

"Have you lost your mind?" I asked Frankie, because she knew darn well that the mere mention of a witch, a kid lugging around a broomstick on Beggar's Night, or even Aunt Jane May dabbing witch hazel on her skeeter bites scared Viv down to the bone, and I mean that quite literally. Because it wasn't the owner of a gingerbread house in the Black Forest or a hag offering a poisoned apple to a beauty that had far surpassed her own that'd traumatized her. It was her own flesh and blood.

Somewhere along the road to dotage, her grandmother, Esmeralda, had gotten it into her superstitious, zealous head that Viv was possessed by the evil spirit of one of their ancestors—a gal by the name of Bridget who'd been found guilty of practicing witchcraft in County Tipperary in the 1800s and was subsequently burned alive in the town square. Granny Cleary had recently taken to keeping a bottle of holy water strapped around her waist and she'd jump out at her granddaughter and douse her in it every chance she got. And whenever Viv stepped out of line—exactly as often as you'd think a kid like her would—anyone within a block of the Cleary house could hear that pipe-smoking shrew yelling at the top of what was left of her wee lungs, "In the name of the Father, the Son, and the Holy Spirit, remove your evil curse from this child! Be gone with you, witch! Be gone!"

When Frankie didn't respond to my scolding, I tried to appeal to her softer side. "Look at her." I pointed across the hideout at Viv, whose normally pale face had gone whiter than her Holy Communion dress. "Please take the dare back."

Frankie got such a sweet look in her eye that for a moment I thought she might do as I'd asked, but her mouth said otherwise. "Forget it," she snarled. "That's what she gets for wantin' to watch those disgusting movies and botherin' us about chasing after Aunt Jane May and some stupid mystery man a hundred times a day. She made her bed."

"I'm begging you." I waved my prayer hands around. "She can't even talk!"

But Viv, a resourceful child who had four obnoxious older brothers to contend with, as well as her fervent granny, proved me wrong when she uttered what she usually did when she needed to distract an attacker long enough to escape from the corner she'd been backed into.

"Don't look now, but . . ." she said and pointed her spindly arm over our shoulders. "The handyman is watching us in the shadows behind the creek."

"No, he's not! You're just tryin' to make me forget about the dare. Admit it!" Frankie said like she was arguing a case in a court of law. "And remember—you're under oath!" She jabbed her finger toward the rusty mark in the middle of the hideout floor like it was damning evidence, which, of course—it was. Because that wasn't any old stain. It was an indelible reminder that the girls and I weren't just best friends. We were family. Blood sisters. That stain was our coat of arms.

Of course, it'd been Viv's idea to perform the ritual we'd seen the natives do in *Voodoo Island*. A goat had been tied to a stake in the movie, so she suggested, "Let's steal a kid from the Erdman farm." Not feeling entirely sure she wasn't referring to one of the Erdman children, I put my foot down. "I'll beat the bongo," I told her, "but that's as far as we're going." And after I grabbed the drum off the shelf, we mumbled some jumbo, lit a few candles, and Frankie used a penknife to prick my finger and then hers. But when she cut thin-skinned Viv's thumb, the blood came gushing, and the stain remained to remind us what we meant to one another and always would.

With my last hope for a night meant to honor my mother's memory and my father's devotion to her destroyed by Viv's baiting and Frankie's dare, I blew a gasket. I got to my feet, drew myself up to my full height, and growled, "If you don't go to sleep, I'm gonna throw the both of ya out the window!" (I could've, if I wanted to. I had five inches on them and the shoulders of an English milkmaid.)

When we were woken the following morning by a cardinal that called the oak tree its summer home, too, and the smell of pork sausage emanating out of the kitchen window of the house, I'd hardly describe the girls and me as bright eyed and bushy tailed. With sweat wiggling down my sides, my stomach complaining, and a hope hangover, I couldn't have cared less which of us went down the wooden steps first, but the two of them picked up where they'd left off the night before, and I had to force them to do our agreed-upon tie breaker.

When Viv lost the rock, paper, scissors shootout, she shrugged it off, but I saw her give Frankie a vengeful look before she picked up the jump rope and shoved it down the front of her shorts. Viv could hold a grudge much better than she could her temper, so I suspected she was up to no good. But as I ran across the backyard to catch up with them, there wasn't a doubt in mind that if the rest of the summer went as badly as our first overnight had, we'd remember it for as long as we lived. If we survived it.

Chapter Three

After Frankie, Viv, and I burst through the squeaky screened door that we were sure Aunt Jane May refused to oil so she could keep track of our comings and goings, we mumbled our good mornings, took our preordained seats at the kitchen table, and awaited delivery of pork sausages, flapjacks with maple syrup, home fries, and the daily lecture she expected us to digest along with our breakfasts.

I felt bad for letting her down and was worried almost to tears that she'd ask if the sleepover had been the kind of respectful evening she'd expected it to be, but all she said was, "'Bout time" and went back to shuffling the silver fry pan across the burner.

She was planted in front of the stove, so the girls and I couldn't see her heart-shaped face, navy-blue eyes, and generous mouth, but the auburn hair she'd stopped winding into a tight bun and begun folding into a French twist was hard to miss. Viv certainly didn't.

She nodded toward Aunt Jane May, raised her eyebrows a few times—Groucho-style—and whispered to me, "I'm tellin' ya . . . hot to trot."

As if the girls and I weren't terrified enough by all the "creature features" we were taking in, we were about to fall into the abyss of adolescence and were pretty fuzzy about where we'd land. We weren't complete ignoramuses. We knew we'd grow breasts and hair in smooth places, and we'd rarely ride past a farm without seeing livestock mounting a barnyard pal. But we mostly had to rely on Doc's medical books—horrifying—and whatever we picked up from girls in town who'd supposedly been around the block. After "Easy Mimi" Kincaid caught us gazing at the sanitary napkin dispenser in the school bathroom like it was the ninth Wonder of the World, she informed us, "One of these nights you're gonna wake up covered in blood that comes from Virginia and you use these pads to clean off the sheets and then ya have a baby."

To further muddy the waters, Viv wouldn't stop spouting off about what she learned from the ladies' magazines in her mother's beauty parlor that she treated like a reference library.

"Don't be disgusting," I whispered back to her at the breakfast table. "She's too decrepit to trot."

With thirty-seven years under Aunt Jane May's belt, I was convinced she was far too long in the tooth for romance. It wasn't that she wasn't good-looking enough to attract a fella. She was. Very. In both face and figure. And her many attributes did not go unnoticed by the bachelors in town. Our elderly mayor had a crush on her and would shower her with compliments, the butcher gave her extra-thick pork chops, and her baker's dozen was always more generous, but their flirtations were met with nothing more than a curt nod and a "Much obliged."

Keeping her eye on Aunt Jane May, Viv slowly tilted my way again. "*True Confessions* says the first things gals do when they're dating a man is freshen their hairstyle, push up their bosom, and show more flesh. And if they get *very* worked up, they wear black stockings with seams, high heels with cleats, and their cheeks look like roses in bloom."

Aunt Jane May's bosom was where it always was, as were the shoes she bought at Harrington's Department Store, the same place the nuns got theirs. Her legs, as usual, were covered in the oatmeal-colored mesh stockings the five-and-dime sold on aisle four, and she wasn't any pinker in the cheeks than she'd normally be on a scorcher of a morning. But I couldn't deny that she *had* changed her hair and she *was* showing more skin, around the house and yard anyway.

"Bare my arms in public?" she'd huffed after I suggested she wear sleeveless tops when the heat came down hard on us. "I'd rather be lyin' in the ground next to your mama than wear an ensemble that'd give the men in this town the idea that I was advertising my wares."

Fat chance, I almost told her.

She maintained the house and garden, and when called on, she'd dust off her nursing skills to assist Doc at his office on Bridge Street. On the evenings she wasn't at a Garden Club or St. Thomas's Ladies Auxiliary meeting, she'd study the words of God and William Shakespeare. She also enjoyed singing along with show tunes on the hi-fi and wouldn't miss the *Gillette Friday Night Fights* and the *Kraft Television Theatre* on our Sylvania set. If the weather was right, she'd sit on the back porch glider, listen to the crickets courting one another, and wait for Frankie's mother to come over after she tucked the Maniachis' house in for the night. When she and Dell let their hair down and drank cooking sherry out of jelly glasses, the girls and I would lie on the hideout floor, barely breathing, so we could hear them talking woman to woman, and we'd gotten an earful one night last summer.

They'd spent some time chatting about the price of beef and whether or not they approved of Elvis Presley before the conversation took a turn. Someone lay on a car horn, so we missed what Dell said, but Aunt Jane May answered, "Before they knew Sophia was born with a birth defect, some of the ladies in the Auxiliary were saying that she and Sally were part of a mob family and she was crippled when she got shot in the back during a bank robbery."

That was news to us, and picturing jolly Sally and bashful Sophia wielding Tommy guns and yelling, "Hand over the money, you dirty rats!" to a bank teller had us rolling around on the hideout floor attempting to smother our giggles.

Sure that Dell'd react the same way we had to that ridiculous gossip, we waited to hear her tinkling laugh coming off the back porch, but you know, it went real quiet back there before she said, "If the truth ever comes out . . . God help us all, Jane May."

The girls and I still weren't sure what to make of that, so we chalked up Dell's comment that night to the cooking sherry. She could go gloomy like that after one too many jarfuls. Frankie called it her Billie Holiday mood.

"This pork could sole a shoe," Aunt Jane May said as she slapped the patties onto the white breakfast plates. "What took ya?"

"So sorry for keepin' you waiting, Auntie," Viv said, because after we performed the ceremony, my blood sisters considered her a relative, the same way I considered their families mine. "It's Frankie's fault."

Looked like she wasn't going to waste any time getting back at her for the witch dare, and, as the peacekeeper of our triumvirate, it behooved me to consider all options. I was almost certain the jump rope Viv'd stuck in her shorts before she climbed down from the hideout figured into whatever revenge she'd come up with, because I'd recently caught her fashioning nooses with it. When I asked her if she was planning on hanging anybody in particular, she had the gall to tell me, "For your information, Elizabeth, I'm working on my knot merit badge," like I'd forgotten she'd been kicked out of Girl Scouts for eating what she was supposed to be delivering. (She had a sweet tooth a mile wide and was unable to resist those chocolate mint cookies.)

"Biz and I got up early to pray," Viv further lied to Aunt Jane May, "but Frankie wouldn't wake-up and—" She yowled. "She just kicked me under the table!"

Brandishing a wooden spoon, Aunt Jane May spun around. "This better not have been how y'all acted last night." She inspected our faces, but we'd practiced looking guileless for many years and our hard work paid off. "And how many times do I have to tell you to sit right in those chairs? Mark my words, you're going to end up lookin' as hunched as Edith Dirks, bless her heart."

Most of her lectures began with "Mark my words" and didn't end with, "And they all lived happily ever after." The second she'd turn her back, we'd smirk at her gruesome warnings the way know-it-all girls of that age do—but not always. Because she and my mother had grown up in a town that had about as much in common with Summit as Mars, there were times Aunt Jane May seemed as strange to us as the aliens that scared us at the movies.

In Little Wildwood, Louisiana, you could be both a Roman Catholic and a believer in voodoo—a burlap doll sat next to Aunt Jane May's missal in the top drawer of her dresser. Folks wrestled alligators in swamps, and because we didn't know what the main ingredient in hush puppies was and were too afraid to ask, we thought they ate shoes down there. It also wasn't unusual in her neck of the woods for a baby to be born on the "right side of the blanket," the way she'd been. She possessed "the gift," or what some folks called "intuition" or "being on God's wave length," and knew things that she seemed to pluck out of thin air.

Steaming plates in hand, Aunt Jane May shouted, "Did you not hear me? Put some starch in those backbones!"

Only after we did would she set our breakfasts down and herself at the head of the table, because my father was already at his busy downtown office. When we finished saying grace, Aunt Jane May snapped open the red clutch purse she'd begun carrying around since the heat flared up, withdrew one of the large, white lace hankies she kept at the ready to dab the "sheen"— never sweat—off her brow, and began her daily lecture.

"Where I come from," she said, "ya know what they like to say when it grows so fiercely and unexpectedly hot like this, girls?"

Like butter wouldn't melt, Viv said, "What do they like to say, Auntie?"

"That Satan knows when there are young souls ripe for the pickin' and in his excitement to gather them, he fled perdition so fast he left the door of the everlasting fires open behind him. So less'n you three are itchin' to spend all eternity burning, I'm warning you to keep your eyes open for lurking evil and trouble of any kind." She swiveled my way. "As always, I expect you to remember that you're a Buchanan and keep these two in hand. Stay away from Broadhurst, don't pester Audrey Cavanaugh, keep your noses out of other folks' business, and,"—she paused to wet her lips— "I want you to quit visiting Earl Spooner's Club. In fact, once the sun sets, I don't want you ridin' over the tracks at all."

When the Northern Railroad came through Summit way back when, they must've been in a hurry, because the part of town she was forbidding us to visit looked like it'd been built on the fly and was aptly named. The sewer system in Mud Town was sub-par and the drainage almost nonexistent. The ground was always damp and smelled freshly turned, and when it rained too much, you could almost feel the place slipping off the face of the Earth. Property went for near nothing and was bought by "colored" families, many of whom were descendants of the men who'd come to town to lay the tracks, and they had every right to set roots, no matter what some of our neighbors thought.

Aunt Jane May wasn't like those folks.

Whatever reason she had for not wanting us to go over to Mud Town after dark, it wasn't because she was prejudiced. She spoke in glowing terms about the brown-skinned women who had tended to the Mathews sisters when they were growing up and her best friend, Dell, wore only white at night to avoid getting struck by a car.

As our mouthpiece, Viv should've been vehemently challenging Aunt Jane May's new rules, but she was as dumbstruck as I was, so it was up to Frankie to say something and she didn't disappoint.

"Pardon me, Frances?" Aunt Jane May said. "You got somethin' to say, speak up."

Too smart to repeat the caustic remark she'd uttered under her breath, Frankie replied, "I said that as soon as we're done here I gotta go clean the wax out of my ears 'cause I thought you just told us that we couldn't go over to Mud Town after—"

"Nothin' wrong with your hearin'," Aunt Jane May spit out, "and nothin' wrong with mine neither."

"But," I said, "we promised Jimbo that we'd—"

"Then you ought to be more careful what you promise," Aunt Jane May barked. "What goes on after dark across the tracks is . . ."

She was searching for the right words, but if I'd been asked to fill in her blank, I would've had no problem coming up with "mysterious" and "delicious" and "religious."

The girls and I had been visiting Mud Town our whole lives and loved it much more than we did Summit proper. If we could manage it, we'd slip out of St. Thomas's Sunday Mass and ride over to Emmanuel Baptist to sit beside Jimbo and Dell and get treated to a lively sermon by Reverend Archie and singing that made our choir sound soulless. We'd play Ghost in the Graveyard in the cemetery on Wickers Avenue with our friends over there, and we couldn't get enough of Jimbo and his front-porch stories. And not only did Earl Spooner's Supper Club serve far and away the best food in town, the back door was left open on steamy summer evenings. The girls and I would eat slices of chiffon pie and watch couples on the dance floor move nothing like the couples at our church mixers. Their hips undulating to that low-down saxophone music made the high insides of my thighs tingle in a way the polka never did, though I couldn't have told you why.

Aunt Jane May flicked her tongue over her lips again and said, "I'm givin' the three of you fair warning. If I should hear from Jimbo or Bigger or anybody else that you were seen over in Mud Town after the sun sets"—she smacked her fist down on the table like it was a gavel—"there will be severe consequences. Ya hear me?"

Frankie nudged me under the table to let me know what she was about to do, then turned to Aunt Jane May and said, "Jesus Christmas, of course we can hear you. Sam Osbourne could and he's been dead and buried for a week."

Now, I gained no pleasure from challenging the powerful forces that ruled our world—our aunt and the Almighty—but if Frankie hadn't distracted her with that blasphemy, I would've placed my hand down on the kitchen Bible and sworn to stay on the straight and narrow and make sure the girls did as well. I would've been lying, of course, and if Aunt Jane May ever found out, she'd kill me. "Spinnin' a tall tale is one thing, and holding back a truth that could hurt feelings is allowable in certain situations," she'd lecture us, "but the Lord detests lying lips, and He and I are on the same page." She meant the page of the Bible she was quoting from. "Mark my words, girls, I ever catch you prevaricating to me I will cook your gooses beyond recognition and bury them under the willow out back."

Since her parenting philosophy was similar to everyone else's at the time: raise children like you would mushrooms—keep them in the dark and feed them lots of bull crap—the girls and I had to rely on our keen powers of observation to determine what future she had in mind for us. A tapping toe promised an afternoon of chores. Calling any of us "Missy" was a lit stick of TNT. And when she gave her lips a tongue lashing? That meant she was hiding something from us, and judging by how vigorously she was going at it that morning—it was something big.

When she finished reprimanding Frankie for taking the Lord's name in vain, she moved on to the Tree Musketeer who'd usually be giving her the business. "You've been suspiciously quiet this morning Vivian," she said. "You got somethin' on *your* mind needs airin' out?"

"Actually, I was thinking these flapjacks are the best I've ever had and . . . oh, yeah." Viv smacked her forehead, like this idea had just dawned on her. "I've been meanin' to tell you how much I love your new French twist. It's very *oo là là*."

Aunt Jane May didn't want to be charmed by Viv, but I saw a hint of a smile coming onto her lips before the grandfather clock in the front hallway chimed a warning that *tempus fugit*. "Lord Almighty," she said, "it's eight already?" She dabbed at her mouth with her napkin. "I have a million and one things to do today and you foolish girls and this heat have me—"

"Fit to be tied?" Viv said as she plopped the jump rope she'd been holding in her lap down onto the table.

Given the mood she was in, I was sure Aunt Jane May would not find that amusing, but she chuckled. With gusto! Even Frankie, who found Viv funny but hated to let on that she did, grinned. I did, too, but only because I was relieved to learn the rope was not intended for Frankie's neck.

Viv was so pleased with herself for pulling that gag off, but she wasn't about to rest on her laurels. Sure now that she had our aunt eating out of her hand, she snatched Frankie's newly created paper fortune teller off the table and impishly asked her, "Three's your favorite number, right?" After she manipulated the paper the requisite number of times and flipped up the flap, she

pretended to read what she found in the mysterious voice gyp-
sies used in werewolf movies to tell fortunes in their caravans in
the woods. "It's a *goood* thing you are *loooo*king like a million
bucks, because you're about to meet a tall, dark, and handsome
man or maybe *yooo*u already have." She dropped the act. "You
got somethin' on *your* mind needs airin' out, Auntie?"

That was so out of line, even for her, that I cringed at the
dressing down she was about to receive, but Aunt Jane May
turned as red as her clutch purse and bolted out of the kitchen
so fast she created the breeze the girls and I had been hoping for
all week.

Granted, she could've just been in a hurry to get to her
chores, but it looked to me like her hasty exit coming on the
heels of the fictional fortune meant that it'd hit a nerve. Judging
by the smarmy look on Viv's face she thought so, too, and given
her passionate desire to catch our aunt in the act, I feared that
trouble was coming our way, just as Aunt Jane May had warned
us it would if we strayed from the straight and narrow.

Chapter Four

Back then, kids were kept under adults' thumbs nine months out of the year, but during the summer, they led their lives and we led ours, and the twain rarely met except at Sunday suppers and in church pews, which is where the girls and I were when we received the news that could put the kibosh on the freedom we'd been enjoying the past few weeks.

Doc, his younger brother Walt, who was the sheriff of Summit, and Aunt Jane May and I were expected to sit in the dedicated Buchanan pew up front. Viv was with her family a few rows behind us. Frankie and the Maniachis back further still. Frankie was a Baptist at heart and would've liked to have been over at Emmanuel Baptist wedged between Dell and Jimbo, but those church busybodies and the group of Germans would notice if the "orphaned relative of the Italians" didn't show up at Mass with them.

I couldn't see how the girls were occupying themselves while Father Casey, the pastor of St. Thomas Aquinas, droned on at the altar, but I was staring at a stained glass window that depicted St. Joan of Arc getting burned at the stake and recalling how Aunt Jane May had told us that the fierce and sudden heat enveloping the town had been Satan's doing. At the time, I had filed that away as just another one of her endless "Mark my words" warnings, but I was beginning to believe her.

Those attending the nine o' clock Mass that Sunday were slippery with sweat and sliding off kneelers left and right. And oh, how the poor choir suffered in those heavy red robes. Their harmonious pleas for salvation drifting down from the loft had sounded unusually authentic before the heat got to one of the sopranos. Aunt Jane May called down to Doc to come quickly and bring his smelling salts, but no sooner had he finished ministering to seemingly always pregnant Mrs. Ellsworth when old Mr. Woolty went woozy in the Communion line and knocked a couple of people standing behind him onto their keesters. After the church ushers helped everyone get recombobulated, Doc stepped up to the altar and suggested to Father Casey that before anyone else succumbed to the heat, he better wrap things up.

Our pastor's cheeks looked like stop signs and his vestments clung to his pot belly, so he readily agreed to Doc's suggestion to cut the Mass short. But before he dismissed us, he made his way to the lectern to deliver what he promised would be a few parish updates.

"There will be a school uniform sale on Friday, a paper drive this Saturday, and if you haven't heard yet, an emergency town meeting has been called for seven o'clock this evening. The president of our Ladies Auxiliary,"—our pastor grinned at Mrs. Mulrooney, who was sitting next to her vile thirteen-year-old daughter Brenda in the pew across from ours—"has brought to our attention a matter of utmost urgency. The topic of tonight's meeting will be 'Broadhurst: Are Our Children Safe?'" There was some grumbling among his flock and a few of them raised their hands, but Father Casey wisely deferred to the experts.

"Mayor Kibler will moderate the meeting, and the sheriff and Doc will be present as well, along with Doctor Cruikshank and Nurse Holloway from the hospital. They'll address your concerns and answer any questions, and I expect each and every one of you to attend."

The girls and I already knew about the rumors Mulrooney was spreading about Hopper, so that came as no surprise. But calling for an emergency meeting to discuss his transfer was, and we were about as pleased with that news as we were with Aunt Jane May's forbidding us to ride over to Mud Town after the sun set.

Because when even Viv's conniving mind couldn't come up with one good reason why she'd forbid us to cross the tracks after dark, we did what we so often did. We ignored her warning. We also paid no mind to the one she'd issued about staying away from Broadhurst. We'd been riding over to the mental institution every afternoon, so about the last thing we needed was Aunt Jane May keeping closer tabs on us, which we could count on if things went sideways at the town hall that night.

She'd think she was keeping us safe because, like most of the folks in town, she didn't understand, the way the girls and I did, that the Broadhurst patients posed no danger, and that would include Hopper. If he did get transferred, the child killer would be locked up on the third floor of the hospital with the other criminally insane patients who'd never feel the sun on their skin or breathe fresh air again.

Frankie, Viv, and I were taking turns kicking an empty Campbell's soup can down the block on our way home from church and bemoaning the meeting the president of the Ladies Auxiliary had called for that night.

"I don't get it," I said to Frankie. "How come, do ya think, Mulrooney is trying to make everyone believe that if Hopper gets moved to Broadhurst he'll escape and strangle some kids?"

"Yeah," Viv said and gave the can a kick that landed halfway down the block. "Since when did that turd turn into the patron saint of children?"

As if she'd already given the matter a lot of thought, Frankie said, "I don't think Mulrooney is tryin' to keep kids safe from Hopper. I think she's got an ulterior motive."

Viv bobbed her head in enthusiastic agreement, but when Frankie hopped forward to give the soup can a swift kick, she whispered behind her hand to me, "What's an ult . . . what she said?"

"An ulterior motive is a secret reason for doin' something," I whispered back.

Viv nodded, squared her shoulders, and said, "Yeah, I got some ideas about what that so-and-so is secretly up to, too, but age before beauty, Frankenstein."

Frankie smiled at the nickname, then said, "I heard Brenda Mulrooney telling some little kids at the park yesterday that they better let her win at hopscotch or her mother'll put 'em in jail after she becomes mayor."

"And you believed her?" Viv let loose with a deprecating guffaw that'd usually be directed at me. "She's as full of it as her ma is."

Frankie shrugged. "It's a free country, so think want you want, but I figure Mulrooney's gonna start saying that if Mayor Kibler was in his right mind, he'd be as worried as she is that kids could be murdered by Wally Hopper."

"And then she'll start tellin' everyone that the mayor should've been the one to call for an emergency meeting instead of her and that's proof he's over the hill and . . . and she'd be the best person to replace him," I said, finally catching on. "Oh, poor Bud. He'll never see it comin'."

We had a soft spot in our hearts for the man who dressed like Count Dracula and gave out all-day suckers on Halloween, and would say, "Why, hello there, Small Fries," whenever he bumped into us. But not everyone regarded Bud Kibler as highly as we did. When he'd been spotted around town mumbling to himself with his barn door open and his silver hair looking like he'd stuck a fork in an electrical socket, there was talk about his arteries going hard on him. Talk started by none other than Evelyn Mulrooney.

Viv raged, "I wouldn't put it past her to start telling everybody again that Bud is goin' feeble, and on top of that our summer is gonna get all screwed up. After she gets everyone worked up over Hopper, grown-ups are gonna start watching our every move and—" She was so frantic that she swallowed her Juicy Fruit and it got lodged in her throat. After I smacked her hard on the back and the wad came flying out, she picked it up off the sidewalk and stuck it back in her mouth. "If Mulrooney gets to be mayor . . . she's gonna act like the goddamn Queen of Sheba!"

"Simmer down," Frankie told her. "I only *think* all of this has something to do with Mulrooney runnin' for mayor. We need proof. Since the whole town will be gathered at the emergency meeting tonight, I bet that's when she'll reveal what she's got up her sleeve."

"You mean what she's got up her sleeve besides her flabby arm and the revenge she came up with for Auntie after the sheriff shot her down at Delson's," Viv groused.

After Widow Mulrooney had completed the requisite year of mourning for her husband, Herbert, who'd been kicked in the head by a cow at Camp's Dairy, she packed away her black mourning dresses, shook out her spring frocks, and informed our uncle, the sheriff, at Delson's Coffee Shop that she'd be willing to attend St. Thomas's May Day Mixer with him. He thanked her for the invitation, told her he was flattered, but, "I've already asked Jane May."

Mrs. Mulrooney seemed to respond to his rebuff graciously enough at the time, but the girls and I suspected that she was so infuriated about getting passed over that she could barely see straight. Of course, she couldn't be blatantly vindictive toward Aunt Jane May. Jealousy was a sin and the president of the Ladies Auxiliary couldn't let her slip show. But if you observed people as closely as we did, you'd learn that no matter how holier than thou they appeared, their oiliness would eventually seep to the surface, and Evelyn Mulrooney's had at that month's church fundraiser, "Pastry for Pagan Babies."

After she strode onto the school's gymnasium floor last week, she appeared to be gushing with excitement when she greeted the crowd who'd forked over five dollars to spend the evening sampling pies, cakes, and cookies and voting on the most delicious, but she didn't fool the girls and me. When Mulrooney leaned into the microphone and said, "May I have your attention, please? The ballots have been counted and Jane May Mathew's devil's food cake has taken top honors. Again," she smiled, but it didn't reach her eyes. And instead of offering hearty congratulations to the winner, she quipped, "But I'm sure we can all agree that an *angel* food cake would've been more in keeping with our Roman Catholic values."

The crowd got a big yuck out of that, but the second that crack came out of Mulrooney's mouth, I told the girls, "Something's rotten in Denmark."

Seemed like Viv barely listened to the Shakespearean passages Aunt Jane May would read aloud to make us more cultured, but she said, "Yeah, but something stinks around here, too, and I think it's the stench of the green-eyed monster comin' off Mulrooney. You see that look she's givin' Auntie? I've seen it a million times on my ma's and granny's faces."

Frankie and I were well familiar with that look. Viv had inherited it.

"We gotta keep extra close tabs on Auntie from here on out," Viv added with a shudder, "because as cagey as she is, she's no match for an Irish gal lookin' to get an eye for an eye."

Frankie nodded in agreement and said, "Dell says all the time that 'Hell hath no fury like a woman scorned.'"

So whatever came out that night at the town hall meeting, if it involved Mulrooney, the girls and I knew it wouldn't be good. We couldn't be sure, of course, because as Frankie said, we had no proof, but it sure seemed like she was up to something that'd put a crimp in our freedom and adversely affect the patients at Broadhurst as well. Not to mention that she might be going after darling Mayor Kibler's job and had something nasty in store for our beloved aunt, too. The Bible taught us to "know thy enemy" and the girls and I thought we did, but what good would it do us if we didn't know her plan?

"I think Frankie's right." I kicked the soup can so hard it dented the tip of my patent leather shoe. "We need to get to that meeting tonight to find out what Mulrooney's up to, but when we ask Aunt Jane May she's gonna tell us to—"

"Mind our own businesses," Frankie and Viv chimed in.

It was a lot for us to take in, and we walked the rest of the way home stewing over the powerful forces we were up against. When we rounded the corner toward home, I could see the rainbow flag attached to the roof of the hideout hanging lifelessly in the still morning and I thought, *That's just how I feel.*

Sensing my despair, Viv reached for my hand and gently ran her thumb across my knuckles. "Auntie forbid us to cross the tracks and warned us to stay away from Broadhurst, but that hasn't stopped us. And if you think I'm gonna let her keep us from goin' to that meeting tonight," she said with a grin, "you're even stupider than you look, ya dumb chump."

Chapter Five

On our walk home from Mass that morning, the girls and I had decided it was pointless to ask Aunt Jane May if we could go to the emergency meeting that night, but Frankie insisted we take a run at her later that afternoon. "We could get lucky," she'd said as we roller-skated past the downtown shops. "She might still be in her church mood."

Sure that Viv already had one foot in hell, Aunt Jane May spent a good part of her day reprimanding her, but deep down? Those two were cut from the same cloth. Both of them were extravagant with their words and their gestures, and what beautiful music they made together. Viv would often slip out of the hideout after she thought Frankie and I were asleep to go sit with our aunt on the back porch glider. They loved Doris Day songs and show tunes like "I'm Gonna Wash That Man Right Outa My Hair," but they harmonized on hymns, too. Their version of "Amazing Grace" just about did me in.

Sure that Viv would have the best chance to win Aunt Jane May over, after we unstrapped our roller skates, we went looking for her and found her on her knees in the front garden. She was snipping roses for that night's supper table.

"Excuse us for botherin' you, Auntie," Viv said, "but we can't seem to agree on what time you said you wanted us to be ready to go to the town hall with you tonight. We wouldn't want to be tardy. Did you say six thirty or quarter of?"

Aunt Jane May leaned back onto her haunches and said, "Vivian Edna, because it's the Lord's day, I'm going to pretend I didn't just hear you ask to attend a meetin' that's none of your businesses."

Repaying the favor, Viv acted like she hadn't heard *her*. She was about to launch into another one of her cock-and-bull stories when our aunt reached into her gardening box and yanked out a few of the tools the girls and I called Satan's pitchforks. "And if I hear one more word comin' out of any of your mouths, you'll be poppin' dandies out of the lawn the rest of the day, I don't care how blasted hot it is. On second thought—" she grinned, not nicely, and tossed the tools at our feet.

Viv protested, "But . . . but it's supposed to be a day of rest!"

"Fifty each, and you can bet I'll count 'em."

We couldn't afford to get on her bad side any worse than we already were, so we did as we were told. But after we'd accumulated half our quota, we took a break from the beating sun beneath the big weeping willow out back. The one Aunt Jane May promised to bury us under if she ever caught us "prevaricating" to her. We were gulping water out of the garden hose, making necklaces with the dandelions we'd dug up, and cloud watching through the tree's dangling emerald branches.

When a chubby cumulus floated by, Frankie tickled my cheek with a blade of grass and said, "Hate to break it to ya, but I think another something Mulrooney's got up her sleeve is the sheriff."

I swatted her hand away. "What d'ya mean?"

"I think she wants to marry him, and Viv thinks so, too."

"What?" The most shocking part of that statement wasn't that that social-climber wanted to become part of the most powerful family in Summit, but that the girls had agreed on something.

I bolted upright and asked Viv, "Is that right?"

She nodded with gravitas, but then said, "Rotsa ruck" and burst into giggles and didn't stop until she wet her pants.

I wasn't concerned I'd ever be asking "Aunt Evelyn" to pass me the meat loaf during Sunday supper either. With a face as plain as butcher paper, a figure that resembled a snowman's, and the personality of a garbage truck, her chances of landing Walt Buchanan were about as good as mine with Rock Hudson. But I *was* surprised to learn that she didn't know that he only went in for pretty gals who were, as Viv described them, "built like brick shit houses." Uncle Walt's dates had to have a lot on the ball and possess a good amount of charm to boot. Qualities that described Aunt Jane May to a T, even that last one, when she wasn't going off on Frankie, Viv, and me, anyway.

"Speak of the devil," Viv muttered when our aunt appeared on the back porch.

"You can finish up tomorrow," she called out. "Biz, come in here now and get yourself cleaned and changed. We have hungry men to feed and this supper isn't goin' to make itself."

* * *

"Ya ask me, this heat is givin' everyone a chronic case of pissy-itis," is how Aunt Jane May characterized the mood that was wet-blanketing Summit as I helped her put the finishing touches on the most important meal of the week. "I swear, I can't go anywhere these days without someone speakin' snippy or acting like they're bendin' over backwards."

She wasn't "whistlin' Dixie." God-fearing people I'd known my whole life, who never raised their voices or uttered a cross word, were on edge. A fight had broken out at Top's Bar and tumbled out onto the sidewalk, and we'd heard that a couple of the nuns from St. Thom's had gotten into a tussle over a pack of fish sticks at Rusty's Market.

"And now we got this emergency meeting to deal with and"—Aunt Jane May looked down at her hours of hard work—"this food is gettin' cold." She untied her gingham apron, snatched up the platter of Southern fried chicken and the tureen of milk gravy off the kitchen counter, and nodded at the remaining bowls. "Set the taters in front of your uncle and the corn bread next to your father."

Doc would usually wear his navy blue suit when we'd gather in the formal dining room on Sundays, but even he was affected by the heat. He looked just as handsome in a starched white shirt and charcoal slacks when he held the chair out for Aunt Jane May, then me, and took his seat at the head of the table.

You couldn't tell he was six foot two when he was seated. Same as me, most of Doc's height was in his legs and I inherited my broad shoulders from him, too. I had my mother's light blue eyes, but his reminded me of my favorite crayon—cornflower. A lustrous chestnut, his hair was combed back from his forehead and held in place with Brylcreem—"just little dab will do ya." And when he finished shaving in the morning, he slapped Old Spice on his cheeks with hands that built hideouts but also healed. That woodsy, cinnamon smell would still be lingering on him the nights I didn't sleep with the girls. I'd strain to hear the sound of our woody station wagon pulling into the cobblestone driveway, the squeak of the back door, his soft footfalls coming up the staircase and then down the second-floor hallway. I didn't want to scare him off, so I'd pretend to be asleep when he came into my bedroom to brush the hair off my forehead and check for a fever that might take me away in the middle of the night, the way one had my mother. That tender act never failed to make me feel less like a consolation prize and more like a cherished consequence and I'd sleep the sleep of angels and dream of Sunday suppers when the man of so few words would say a little something to me. When he'd told me a few weeks ago that he thought I'd grown and he'd get the yard stick out after dessert, I couldn't spoon what remained on my plate down fast enough.

After Doc gave thanks to the Lord for the food we were about to receive, he commented on how lovely the table looked, thanked Aunt Jane May for preparing the meal, then turned to me. "Are you and your friends enjoying your summer vacation, Elizabeth?" he asked.

"Yes, sir. We're having a swell time," I said, but I thought how quickly that could change if Evelyn Mulrooney got her way at the emergency meeting.

The girls and I were so desperate to head over to the town hall after supper that I was tempted to ask Doc for permission, but Aunt Jane May would go purple in the face if I undercut her and would strongly "suggest" we meet out in the kitchen. I could find myself washing dishes and polishing silver for the rest of the night and I couldn't risk that. Frankie, Viv, and I had plans. Big plans. I already saw myself as the weakest line of our threesome and I couldn't bear being the one who threw a monkey wrench into them.

From his seat next to mine, the sheriff of Grand County tucked his napkin into the top of his tan uniform shirt and said to me, "A penny for your thoughts."

I grinned at what he'd been saying at the start of Sunday supper as far back as I could remember, then told him what *I* always had, "Make that a nickel and you got a deal."

"You drive a hard bargain, kiddo," he said as he produced one from behind my ear.

Good looks ran in our family, so he turned heads. He had the same coloring as his brother, but he was an inch taller, with a much more powerful physique. He also had darling dimples, was good with a gun, and had a rough-around-the edges way about him that the single ladies in town seemed to find irresistible.

Frankie thought the sheriff did a good job of keeping the peace and treated Mud Towners more fairly than many in town did, but she didn't care for how opinionated he could be. Viv thought he was a barrel of laughs and got a kick out of his magic tricks. I adored every inch of him except for how he thought of Broadhurst as a dent in the otherwise shiny exterior of our town. Viv was right. He could be so charming. But Frankie was right about him, too. He was a loudmouth, that's for sure.

I would've wagered the nickel he gave me that at some point during the meal he'd start spouting off about one of his favorite topics and reveal some much needed information about tonight's meeting that might be useful to the girls and me. It wouldn't take much to get him going. All I had to do to nudge him onto his soapbox was mutter into my napkin just loud enough for him to hear, "Broadhurst."

"That hospital might look good on the outside, but it's nothing more than a fruitcake factory, am I right, Biz?" Uncle Walt circled his finger around his ear and waited for me to do the same because, even though we weren't, he thought we were on the same wavelength. "But," he added with a grin, "if tonight's meeting goes like I think it will, that could soon change."

Oh?" Doc looked up from the piece of cornbread he was buttering. "Why's that?"

"Evelyn Mulrooney has assured me that she'll convince folks once and for all that those lunatics are a danger to the town. For God's sakes, Martha Winchell barely survived that car crash."

That wasn't true. That was just one of his big blusters.

Mrs. Winchell was only shaken up the morning she was on her way home from the library when one of the Broadhurst patients popped up in the back seat of her Rambler, pointed at the book she'd checked out, and told her how much he'd enjoyed *Gone with the Wind*. It wasn't his fault Old Lady Winchell goosed the gas and ended up in the Schroeders' front yard with their bird bath doing double duty as a hood ornament.

"Cruikshank acts like my men and I have nothing better to do than round up those escaped patients and drive them back to that loony bin," the sheriff complained as he carved into his chicken breast with too much vigor. "And the mayor won't act on my complaints." He reached for the bowl of mashed potatoes and slapped a generous scoop down onto his plate. "I know you don't agree with me, Doc, but I'm not the only one in town who thinks it's time for Bud Kibler to retire. Evelyn Mulrooney is running against him come September, and if she wins, she's planning to do all she can to shut the hospital down."

I almost choked on my string beans because that was almost verbatim what Frankie had told Viv and me on our walk home from Mass that morning—only much worse. Not only had Mulrooney scared our neighbors into believing that if it wasn't for her diligence, they wouldn't have known Hopper could be headed our way to murder their children, she wanted to further convince them of her mayoral worthiness by leading a charge to close Broadhurst down.

This was such life-changing news, not only for the girls and me and poor Bud Kibler, but for the patients we'd grown to care about. I was dying to hear more, but Uncle Walt was ready to move onto another one of his favorite Sunday supper topics—Aunt Jane May's home cooking.

He leveled his bachelor blues at her and said, "Janie"—that's what he called her—"nobody does spuds half as good as you and they're especially fine tonight."

Aunt Jane May had an aversion to bragging, but being from the South and all, hospitality was her Eleventh Commandment, so I expected her to politely thank him for the compliment and quickly move onto another topic. What I hadn't anticipated was seeing a rosy blush rise up from the scooped collar of her pretty lilac dress when she told him, "I tried foldin' in a cup of sour cream this time. Glad you like them."

She was humble, but not the demure type, and as I watched that blush crawl toward her neck, I wondered what the heck was going on. A few weeks ago she'd turned the color of her red clutch purse at the breakfast table, and here she was almost fuchsia at the supper table. Is she allergic to cooking? Does she have scarlet fever?

But that was stupid. That didn't make sense.

She'd been cooking her whole life without a deleterious reaction, and a nursing diploma from the University of Mississippi hung on her bedroom wall. She knew scarlet fever was contagious and wouldn't think of spreading it around, and she didn't appear to have any other symptoms. Her appetite was hearty, and she wasn't listless or glassy-eyed. Other than the blush that'd charged all the way to her cheeks, Aunt Jane May looked like a million bucks. Just like Viv told her she did the morning she'd read her that pretend fortune about Mr. Tall, Dark, and Handsome and . . . O, Mary, sweet mother of God.

That could not be a coincidence.

Had Aunt Jane May been trotting hotly with a man who was no longer a mystery because he was sitting next to me at the dining room table? Did she forbid the girls and me to ride over the tracks because she and Uncle Walt had been secretly meeting at Earl Spooner's Club after dark? Was that her lip-licking secret?

Of course, I was completely bowled over by that possible turn of events and reversal of roles, but I understood why she'd want to keep that from us. Frankie and I would keep our traps shut, but Viv had been acting so impetuously that she couldn't be counted on anymore to keep a secret. And given what the girls told me that afternoon about Mulrooney setting her matrimonial sights on Uncle Walt, if Viv found out that he and Aunt Jane May were dating each other, she might tell Mulrooney for the pure satisfaction of seeing her suffer, and that wouldn't work out so hot.

Snug in the hideout, Frankie, Viv, and I had heard the president ranting during one of the Auxiliary meetings held in our living room, "I've been told they're dancing to jungle music at that club across the tracks. The Lord wants us to do something about that, ladies. We'll be making picket signs at the next meeting. We need to close that place down."

If any of those purported do-gooders should happen to march in front of Earl's back door and see Aunt Jane May dancing the night away with Uncle Walt, that'd be disastrous. She'd get kicked out of the Auxiliary. Blackballed. The same way Mrs. Joan Abernathy had been when, after one too many cocktails at the church Christmas party, she'd sashayed over to Father Casey, undid the top buttons of her Peter Pan blouse, and asked him if he'd like to take a peek at Never Neverland.

The girls and I thought that was hilarious, but the religious ladies weren't known for their sense of humor. They started one of their whisper campaigns, and by the time they got done putting Mrs. Abernathy through the wringer, she couldn't show her face in town. She and her family had to move to Port Washington.

That's not the fate that'd befall Aunt Jane May, of course. As powerful as Mulrooney was, she'd never get rid of the matriarch of the Buchanan family. But she *would* do all she could to tarnish our aunt's sterling reputation. Nobody looked down on a man who sowed his wild oats before he tied the knot, but a single gal like Aunt Jane May was supposed to stay unplowed. Mulrooney would drag her name through the mud—in the name of Jesus Christ, of course—if she found out that my aunt and uncle were pressing against each other at Earl Spooner's Club. She could even spread around what her daughter Brenda had told the girls and me at the park yesterday after I beat her at tetherball, "You think you're such a big deal, Buchanan, because your relative discovered the town, but my ma thinks your aunt is doin' unnatural acts with your uncle and she's gonna tell everyone in town."

I could tell by the venom in her voice and Viv's volcanic reaction that she had insulted and threatened our loved ones, but I had no idea what she meant by "unnatural acts," so Frankie had to keep Viv from gouging Brenda's eyes out and explain to me at the same time, "Her mother told her that Auntie and Uncle Walt are . . ." she thrust her pelvis forward and backward a bunch of times.

"Hula-hooping?" I guessed, because that's what it looked like and it'd be a pretty unnatural act for them to do.

"For the love of God!" Viv yelled as she struggled to get free of Frankie's grip. "This little shit is sayin' that her ma is gonna tell everyone that Auntie and Uncle Walt are doin' what the Willis's and the Harris's dogs are always doin' and—let me at her!"

Then again, I thought, as I went back to studying Aunt Jane May across the dining room table on the night of the emergency meeting, I might be making a big deal out of nothing. She'd just finished slaving away in a steamy kitchen during record-breaking heat, so her rosy cheeks could be nothing more than a prickly rash. And even if my uncle raved about her cooking, enjoyed watching the *Gillette Friday Night Fights* with her and, by all reports, had a ball twirling her around the dance floor at the May Mixer, that didn't mean they were in love.

Did it?

I'd lost my mother, and my father wouldn't dream of replacing her, so I never had the opportunity to watch a man and woman romance each other close-up. But I had observed enough couples holding hands or snuggling during a Music Under the Stars concert or smooching in the balcony at the Rivoli to know that kind of love could be a many-splendored thing.

But then, what about Mrs. Merchant, who used to show up on our front porch in the middle of the night when her husband busted her nose or broke her rib? And no matter how many shifts Mr. Ellis worked at the dairy, his wife shared her displeasure on payday with anyone who was within screaming distance.

I guess about the only thing I knew for sure about love and marriage was, *if* our aunt and uncle had fallen for each other, the girls and I wouldn't be trying on flower girl dresses at Suzy's Bridal Shop. Aunt Jane May would never say "I do" and move into his bungalow on Chestnut Street, not in the near future anyway. She'd stepped into her sister's shoes to raise me and tend to her brother-in-law's hearth and home and she'd never relinquish those commitments.

And what would happen after she said no to Uncle Walt's proposal? Would he drop her and break her heart? If another man pulled a stunt like that, the Tree Musketeers would come up with a suitable punishment for the louse, but would that same principle apply to a member of our family? Who would the girls and I owe our allegiance to? Both of them? If so, that could turn into a mess of biblical proportions. I could almost see Solomon's sword hanging over—

"Elizabeth Augusta Buchanan!" Judging by how hard Aunt Jane May kicked my foot under the dining room table, it wasn't the first time. "Have you gone stone-deaf?"

I snapped to. "No, ma'am."

"Then do what I told you to."

I'd been a million miles away and had no idea what she was talking about. I was tempted to compliment her, the way Viv would have, but I wasn't fast on my feet like she was. "Sorry," I said. "Come again?"

"We're waiting on you to fetch the pie from the kitchen," Aunt Jane May said through clenched teeth. "The way I asked you to five minutes ago and three before that."

I should've been mortified that she'd reprimanded me in front of my father and uncle, but I was grateful she'd brought me back to the here and now, and I jumped out of my chair and said, "Back in two shakes!"

I'd spent entirely too much time plying my uncle for information about the emergency meeting and imagining a dire future for Aunt Jane May, and not nearly enough time rehearsing my lines for a command performance that might take place after supper. If I didn't play my part to Viv's satisfaction, she might start practicing her noose-making again. Only this time, she'd have my neck in mind.

Chapter Six

❧

Despite the unpredictability swirling around the girls and me, there were some things we could still count on.

We knew that once Doc and Uncle Walt made quick work of their cherry pie slices, as was their custom after every Sunday supper, they'd excuse themselves. They'd go out back to smoke cigars and talk brother to brother in bentwood chairs set beneath a sycamore tree because Aunt Jane May wouldn't let them smoke in the house.

Soon as they were out of the picture, I did what I'd promised the girls I'd do before we parted ways that afternoon. After Aunt Jane May and I cleared the dishes off the dining room table, as was our custom, she filled the kitchen sink with hot water, and I got busy trying to change her mind while she washed and I dried.

"Father Casey told us at Mass this morning that he expected *everyone* to attend the emergency meeting and . . . what if one of us gets run over by a car when we're playin' kick the can tonight?" I said. "We'd go straight to hell for disobeying a direct order from a priest. You don't want that on your conscience, do you?"

Aunt Jane May nudged a curl off her cheek with the back of her soapy hand and said with a bemused snort, "Think you girls will ever get it through your heads that when I say no I don't mean maybe?" She passed me a slippery china saucer. "That day ever comes, be sure to let me know, all right? I'm plannin' on contacting *Ripley's Believe it or Not.*"

About the time I was stacking the last of the dishes, Frankie and Viv must've smelled Doc's and Uncle Walt's smoke signal. Usually, when the cigar fumes floated over to their yards on Sunday nights, they'd come grab me, and we'd play a board game in the hideout until Ed Sullivan's show came on because we really liked jugglers and Viv was trying to learn ventriloquism from Señor Wences.

But that Sunday night, the girls were standing outside the screen door to find out if I'd succeeded in obtaining Aunt Jane May's approval to attend the town hall meeting. After I snuck my hand out from behind the dish towel and gave them the thumbs down, the plan Viv had come up with to discover what Mulrooney had up her sleeve was set in motion.

Besides striking beauty and a superior intellect, Frankie had better than twenty/twenty vision, so she always served as our lookout and scout. She jumped off the back porch and skipped toward the tire Uncle Walt had hung from a branch of the hideout tree with a thick nautical rope. Per Viv's direction, Frankie was to act like she was having a gay old time, but what she was really doing—her ulterior motive—was keeping her eye on the Buchanan brothers. When they snubbed their cigars out, it'd mean they were about to head back to Doc's study for their post-dinner whiskey before they left for the meeting. Frankie's job was to let Viv and me know when they were on the move. If we heard her whippoorwill whistle, we were to drop whatever we were doing, meet her out front of the house, and run like hell.

Viv's role was to mislead Aunt Jane May about where we'd be when she and Doc and the sheriff were at the meeting and our little actress played it to the hilt. She came bursting through the screen door, snatched a shortbread cookie out of the jar, and delivered her opening line with one of those toothy smiles of hers. "Mmm . . . mmm . . . mmm. If you don't enter these cookies in the County Fair this year, Auntie, I swear I will." She turned toward me then and said so smoothly, so convincingly, that for a moment I thought she'd called the plan off, "I heard the Olly Olly Oxen call on my way over here. If we don't want 'em to start without us, we gotta get a move on. Go change your clothes, and I'll grab Frankie."

We couldn't risk my family seeing us heading downtown instead of up the block, so the next part of Viv's plan called for us to say our good nights and then conceal ourselves behind the six-foot hedge that separated the Buchanans' property from the Maniachis'. After we heard Aunt Jane May, the sheriff, and Doc leave for the town hall, so would we.

That all went without a hitch, and we were so pleased with our efforts that instead of staying focused on the job at hand, we acted like the three eleven-year-olds we were. We were doing this little celebratory bunny hop dance we did after things went our way when Viv suddenly stopped, pointed toward the lush vegetable garden in the Maniachis' backyard, and said, "Aww, damnit to hell and back. I forgot about Uncle Sally."

Not factoring him into the plan was flat out negligent on Viv's part, and Frankie and I should've taken him into consideration, too, because it wasn't like he'd ambushed us. During the warm months, we could almost always find him in his backyard garden that time of night watering or pinching suckers off his tomato plants and singing an Enrico Caruso aria or an Ole Blue Eyes tune.

With his wavy dark hair and wide shoulders, Sally Maniachi bore a strong resemblance to Aunt Jane May's favorite boxer Rocky Marciano, only he liked to eat more than fight. I'd seen folks sitting next to him at church change pews because they found his ever-present pungent aroma off-putting, but the girls and I thought that on the off chance a vampire did show up in the hideout and our crucifix didn't do the trick, we'd run next door and his garlic breath would be our saving grace.

Of course, I was quite fond of Sally and grateful to him and his twin sister, Sophia, for taking Frankie in and pretending to be her relatives. And when the church spinsters and that group of Germans grew suspicious of the little newcomer to town, I greatly admired how he shut them up by writing a check for a new church roof because, "Nothing talks louder than money, girls." And what a kind and understanding employer he was. On a night I was restless and thirsty in the hideout, I was on my way back to the house to get a glass of lemonade when I heard some whimpering coming from the Maniachis' backyard. I thought Sophia might've fallen out of her wheelchair and needed help, but when I looked around the bushes, I could see that Sally was letting Dell cry on his shoulder, probably about how much she could use a new vacuum cleaner because he gave her a Hoover 800 a few days later that she really loved.

After Uncle Sally spotted us the night of the emergency meeting, he smiled and waved enthusiastically with both of his arms, which is how he always greeted us. Like we'd just disembarked from a cruise ship that'd docked in Sicily and he was a tour guide who couldn't wait to show us a good time. He'd usually shout at us, "*Ciao, bambinas,*" in his booming voice, but if he did so that night my family was sure to hear, so Frankie had to act fast. She locked eyes with Sally and ran her finger across her throat—Italian sign language for "Keep your mouth shut or you'll be taking a long walk off a short pier." Of course, we hated to see his welcoming face turn into a wounded one, but we knew he'd do as Frankie asked because he adored her, and if there was anyone in Summit who appreciated the importance of a well-kept secret more than we did, we were looking at him.

But we weren't home free yet.

When the church bells announced that if you intended to attend the meeting at the town hall, you better get on the stick, we had been crouching behind those prickly bushes for a good fifteen minutes. When God passed out patience, Viv and her tiny bladder must've been in the bathroom. She was growing more restless and testy by the minute. Frankie was doing her best to keep her occupied with a game of cat's cradle, but Viv had been on such a losing streak that when the string slipped off her fingers, I was sure she'd lose one more thing—her awful temper. If she went off on Frankie, she would give away our hiding spot, and it looked like she was about to do just that when we heard voices on the other side of the hedge, and a few moments later, the doors of the sheriff's county car slammed shut and the engine roared to life.

Soon as Doc, the sheriff, and Aunt Jane May were halfway down Honeywell Street, we shouted *"Arrividerci"* to Uncle Sally, promised we'd come *mangia* with him and Sophia real soon, and ran across the backyard of my house at full speed, praying the whole time that we'd make it to the town hall before my family did.

After Frankie, Viv, and I hopped over the stepping stones behind the hideout, we ran down an alley, jumped the Wellners' fence, sped down Main Street, and arrived at the square in the nick of time. Seconds after we concealed ourselves behind one of our favorite downtown observation points—the storage shed adjacent to the town hall—the sheriff pulled into his reserved spot in front of the building.

The hall was primarily used for government meetings, beauty pageants, holiday plays, and whatnot, but there was no jockeying for position or buzz of anticipation that night. Parents who'd been planning on distracting themselves from the punishing heat by sitting out on their front porch steps and talking about the Milwaukee Braves' winning season with a cold bottle of Pabst Blue Ribbon were not happily chatting or stepping lively. They were shuffling along the sidewalk and milling outside the front doors of the town hall looking so lifeless that my first panicked thought was that the search the girls and I had done around town for pods incubating soulless aliens after we'd seen *The Invasion of the Body Snatchers* hadn't been thorough enough.

The next part of Viv's plan called for us to hurry to the spot that we'd watch the meeting from. Considering the split-second timing it'd take to beat my family to their seats, we probably should've called the whole thing off, but with the lives of so many people we cared about at stake, the girls and I had no choice but to put our guts where our hearts were.

"One for the money," I said, and Viv piped in, "Two for the show," and after Frankie capped off our call to action with "Three to get ready," our voices rose together in a quiet but determined "Go, Tree Musketeers, go," and we took off toward the town hall.

Chapter Seven

～

Children weren't always seen and not heard in those days—mostly we weren't seen *or* heard—so we weren't concerned that our presence outside of the town hall that night would be noted by anyone other than Doc, Uncle Walt, and Aunt Jane May. We knew our neighbors would be far too preoccupied with their heat discomfiture and the provocative topic of the evening to pay us a lick of attention.

When we skirted past them and reached the door we planned to enter the building through, I was surprised to find it locked, but that wouldn't stop us either.

After we'd seen Vincent Price doing his dirty work in the *House of Wax*, we got the idea to at least try to get a peek inside the locked basement room at Broadhurst that we'd begun calling the Chamber of Horrors after the one in the movie. To facilitate that goal, Viv had donned Frankie's Girl Scout uniform—she set hers on fire and toasted marshmallows over it after she'd been kicked out of Troop 333—and paid the town locksmith a visit at his shop on Ivy Street to convince him that she was working to earn something she'd called a "Disaster Badge." She explained to former Eagle Scout Ed Gracker that she knew how to use a tourniquet on deep wounds and suck poison out of a snake bite, but she needed him to provide her with the means to get into a locked building that'd gone up in flames so she could save anyone trapped inside. Ed was a good egg, but not the brightest, none of the Grackers were, and he was certainly no match for a kid who'd grow up to be an Emmy-winning actress. He ended up cutting Viv not one key but three that day, and she never left the hideout without them in her pocket or hanging around her neck. "Because," she said with a sly grin as she slipped one of them into the lock on the town hall door the night of the emergency meeting, "it always pays to be prepared."

Frankie went first to get the lay of the land. When she returned a few minutes later and gave Viv and me the okay sign, we tip-toed inside, concealed ourselves behind the maroon velvet curtain at the back of the stage, and gingerly moved along the wall until we reached the metal ladder that led up to the catwalk.

It was the ideal spot to watch the meeting from. Angled enough that we could see anyone on the stage, as well as the audience, but I could've kicked myself for not bringing our binoculars along. I would've liked to get a closer look at a couple of faces. Knowing how someone felt about the issues to be discussed that night might come in handy at a later date, I thought.

Peacekeeping Uncle Walt, who was expected to show up at all town functions, was the first to walk onto the stage and take a seat below us. Next came my father. Doc was not involved in the inner workings of the town, but he often tended to the physical needs of the patients at Broadhurst and was thought of as an expert at dealing with emergencies of all kinds. One of the other empty chairs was reserved for Mayor Kibler, and I thought the other must be for Dr. Cruikshank's assistant, Nurse Holloway.

The girls and I were shiny with sweat and smelled as coppery as pennies held in a fist too long, and the crowd below wasn't faring much better. The wimpy breeze created by the fans set around the windowless room wasn't making much of a dent in the temperature or the cigarette smoke that billowed like ghosts above their heads. The gals in their pastel shirtwaist dresses were fanning themselves or powdering their noses, but their husbands were acting like letting on that the heat was getting to them would make the hair on their chests fall out.

Unlike town gatherings like the Fourth of July parade and the County Fair, this was not a mixed group. Just as Father Casey had informed his parishioners of the meeting that morning, I was sure Reverend Archie had told his congregation at Emmanuel Baptist. I was equally sure they didn't shout back at him, "Hallelujah." It troubled me that Mud Towners never showed up at these types of events, so I asked Jimbo about it. "Us givin' our opinions to those in charge is 'bout as useful as throwin' a T-bone to a toothless dog," is what he told me.

Far as I could tell, the only other kids at the meeting were the Jessop brothers and surely not willingly. They were probably forced to accompany their mother because everyone in town knew how wild those boys were, which, of course, meant that Viv found Petey and Pauly irresistible. "Double your pleasure, double your fun," she'd say with a cat-bird smile whenever we ran into them.

I didn't think Viv had spotted the Jessop boys, but in case she did, I cautioned her. "If you got anything to say, keep your voice down or someone on the stage might hear you."

Frankie leaned across me and whispered more firmly to Viv, "Settle down. This board's a lot wigglier than when we were up here for the Miss Firecracker contest. If you go antsy, we could fall off. Pretend you got polio."

I'd usually say "Ditto" when Frankie issued a warning to Viv to sit still, but I couldn't blame her for being excited that night. I was barely able to contain myself either. We'd never seen the head of the mental hospital in the flesh, only heard stories about Dr. Cruikshank from Jimbo, Albie, and Bigger Dolores. I'd also recently heard something about the psychiatrist from someone I respected and trusted above all others: my father.

Shortly after the heat wave started, I'd awoken in the middle of a night that was so suffocating and oppressive that I made my way down to the kitchen to stick my head into the refrigerator for a breath of fresh air. St. Thom's bells had just struck twelve, so I thought Doc and Aunt Jane were asleep, but when I came down the stairs, I heard the tail end of a conversation they were having at the kitchen table. "Arthur Cruikshank calls his treatments innovative, but to my way of thinking," my father said in a world-weary way that was unusual for him, "some of them do not adhere to the Hippocratic oath."

A physician promised to "first, do no harm" and it sounded like Doc thought that Cruikshank was falling down on the job. I didn't know if he was referring to the cattle prods, straitjackets, hot baths, and powerful medications some of the patients at the hospital could be subjected to, or if he meant something else. I was dying to waltz into the kitchen and ask him, but even if I'd had the guts to, he wouldn't have told me. My father took patient confidentiality as seriously as a priest took the confessional vow of silence.

Once everyone at the emergency meeting found a chair or section of wall to lean against, the president of the Ladies

Auxiliary made a grand entrance to applause led by her followers, who were looking at her like they had first-row seats to the
Second Coming of Christ.

"Good evening, everyone," Mrs. Mulrooney announced
into the microphone. "I'll be acting as your moderator tonight
because Mayor Kibler is unable to join us." She pivoted and
pointed toward the empty chair next to Doc. "He's indisposed."
She followed that up with a "Tsk, tsk" that made it clear what
she really meant: *Bud has gone so far over the hill that he's forgotten about this very important meeting. Isn't it just so sad when
someone's arteries go hard on them? When the next election rolls
around, vote for me!*

Viv whispered to us, "Indisposed? Disposed *of* is more like
it." She made a disgusted snort. "I thought I heard scratching
inside the storage shed when we were hidin' behind it. Mulrooney outweighs the mayor by a good fifty pounds. I bet she
locked him in there. We better swing by after the meeting and
make sure he's still alive."

"So, without further ado," Mrs. Mulrooney continued, "I'd
like to introduce you to our speaker this evening, *Doctor* Arthur
J. Cruikshank." I couldn't see if she rolled her eyes, but she made
it sound like the psychiatrist was akin to a snake oil salesman
and anyone in the audience who fell for his spiel must've been
born yesterday. "Accompanying him this evening is his assistant
and head nurse at the institution, Miss Ruth Holloway."

When the two of them walked onto the stage, I was surprised by how different they looked from the way I'd been picturing them.

Doctor Cruikshank was around my father's age but didn't
have anywhere near his stature or good looks. His face ran long,

with features too closely spaced together, and his bushy black mustache didn't match the fringe of brown hair that ran around his head like the bric-a-brac Aunt Jane May sewed onto throw pillows to give them more pizzazz.

And Nurse Holloway didn't look nearly as bad as the stories we'd heard about her. She wasn't going to win any beauty contests, but she wouldn't leave with the booby prize either. I thought she probably didn't attend these kinds of meetings very often because she was wearing a garish flowered dress that'd be more suitable for a garden party when she took the empty seat next to Uncle Walt.

Dr. Cruikshank nodded at Mrs. Mulrooney, then stepped up to the microphone and said, "Thank you for attending on an evening I'm sure you'd rather be spending somewhere else." There was a smattering of laughter from the audience, but it was guilty sounding because they were courteous people who felt uncomfortable for putting him in the hot seat. "In the interest of moving things along, I'd like to immediately address your concerns about Wallace Hopper." He paused to survey the crowd. "As some of you might have heard, he will be transferred from Milwaukee County Hospital to Broadhurst in the upcoming week."

When the room erupted in angry mumbles, the sheriff sprang to his feet to remind everyone to mind their manners, which must've pained him considering how much he disliked Dr. Cruikshank.

"I understand your concerns, but I assure you, Mister Hopper poses no danger to your children's safety," the psychiatrist hurried to say. "We'll take every precaution to keep him secured behind—"

"Stop right there," Mr. Willis, owner of the Rivoli Theatre and father of four young girls said as he leapt out of his chair. "We've heard you allow patients to run free in a yard, and if you think you're going to keep that child killer secured behind that wrought-iron fence, I've got news for you. My grandfather built that fence. It's decorative—nothing more than a boundary marker. Hopper would have no problem scaling it."

While the owner of the Rivoli Theatre was partially correct—Frankie, Viv, and I had climbed that fence many times—he had to calm down. He was huffing and too red in the face, not good signs for a man with a heart condition.

Of course, Mr. Willis's health concerns weren't public knowledge, but when you're the child of a physician you don't get to see all that often, and when you do he doesn't talk to you much, you might resort to drastic measures. When I stumbled across the key to Doc's file cabinet Aunt Jane May had hidden under a lamp in his study, I felt grateful for the opportunity to learn more about him and his work. My prayers had been answered is how I chose to think about my snooping.

"Patients with criminal histories like Mister Hopper's are *not* allowed access to the recreation yard," Cruikshank told Mr. Willis in a soothing voice that reminded me of the commercial pitchman who made cheddar cheese sound like caviar during the *Kraft Television Theatre*. "The hospital has the legal responsibility to keep him confined in a locked cell on the third floor and behind—"

Like a special effect in one of our horror movies signaling impending doom, the overhead fluorescent lights flickered a few times and settled at half power, and the fan blades neared to a stop.

All the heads in the room swiveled off the psychiatrist toward Lance Howard, who was slouching against a doorjamb to the left of the stage. He used to operate the Camelot Ferris wheel at the traveling carnival that was part of the County Fair, but he was fired last summer. Our kind-hearted mayor felt sorry for him and gave him a job maintaining the town buildings and grounds, and Dr. Cruikshank had hired him to do the same kind of work at Broadhurst. The kids in town liked the handyman because he'd pass out saltwater taffy, but not the girls and me. He made Frankie's and my skin crawl, but Viv was particularly put off by "Sir Lancelot," which was Howard's carnie handle and what he wanted all of us to keep calling him. Whenever we'd ride past him mowing the park grass or see him working around the mental hospital, Viv would grimace and say, "Sir Lancelot, my foot," because he didn't look anything like a knight in shining armor. He looked like all those carnival roustabouts did. Like sacks of bones in need of a dentist and a sly look etched on their faces that made you think they couldn't wait to close the carnival down for the night so they could get busy doing what good-hearted men had no idea existed.

"Mister Howard?" Mrs. Mulrooney called over to him. "The lights? Could you check the fuse box?"

He was cleaning his fingernails, and when he slowly drew his eyes up to the fluorescents like he hadn't noticed they were on the blink, the absolute worst happened. He and I locked eyes. I couldn't imagine the awfulness that'd ensue if he pointed up at the catwalk and shouted the alarm, but all he did was wink at me. I was so relieved that I thought one kind deed deserved another. Instead of turning our backs on him the next time he waved us over, I'd call him Sir Lancelot, take a piece of his taffy, and make sure the girls did as well.

While the crowd waited for Lance Howard to return from the basement with a verdict about the lights, they talked among themselves. Dr. Cruikshank used the pause in the proceedings to pour himself a glass of water and confer with Nurse Holloway, and Doc and Uncle Walt put their heads together. I searched the faces below for Aunt Jane May's. I was curious to see how the meeting was affecting her, because she never said much about the Broadhurst patients other than calling them "those poor, tortured souls" and telling Frankie, Viv, and me to "leave them be."

The moody lighting and the hazy clouds of cigarette smoke made it hard to see, so it took me a few minutes to spot our aunt in the last row. I only did so because her rigid posture, auburn hair shot through with gold, and pretty lilac dress were real standouts. I'd understand if Uncle Walt was in love with her, because she was a real knockout. Especially in comparison to the rumpled gal she was sitting next to. The two of them reminded me of those before and after snapshots Viv's mother tacked to the House of Beauty bulletin board to show off her skill at turning plain Janes into Jayne Mansfields.

The church gals played Bingo on Tuesday nights to raise money to send to Father Damien's lepers, sold pastry to help out pagan babies, and donated their kids' outgrown clothes to the Burkes, a family of fourteen, but when it came to other gals' appearances? They weren't so charitable. Aunt Jane May's seatmate had to know that wearing a shapeless beige shift and a battered hat pulled down too low on her face would make her an object of ridicule at the coffee klatches for the next week. To show up at a town function looking like she didn't give a hoot what anyone thought of her? That took the kind of moxie I wished I had more of and I wondered—who *is* that?

Like she read my mind, the gal plucked the ratty straw hat off the top of her head, began fanning herself with it, and when I saw who it was, I almost tumbled backward off the catwalk.

What in God's name was Audrey Cavanaugh doing at a town hall meeting?

Was she with Aunt Jane May or was the seat next to her the last one up for grabs? The Summit Witch didn't seem to care about anything else that went on in town, so why'd she care about what went on at Broadhurst?

The girls and I had never seen her out and about and we always kept an eye out for her, for Viv's sake. But plenty of other kids bragged that they'd spotted her skulking around the woods that encircled Broadhurst when they were playing hide 'n' seek or cowboys and Indians up there. The latest word at the fountain counter at Whitcomb's Drugstore was: "I'm tellin' ya, I seen that witch with my own eyes. She had scraggly hair and she was holding a big, long knife in her talons. If I hadn't gotten away, she was gonna drag me back to her house, chop me up, and throw me into her bubblin' cauldron 'cause . . . witches can give harelips to unborn babies after they eat a kid's heart out!"

The girls and I were entertained by the ghastly descriptions of Audrey Cavanaugh that we heard at the fountain counter, but we didn't believe them, because we knew what she really looked like. I caught a glimpse of her about a week after she moved into the old Jenkins place down the block from us.

I was trying on my trick-or-treat costume that morning and having no luck gluing the bolts I'd fashioned out of empty toilet paper tubes to my temples and the Aqua Net spray was refusing to make my hair stand on end—I was planning to beg for candy that night as the bride of Frankenstein—so I was in a foul mood. To add insult to injury, after I came downstairs and took my seat at the kitchen table, Aunt Jane May set my breakfast in front of me and said, "Eat fast. I want you to deliver a housewarming gift to Miz Cavanaugh on your way to school."

I snapped at her, "Do I look like the Welcome Wagon?"

"Do I look like I'd tolerate that tone of voice?" she snapped back. I thought she might haul off and swat me one, but what she did hurt even worse. She looked disappointed. "Your mama would be appalled if . . . have I not done a better job raising you? Miz Cavanaugh is a widow who moved here all the way from Chicago and she doesn't know a soul. She could use a slice." The woman who thought baked goods were the first course of treatment for many of life's ills set a white bakery box down in front of me. "And y'all can forget about helpin' yourselves to the pie, sticking the box down the sewer drain, and using the string for cat's cradle." As upset as I was, I couldn't help but be impressed—and horrified—because that's exactly what was on my mind. "Less'n you want to spend tonight saying a rosary instead of going door to door and askin' for sweets, missy, you'll drop that pie off and be quick about it."

Of course, the girls questioned why I had a bakery box lying on top of the books in my arms when I joined them out in front of the house for our daily walk to school. After I explained what Aunt Jane May was forcing me to do, Viv's eyes turned the size of poker chips, so Frankie ushered her around the corner and kept her company while I ran up the house steps and set the pie on the Summit Witch's front porch.

I really hated to see our vivacious girl a slave to her fear, so I'd been searching Doc's medical files to find something that might cure her. What I'd learned was that what Viv grappled with was not an ordinary fear, like being afraid of the dark or the bogeyman. She had something called a "phobia." Town clerk Lester Maddox had one, too. Only, instead of witches, Lester told Doc he was terrified of falling into quicksand because "You try to fight, you sink, and if you don't fight, you still sink." Doc pointed out to him numerous times that there was no quicksand in Summit and tried to reason Mr. Maddox out of his fear, but ended up noting in his file, "The patient does not respond to logic."

By the time I caught back up to them, Viv's breathing was coming too fast for her to quiz me, but Frankie couldn't wait to learn more. "Did you get a look at her?" she asked.

"She walked past the door, but . . ."

Viv was making such a wheezy racket that I told her to put her hands over her ears so she'd be spared further description, but I knew she'd probably eavesdrop on us anyway.

Once Viv was squared away, Frankie asked me, "Did you hear her cackle?"

"Nope."

"She got a humped back like Edith Dirks, bless her heart?"

I shook my head.

"Talons?

"Uh-uh."

"What about the cat? Charlie Fleming said at the drugstore that it had rabies and—"

"No cacklin', no hump, no talons, no cat frothin' at the mouth—nothin' like that," I told Frankie. "From what I could see, she didn't even look witchy except for her hair."

As I suspected, our little gossip monger *had* been listening in, because no matter how terrified she was, Viv couldn't bear not knowing something Frankie and I knew. She was probably picturing the Summit Witch's hair to be "puke green and made out of snakes," like Mickey Hodges had told everyone at Whitcomb's.

"What's . . . wrong . . . hair?" Viv struggled to ask between breaths.

"It's black, but she's got this wide white streak that starts right here," I pointed at my widow's peak, "and runs down the middle, so her head kinda looks like . . ." I closed my eyes and pictured what I'd seen through the gauzy curtain covering her door window, "the stretch of County C that runs past Broadhurst."

That's when Viv crumpled to the ground and passed out cold on the Henderson's front lawn and Frankie gave her the "kiss of life" whether she needed it or not.

Of course, I desperately wanted to avoid a repeat of that chaotic scene during the emergency meeting, but if Viv's eyes landed on the Summit Witch fanning her face in the back row, her fight-or-flight response would kick in and there wouldn't be a thing I could do to stop it. If she fainted or tried to scramble off the wiggly catwalk in an attempt to put as much distance as she could between herself and the source of her anxiety, the three of us would slip off and tumble down to the stage. Never mind the broken bones or bumps and bruises—they'd be nothing compared to the pain Aunt Jane May would inflict on us. She'd be "angrier than Jesus at the Temple" that we'd disobeyed her order to stay away from the meeting and mortified that we'd caused a scene in front of Doc, Uncle Walt, and the rest of the town. The girls and I could find ourselves up shit creek without a paddle trying to navigate the "severe consequences" she'd warned us about.

My knee-jerk reaction was to hope that Lance Howard would be unable to fix the lights, so the meeting would be called off, but deep down I knew something that miraculous only happened to Nancy Drew or some kid in the Bible or Timmy from *Lassie*, not me. *Viv's right,* I told myself. *I am a dumb chump. I need to stop waiting for hope to throw me a bone and take matters into my own hands. Or better yet . . . pass them on to hands more capable than mine.*

Frankie was the best at riling Viv up, but she was also the best at soothing her ruffled feathers. If Viv had spotted Audrey Cavanaugh sitting in the back row next to Aunt Jane May, Frankie would know what to do. But I didn't want to scare her, too, not until I knew for sure where we stood, so I stole a quick peek at Viv to see if she was exhibiting any of the early symptoms of panic.

Her chest was heaving slightly and her breathing was a tad gaspy. Her green eyes were wider than normal and her nostrils were flared, but . . . if she was truly scared out of her skull, she would've looked like she did when the Wicked Witch of the West appeared on the screen at the Rivoli and she didn't. Viv looked the same way she did when she'd stare at a box of chocolate mint Girl Scout cookies, and I thought, *Lord Almighty. She's seen the Summit Witch and gone straight into catatonic shock!*

I was just about to lean over and whisper *Help!* into Frankie's ear when, out of the corner of my eye, I noticed the curve of a mysterious smile appear on Viv's lips. At first, I thought this was another symptom of losing her grip on reality, but when I followed her line of sight, she wasn't staring at Audrey Cavanaugh. That little vixen was locking eyes with the "double your pleasure, double your fun" Jessop twins in the third row!

Glad that I hadn't alerted romance-hating Frankie and grateful that God had not answered my prayers beseeching Him to cure Viv of her boy craziness, I was wondering if hope was suddenly on my side when the lights bloomed back to full power. Dr. Cruikshank broke away from Nurse Holloway to resume his position behind the podium, and those in the audience who'd risen to stretch their legs or visit with their neighbors returned to their seats.

Picking up where he'd left off, the psychiatrist turned to Mr. Willis. "I assure you that dangerous patients are *not* allowed in the recreation yard," he said. "They're confined to the top floor of the hospital and locked in cells. The patients who *are* allowed time outside each day are harmless. They are their own worst enemies."

That was true, but the doctor would have a hard time convincing the audience of that. Since the bulk of their knowledge of mental illness had been garnered from movies and books in which the mentally ill were almost always portrayed as deranged monsters, I was fairly sure that everyone in the hall was envisioning the Broadhurst patients as vultures circling the countryside for their next meal instead of sparrows who'd had their wings clipped.

But even people you think you know inside and out can surprise the heck out of you sometimes, can't they. When I looked into the crowd to assess their reaction to Cruikshank's words, many of our neighbors were staring at him less skeptically.

Judging by the desperate look on Mulrooney's face, she might've sensed the tide was turning in the psychiatrist's direction as well. Anyone else might've given up at that point, but even if she wanted to, she couldn't. Not if she wanted to be mayor, and impress the sheriff into marrying her when she closed Broadhurst down. If Summit had a town motto, it would've been "Hard work pays off," so perseverance wasn't just a highly regarded quality in a candidate running for office—it was a prerequisite.

To convince the crowd of her grit, Mulrooney dug deeper into her bag of tricks and said to Cruikshank, "But what if one of your so-called harmless patients *did* get it into their twisted mind to climb that fence and head into town to do our children harm?"

Over an escalating buzz, Cruikshank rushed to say, "As an additional safeguard, a siren alerts the staff if one of the patients should attempt to leave the grounds, which I assure you, they have no desire to do. Any more than any of you would if you had a serious illness and were receiving excellent care."

Viv was still focused on the Jessop boys, so she hadn't heard what Cruikshank said, but Frankie and I gave each other knowing smiles because we knew of at least one patient who did want to escape the hospital and had. Mr. Ralph Greer pulled off a disappearing act that would've humbled Houdini and what a story that was.

"Tell me, Doctor, if, as you say, the patients don't wish to escape," Mulrooney spun around to face the crowd, "then how do you explain the ones we've found wandering our streets countless times?"

On account of Jimbo's stories and all the time the girls and I spent up at Broadhurst, we knew the patients who wandered around town sometimes were harmless, but Mulrooney's attempt to antagonize the less informed crowd had the desired effect. When a handful of men leapt to their feet, raised their fists, and yelled, "Yeah, yeah!" it reminded me of the scene in *Frankenstein* when the villagers came hunting for the monster with torches blazing and pitchforks waving.

As much as it must've irked him, the sheriff rose from his chair again and told the crowd to quiet down, but the psychiatrist didn't need his help. He was an old hand at dealing with the emotionally unstable.

"Those patients have not escaped the hospital grounds," Cruikshank reassured everyone. "They are cured individuals who are being reacclimatized to the outside world before their approaching release dates. And yes, a few of them have become overwhelmed by the unfamiliar sights and sounds of your fine town, but"—he looked over at the sheriff like he wanted him to pay special attention to what he was about to say—"there will be no more incidents of that sort. Our escorting staff has recently undergone advanced training and will deal more effectively with panicked patients in the future."

When the lights flickered again and couldn't seem to find the energy to restore themselves, Lance Howard announced to the room, "It's them fans. They're drainin' the power. Ya want, I can close 'em down."

Nobody, not even the farmers, the toughest among them, would remain in that room without ventilation, and when everyone began to gather their belongings, Dr. Cruikshank quickly wrapped up his presentation.

"Your commitment to your community's well-being is admirable," he said, "and should you think of any other questions, or if you'd like to pay a visit to the hospital to put your minds further at ease, please do not hesitate to contact Nurse Holloway." When he pivoted toward her, she nodded and left the stage. "She'll be happy to arrange a tour at your convenience."

For the first time that evening, he smiled, or at least I thought he did. It was hard to tell what was going on underneath the handlebar of hair above his lip, but he must've felt pleased with himself. Doc told Aunt Jane May that he'd received his degree in psychiatry from Harvard Medical School, one of the best in the country, so given the crowd's fear of mental illness, Cruikshank must've known that no one would take him up on his offer. Except for the girls and me. We would've begged, borrowed, and stolen to take one of those tours that might include a visit to the Chamber of Horrors.

"Again, thank you for attending and allowing me to address your concerns," the doctor said to the dispersing crowd. And then, like he was Pavlov rewarding dogs for good behavior, he added, "Please be sure to help yourselves to the complimentary refreshments Nurse Holloway has laid out near the doors."

Evelyn Mulrooney and her followers left the meeting in a huff, likely because it'd not gone anything like she'd envisioned. Her efforts to impress Uncle Walt and close the hospital down fell flat, and the townspeople had not lifted her onto their shoulders and paraded her around the hall calling for her to be our next mayor. But when Doctor Cruikshank strode off the stage, it was to a round of applause and our neighbors emptied out of the hall in a much livelier way than they'd entered it.

In fact, he'd done such a good job of assuring them that their fears about the Broadhurst patients were unfounded that after the good folks of Summit bid good night to one another and returned to their homes, they made their way out to their front porches and allowed the soothing sounds of a hot summer night and a bottle of cold beer further convince them that they were a lot safer than they were.

Chapter Eight

❧

That unforgettable summer wasn't the first one the girls and I had spent time at Broadhurst.

We'd started pedaling up there the year before, shortly after we'd seen *The Snake Pit* at the Rivoli. We didn't know it was about mental illness, of course. Hollywood was releasing movies left and right with insects and reptiles that'd been exposed to radioactivity, so the girls and I assumed it was about a gigantic snake squeezing the life out of Pittsburgh and Mr. Willis had just run out of room on the marquee.

When Frankie and Viv exited the theatre that afternoon, they were quaking in their boots, I mean, really shook up. Not me. *The Snake Pit* fueled my interest that had already been piqued by Jimbo's marvelous porch stories and I rushed straight home to page through Doc's medical books. Mental illness was covered, but only briefly and in terms I didn't understand, so that left only one other resource at the time—the Summit Library.

Unfortunately, the only relevant information I could find in the children's section was *The Tale of Samuel Whiskers*, in which Tom Kitten developed a paralyzing fear of rats, and I had to send Frankie and Viv over to distract Edith Dirks so I could sneak upstairs and search the adult section. Years later, I'd write stories about mental illness, but at the time, the mostly taboo subject was rarely tackled. I found a few novels, but I was a kid and wasn't allowed to check them out. Unless I stuffed *The Three Faces of Eve* or *Rebecca* down my shorts and ran out of the library—Viv's suggestion—I had to resort to camping out in the stacks to read them. All by my lonesome. It wasn't until I harped about being all for one and one for all for a couple of days that Frankie and Viv began to see things my way.

Sort of.

"I need to know more about the Broadhurst patients," I told them in the hideout after the Fourth of '59 fireworks show.

Viv, who'd hidden her face on Frankie's chest for most of *The Snake Pit*, predictably shuddered. "That movie scared me almost as much as *The Wizard of Oz* did. How come you wanna know more about somethin' awful like that?"

That was a $64,000 question I didn't have an answer to at the time, so I told her, "I don't know, but I really, really do. I've read all of Doc's books and the files of the patients he treats up there and everything I can get my hands on at the library, and I've asked Jimbo a million questions. The only way I can learn more is by seeing people act crazy with my own eyes. I wanna go up to the hospital and watch them after they get turned out in the recreation yard, and I wanna to do it tomorrow." I pointed to the "Keep Out" sign hanging by the door. "No ifs, ands, or buts."

Considering how poorly the two of them had reacted to *The Snake Pit* they were reluctant, to say the least, to spend time at Broadhurst, even if it didn't look anything like the Juniper State Hospital, the asylum in the movie. It looked like a beautiful mansion because that's what it was before beer baron Mr. Patrick Broadhurst had it converted into a mental institution in 1952 when his wife hung herself in a tree on the estate after their only child, a little girl by the name of Charlotte, died of measles.

On our ride over to the hospital the next day, Viv called me a dumb chump a record number of times and Frankie never told her to shut up, but what a turnaround they made when we stumbled upon a massive oak that sat on the edge of the fifteen-acre property outside of town. The surrounding woods were mostly high pine or scrub, but this tree was so tall and the spread of its boughs so lush that when the girls and I stood at its base and cranked our necks back it felt like we'd received an invitation to climb a stairway to heaven. As fanciful as we were, we had no problem convincing ourselves that the magnificent oak had to be the very tree Katherine Broadhurst had ended her life in, and from that afternoon on, Frankie and Viv got as big a thrill out of spending time in what we called the "Hanging Tree" as I did.

I'm ashamed now by our insensitivity and can only offer up the ignorance of the times, our youth, and our penchant for scary movies as excuses, but the girls and I would watch the patients during their time in the hospital's recreation yard with the same jaw-dropping looks we'd get on our faces during the Saturday afternoon creature features at the Rivoli.

I should've been pleased that I'd gotten what I wanted and I was at first, but after a few weeks, I found that observing the patients had left me wanting more. "Watching them from up here has been really interesting and I've learned a lot," I told the girls on our special branch in the Hanging Tree. "But it's sorta like . . . like eating candy with the wrapper on."

Viv whipped my way and said, "Are you razzin' me again?"

Frankie said, "She doesn't mean the time you and me were fightin' over that piece of butterscotch and you stuffed it in your mouth without taking the cellophane off, numnuts. She's saying that she wants to do more than just look at the patients. She wants to meet 'em and she's not kidding around. Look at her chin. See how it's juttin' out the same way Auntie's does when she digs in? We got to give her what she wants or she's gonna hang up the "Keep Out" sign."

Those were different days. Our churches weren't locked and rarely our homes. And other than a few pranks on All Hallows Eve and April Fool's Day—bags of dog poop set aflame on porches and shop windows soaped—vandalism was unheard of, and no one stole from another. There wasn't a "No Trespassing" sign posted on the Broadhurst property line, no guards walking the perimeter or barbed wire strung atop the wrought-iron fence, so there was really nothing stopping us.

"I don't wanna meet the patients," Viv whined. "I wanna go to Whitcomb's. Talkin' about candy made me want something sweet and I got to pee."

"Got any other news, Walter Cronkite?" Frankie said. "You always want something sweet and you always gotta pee and . . . hey, wait a minute." She grinned. "You're not chicken, are ya?" She stuck her fists in her armpits and flapped. *"Bawk, bawk, bawk."*

"Ha!" Viv fired back and got into position to jump off the branch.

I yanked her down and said, "Cool your jets."

"We can't just waltz up to the fence and start chatting with them," Frankie told Viv. "Remember how Jimbo told us that their families can't even visit or talk to them? We need to find a place where we won't be seen by someone from the hospital and get into trouble. Give me the binoculars, Biz."

After I handed them off, Frankie used them to inspect the perimeter of the property until she came to rest on the northern-most boundary of the recreation yard, where old growth pine trees loomed.

"That'd be a great spot," I said with a sigh, "but we'll never get through those scratchy boughs without bleeding to death."

"Might not be as bad as you think." Frankie passed back the binoculars, placed her hands on the side of my head and tilted me toward where she'd been looking. "See the cardinal in the tallest tree? About halfway up?"

I nodded, because I'd already noticed it. After I told Aunt Jane May that a cardinal had begun sharing the hideout with us every summer, she smiled and told me, "When red birds appear, angels are near," so I always kept my eye out for them.

"Good. Now move a whiff to the right," Frankie coached. "See the gap?"

Barely.

The girls and I were experts at wedging into tight spots, and the pines would offer good cover, but we couldn't tell from up in the Hanging Tree if the clearing would give us access to the patients.

"Let's check it out," Frankie said.

We took the path that ran along that perimeter of Broad-hurst until we reached the edge of the property that we'd not explored before. The smell was almost intoxicating and the trees created what looked like an invincible green wall. It was hard to get our bearings until I spotted the red bird we'd seen in the

Hanging Tree still perched in a pine. It looked like it was book-marking the spot, so I thought we might be getting a thumbs-up from on high, maybe even from my mother.

After the girls and I scrabbled around the buckthorn, we made our way through the scratchy pine branches with minimal damage, and slipped into the gap Frankie and I had spotted through the binoculars. We ended up in a circular patch of dirt with a sawed-off stump in the middle that made me wonder if the tree had been cut down on a long-ago Christmas Eve before Mrs. Broadhurst had killed herself.

Not much of the wrought-iron fence was exposed—say, a few yards—but Frankie nodded in approval and said, "Good enough. Now all we got to do is get Jimbo's and Albie's permission."

Viv, who'd been reluctant to visit with the patients and was complaining about a couple of bloody scratches on her arms, suddenly perked up. "Pie and a pee? Count me in! Last one to Earl's eats a bowl of grits!"

* * *

Mud Towners weren't forbidden to eat in Summit proper, but they weren't welcomed with a smile either, so between the hours of 6 AM and 2 PM Earl Spooner served breakfast and lunch at his club. You could order eggs done any way you wanted, and there was an array of sandwiches to choose from that outshone anything they served at Chuck's Café on Main. Sweet apple barbecued pork piled high on a hard roll with a scoop of potato salad on the side, a sweet pickle, and a slice of baked-that-morning fruit pie with a scoop of vanilla custard was my go-to favorite.

Few with skin the color of ours felt comfortable frequenting Earl's place—aside from Aunt Jane May, who loved the home-style food, and Doc, after he made a house call. The sheriff would stop by, too, and our mayor could often be found enjoying a ham hock—so the girls and I stood out when we came through the screen door that afternoon, but did not feel unwelcome.

The same customers we'd watch sway to live music in the wee hours were hunkered down in booths with their lunches, listening to bluesy, juke-box tunes. Day or night, didn't matter, the place was always packed, but we had no problem spotting Jimbo. It would've been like overlooking Mount Kilimanjaro. He took most of his meals at Earl's because not only did the club have the best food in all of Summit, he'd get a discount for the evenings he'd be called on to use his orderly skills. "Liquor and trouble are married to each other 'til death do them part," he would say about the belligerent customers who didn't know when to call it quits.

Jimbo's coworker at Broadhurst, Albie Johnson, was sitting next to him in the booth enjoying his lunch at a reduced rate, too, because his girlfriend, Bigger Dolores—there was another Dolores who worked as a cigarette girl at night and was as tiny as the outfit she wore—was Earl Spooner's sister.

Both men were in their early thirties, had full faces, and deep brown eyes, but that's as far as the resemblance went. Jimbo's hair was close cropped and springy, and he smelled like grass clippings. Albie kept his hair smoothed into a flashy style Dell called a "conk," and he smelled of something cheap and store bought. Hardworking Jimbo was well read and a rickety bookcase in his living room was stocked with the classics. Albie, on the other hand, found applying himself to anything other than gambling and alcohol was more trouble than it was worth and his lips moved when he'd read the *Superman* comic book he always had sticking out of his back pocket. But what Albie lacked in initiative and intelligence, he made up for in style. He had this loose, lackadaisical way about him, walked to a beat only he heard, wore what he called "high-tone" city clothes and, Lord, was he ever vain. Never met anybody who liked that man half as much as he liked himself—except for Bigger Dolores, and the girls and I were doing all we could to remedy that situation. We knew Jimbo was carrying a torch for her because he'd break into a sweat and get a shy smile on his face whenever her name came up. So whenever we snuck into the Broadhurst kitchen to help Bigger out, we'd remind her that Albie walked on the wild side so he probably wasn't long for this world, and then we'd brag on Jimbo.

After we said our hellos to the patrons we'd known all our lives, Viv ran to the "Dolls" bathroom to empty what Aunt Jane May called her "thimble" bladder, and Frankie and I made our way to the back booth. When we sat across from Jimbo, he gave us a broad smile. Albie was less thrilled, but not rude. We talked about Dell and Aunt Jane May and how the heat was killing the crops and other town news, until Viv joined us and ordered a bowl of grits for me and a piece of pie for herself from a cute waitress named Hazel.

The stakes were high that afternoon, but I wasn't nervous when I explained to the two orderlies what we were hoping to do at Broadhurst. I saw seeking their permission to spend time with the patients in the recreation yard as a formality, really, just plain good manners. Maybe Albie wouldn't be as quick to jump on the bandwagon as I hoped, because I suspected that he knew the girls and I weren't members of his fan club, but he knew we'd complain to Bigger Dolores if he gave us any grief. Not once did it cross my mind that when I finished my pitch that it'd be Jimbo who'd crinkle his forehead and say, "Don't know 'bout that, Bizzy."

"But—"

"The woods belong to the town, so you girls been all right in that tree watchin', but ya get right up close to the fence, you'd be trespassin' on private property," Jimbo explained.

"Not sure what Cruikshank would do if ya got caught," Albie threw in, "but if he didn't call the sheriff, that bitch Holloway sure would."

"He's right, honey," Jimbo said softly to me. "I don't gotta tell you how your family'd feel about you breakin' the law. Same goes for you, Viv." When he turned to Frankie, there was such love and concern in his eyes. "And you know how Dell frets, baby."

The only Buchanan who was supposed to be familiar with the insides of a police station was Uncle Walt. If the girls and I got caught trespassing, that'd be big news in Summit. My family would be horrified, and Viv's parents, who owned both Cleary's Funeral Home and House of Beauty, relied on good word of mouth to keep their businesses afloat. But Dell would be the hardest hit. "You girls got to be more careful," she'd caution us after we'd gotten ourselves into a scrape. "There's folks in this town who're still suspicious that Frankie showed up out of nowhere with skin darker than their own. You get them talking, there's no knowin' where it'll lead."

By "them," Dell meant the small group of Germans who were very proud of their "Motherland." While they weren't the only prejudiced families in town, they were the most vocal and dedicated to keeping Summit white on our side of the tracks. Every so often, they'd still give the evil eye to the Maniachis and Frankie after Mass on Sunday, probably questioning whether all three of them were "*Schwarze.*" And we heard Dell tell Aunt Jane May during one of their back porch meetings that Mrs. Schmidt, who owned the bakery, called her a "jigaboo" and wouldn't sell her a coffee cake with streusel topping. And none of those Germans hired day workers from Mud Town to wash their cars or mow their lawns.

So Jimbo had a right to be concerned, but I couldn't recall him ever refusing a request we'd made, and I couldn't believe he'd chosen to nix this one. Not everyone who worked at Broadhurst cared about the patients, but he treated them with TLC. He thought it was wrong that they weren't allowed to talk on the telephone, even to their families. And he didn't like that when loved ones wanted to pay a visit that it had to be scheduled a month in advance, and how when the day drew near, someone from the hospital would inevitably cancel the get-together for the "good of the patient."

"But," I told Jimbo, "you tell us all the time how you think they'd get better faster if they had more contact with regular people."

It seemed to take him forever to weigh the pros and cons of my request before he reached down to his lap, plucked up the white napkin, and waved it in mock surrender.

"All right, all right," he said. "I can see how important this is to you, and I do believe it'd be good for the patients to spend time with the three of ya." He tilted his head toward Albie. "But it needs to be fine with him, too."

Far as I could tell, Albie didn't care about much of anything except for how he looked, *Superman* comic books, throwing dice in the back room of Chummy Adler's bar, Jack Daniels, the fancy Chrysler he'd been driving around, and staying on Bigger Dolores's good side, so he responded about the way I thought he would.

"Bigger is fond of you and she'd like it if I helped you girls out," he said, like she might give him some kind of reward. "But you gotta agree to a few rules first." He took his sweet time sucking the last of the meat off a rib bone, and carefully placed it on top of the pile on his plate like he was putting the finishing touches on a sculpture. "When you're talkin' with the patients, you can't say nothin' about their conditions, and whatever you do don't touch 'em. That can set some of them off real bad and I don't wanna have to use the siren."

Housed in a gunmetal-gray box next to the front door of the hospital, the siren made this unearthly screeching noise to let everyone on the grounds know that things had gotten to the point-of-no-return in the recreation yard and reinforcements were needed ASAP.

"Cruikshank got real mad the last time I pulled it and if I gotta haul my hind end up to his office and tell him I lost control of the yard again, he could call me a derelict of duty and fire me," Albie added. I couldn't tell if he said that to make sure we followed his rules or whether he wanted us to know that he was putting his job on the line for us and we owed him one, but I suspected it was the latter. "You also got to be real careful about gettin' seen 'cause there's eyes everywhere."

That shot a shiver through me because it reminded me of this movie the girls and I had seen called *The Crawling Eye*—if you think it'd be easy to outrun a slow-moving but deadly eyeball, boy, would you be wrong. "Uh . . . what kind of eyes do you mean exactly?" I asked him.

When Albie drew closer, his breath smelled so warm and saucy it made my eyes water.

"Bigger and me, we used to like to meet up in the kitchen cooler durin' lunchtime. We was real careful," he said, "but somehow Holloway found out were in there ballin'. Jimbo don't agree with me, but I think Cruikshank might got cameras hidden all over the hospital and grounds so he can keep his eye on us. You don't want no picture of the three of ya sneakin' 'round the property," Albie said.

He was just trying to scare us into being more careful when we were visiting with the patients so his rear end wouldn't end up in a sling, and it wasn't even a very good lie. Telling us that he and Bigger were "ballin'" in the kitchen cooler was too ridiculous to believe. Hanging out close to the food and refrigerated air seemed right, but no way would those two play catch in there. Neither one of them were at all athletically inclined.

"And the most important rule of all is, if ya get caught, ya gotta take your licks," Albie said. "You can't tell *nobody* that Jimbo and me told ya you could visit with them." He sucked the spicy, peach barbecue sauce off his fingers, then slid one of Earl Spooner's bumpy red menus out from behind the napkin holder. "Set your right hands down and swear, or no deal."

Albie spent a lot more time eating than praying, so the menu was his version of the Bible, I guessed, and I did what he asked and so did Frankie, but I had to elbow Viv and say, "Swear."

"Nobody's better at sneakin' around than us," she said with a mouthful of pie. "And we found that good hiding spot in the trees and—"

"What d'ya mean *we?*" Frankie said.

When Viv grinned, we could see the cherries stuck between her teeth. "Why jinx it with a swear? We won't get caught."

Jimbo reached across the table, plucked the fork from Viv's fingers, and cradled her pale white hands in his dark ones. "Don't be so sure 'bout that, baby."

After Albie washed down his last rib with what looked like whiskey, he peeked over his shoulder to make sure everybody in the club was more interested in their lunches than what he had to say. "There's mysterious goin's on at the hospital. Private things they don't want nobody knowin' about."

"Private things" was what the girls and I called whatever it was that was going on between our legs, so Viv thought he was going to say something naughty, and she slapped her hand down on the menu and was almost drooling when she asked, "What kind of mysterious and private things?"

"Patients get transferred, files go missin', there's that locked room in the basement, and I seen lights in the woods when I pull the night shift," Albie said.

Seemed like there were an awful lot of reasons for us not to visit the patients, so my heart and mind were in a tug a war. When I'd first got the idea, I hadn't thought it through any more than any other kid my age who got enthused about an exciting new adventure would. Getting confronted that afternoon in the back booth of Earl's with how my desire to speak with the patients might expose Frankie's secret, get Jimbo or Albie in trouble, or embarrass our families was a real slap in the face.

Because I couldn't make up my mind whether we should just forget the whole thing or go full steam ahead, I decided that what we'd do would depend on the answer to my next question. One I wasn't sure at all I wanted to hear the answer to.

"I don't think anybody from the hospital will catch us 'cause Viv's right. We're really good at sneakin' around and we'll keep our eyes out for those hidden cameras," I told Albie, to placate him. "But what if one of the patients reported us to the higher-ups?"

Albie grinned and said, "Don't got to worry 'bout them none, sugar. Nobody believes a word they say." He drained another shot of whiskey. "They's always conversatin' with outer-space people or saints, or tellin' ya that they're the king of England or Marie Annette. Like that new fella they just locked up on the third floor." He nudged Jimbo. "His chart says he's John Johnson, but what's he call himself?"

"Leo," Jimbo said.

"Yeah, that's right." Albie reached back and removed from his pants pocket the newest *Superman* comic the girls and I had picked up for him at Whitcomb's. They had a spinning red rack of them over there and once a week he'd give us a dime and tell us to fetch one for him. "Mitch, the orderly on the third floor, he told me this Leo goes on and on about bein' a newspaper reporter, and he offered him cash money if he'd call his boss." He tapped his manicured finger on the cover of the comic book. "He's actin' like he's Clark Kent from the *Daily Planet* tryin' to get in touch with Perry White." He'd gotten tipsy from the whiskey and he belly-laughed loud enough to draw attention. "Tell ya what. You girls keep bringin' me my Man of Steel books, remember the rules ya just swore to, tell Bigger every so often what a catch I am, and everything should be just dandy."

And, you know, from his mouth to God's ear—it was. Getting to know the patients from the spot behind the fence that summer turned out to be more than even I could have hoped for, and I looked forward to doing so for many more summers to come. But then Viv had to go and ruin it all a year later when she did something reckless that'd end up almost costing us our lives.

Chapter Nine

During the last weeks of June, when Aunt Jane May wasn't lecturing us about staying on the straight and narrow or keeping us busy with enough chores that might ensure that we did, the girls and I traded gossip at Whitcomb's Drugstore, did swan dives off the high board at the community pool, and worked on ticking adventures off our list.

Summer 1960

1. *Visit Broadhurst and try to sneak into the Chamber of Horrors.*
2. *Scary movies on Saturday and a romantic one if Viv won't shut up.*
3. *Are Aunt Jane May and Uncle Walt in love?*
4. *Stop Mulrooney.*
5. *Fourth of July*
6. *The County Fair and Carnival.*
7. *Watch out for Dutch Van Heusen and Elvin Merchant, who are hell-bent for leather.*

I had to add number 7 to the list after juvenile delinquent Herman "Dutch" Van Heusen cruised past the girls and me when we were on our way to the library to pick up the newest Nancy Drew.

He yelled from his Chevy car, "I'm gonna getcha for what ya did to me, ya little shits," which was a shocker, honestly. I thought he'd forgotten about how we almost drowned him.

I added the leader of those JDs—Elvin Merchant—to the list, too, after we spent some time at the drug store's fountain counter the next afternoon. Frankie, Viv, and I already knew that besides working at the family service station, he'd gotten a job collecting money for Chummy Adler. Merchant was warning folks in Mud Town, like Albie, that if they didn't pay their gambling debts, he'd make them pay with broken arms and teeth. But what we found out about him that day at Whitcomb's was even worse. All the kids were talking about the awful thing Merchant had done to Cindy Davenport, which *wasn't* that much of a shocker, honestly. He had always been the worst of the bunch. The kind of boy you just knew folks would read about in their newspapers someday and say about whatever atrocity he'd committed, "Anyone with half a brain could see that coming from a mile off."

The girls and I had been giving most of our attention to number one on the list, but we'd not had a chance to sneak down to the secret room in the basement yet, and we never went up to Broadhurst on Saturdays. That was the day we worked on number two.

We hardly ever argued about what movies we'd see, but in keeping with Viv's newfound fixation on romance, Frankie and I had to appeal to her sweet tooth to see things our way. We told her that if she'd quit barraging us with dumb ideas about how we could sneak into the Starlight Drive-In to see a *Summer*

Place, we'd buy her whatever candy she wanted when we went to see the new horror movies at the Rivoli. She eventually gave in, but that turned out so bad that I wished she'd stood her ground.

The three of us and the other kids in town got a big kick out of *The Amazing Colossal Man*, but Viv, who was growing more boy-crazy and impetuous by the day and was somewhat ticked off that she'd miss seeing that movie with Troy Donahue and Sandra Dee, did something we'd lived to regret during *The Incredible Shrinking Man*. She leaned over her seat and planted a juicy kiss on Norman Wilkes's neck. Girls weren't supposed to do those sorts of things and Viv could have earned a bad (worse) reputation overnight. The way "Easy Mimi" Kincaid had after a few of the boys let it be known that she was willing to satisfy their curiosity. Some of the girls now said, "P.U." and held their noses when they walked past Mimi and called her mean names. She was a sweet kid who just couldn't say no and was crushed when she was shunned and insulted, but if those snots tried something like that with Viv, she wouldn't have taken it lying down.

Because Frankie and I didn't want to spend the rest of our vacation burying the bodies our little hellion would leave in her vengeful rampage, I ran out to the concession stand and bought three Sugar Daddys to make Norman forget the kiss that Viv had laid on him. But Frankie, who'd learned how effective strong-arming could be from watching Jimbo at Earl's Supper Club, shoved her fist into his face and hissed, "You tell anybody Viv slobbered on ya, I'm gonna punch you in your Adam's apple so hard that your puny voice will go even higher . . . *Norma*." The poor boy was already getting teased for having to sing with the girls in choir, so he readily agreed to keep his mouth shut.

But the rest of the kids in the balcony that afternoon didn't, and in a matter of days, everyone started calling him "Norma." He vowed revenge against us, of course, but we weren't losing any sleep over it. He was small potatoes compared to Dutch Van Heusen and Elvin Merchant, and the other big problem we'd suddenly come face-to-face with.

The girls and I had been so busy we hadn't noticed that June had turned to July and number five on our list snuck up on us.

I'd like to blame our lack of preparation for the big day on all the chatter floating around town about how that year's Fourth of July festivities might get canceled for the first time in history on account of the heat wave, but the girls and I knew that was just folks blowing off steam. Only those on their deathbeds, the perpetually overdressed Montgomery sisters, and anyone willing to be mocked for months for being "city soft" would've skipped the town's annual patriotic merrymaking. And now, it looked like the girls and I would be sitting on the sidelines, too, if we didn't immediately get on the stick.

Aunt Jane knew we'd usually count down the days to the early morning parade down Main Street, and the races, games, picnic, and fireworks that'd be held at Grand Park afterward, but it was a few days before the big shindig, and she hadn't said a word to us. That was *very* unlike her, which is why I asked the girls that night in the hideout, "Don't you think it's kinda weird that she hasn't asked to inspect our bikes the way she always does?"

"It's 'cause she's on cloud nine, which, for your information, is something else that happens when you're trotting hotly," Viv told us as she paged through a *Photoplay* magazine on her sleeping mat.

Frankie and I were playing go fish, and the cards in my hand started quivering when I said, "We're gonna be in such deep doo-doo when she sees we haven't a lifted a finger. She'll know that we've been up to no good."

Viv said with a laugh, "Don't sweat it. I'll come up with some baloney to tell her."

In the middle of rearranging her cards, Frankie jerked her head up and said, "Did you hear that? That squeak? I think she's on the move."

Aunt Jane May looked forward to squirming out of her girdle and letting her hair down after she put the house to bed for the night, and would only leave the premises if she was called on to assist Doc with a medical emergency or if a member of our parish needed hand-holding.

If the girls and I were in the hideout and not out gallivanting, we'd know when she'd been called to help someone in need if we heard the telephone ringing, the kitchen screen door slamming shut a few minutes later, and her hollering up at us, "Don't get any bright ideas."

So when Frankie heard that squeak from the screen door, without any of the other rigmarole that'd let us know she was on one of her missions of mercy, we got suspicious and peeked out the hideout door to see what was what.

The globe light above the screen door hadn't been turned on, the way it usually was, and it was a moonless night, so it was hard to tell who was back there. I thought it might've been Doc coming home from the office until our aunt's velvety bass reached our ears. Only she wasn't warbling one of her favorite hymns or "I'm Gonna Wash That Man Right Outa My Hair" or "Que Sera, Sera." This tune sounded familiar, but the way she was humming it so low down with a lot of bluesy rhythm, I couldn't place it. But I had no problem figuring out what the *tap tap* noise she was making was. She was walking down the cobblestone driveway in high-heeled shoes. With cleats.

"Told ya so!" Viv crowed. "I bet she's got on black stockings with seams and a dress tight enough to show off her bosom, probably red, because that's Uncle Walt's favorite color. I bet she's meetin' him at Earl Spooner's Club." She jammed her feet back into her sneakers and grabbed the binoculars off the brass hook before she noticed that Frankie and I hadn't made a move to toss our cards down and join her. "Get the lead out! You told me that if I got some proof that we'd spy on her and she's gettin' away!"

Every night that week we'd ridden over to Jimbo's to hear a story about the Broadhurst patients or play ghost in the graveyard with our friends at Mud Town Cemetery. Afterward, we'd cooled down with slices of chiffon pie on the back porch of Earl's and watched the dancers. So far, nobody had reported seeing us to Aunt Jane May and I didn't want to push our luck. But that wasn't the only reason I told Viv, "I don't want to go over the tracks tonight. I want to play cards."

Viv looked at me like I was a cat box overdue for a cleaning, then nudged Frankie with the toe of her red high-top. "But you're comin', right?"

Normally, Frankie would jump at the chance to spend time alone with Viv, but she said, "Got a blister on my heel. Go fish, Biz."

Once Viv got a plan set in her mind, she hated for it to go off the rails, and after she called us every name in the book, she hollered, "Who needs ya? I'll go after her alone."

Pretty sure she wouldn't, not after hearing the recent reports circulating around the drugstore about the Summit Witch doing her best hunting at night, I shrugged and said, "Suit yourself."

Frankie called her bluff, too. "Don't wake us up when you get back. Any jokers, Biz?"

"You . . . you . . ."—Viv ripped off her high tops and threw them at us—"stinkin' party poopers! I'll get you for this."

That threat would usually spur me into action, but her fury couldn't trump my fear that night. I was too scared to follow Aunt Jane May because what if Viv was right and she *was* meeting up with Uncle Walt at Earl's? If they got spotted wiggling their hips on that dance floor, you best believe that'd get back to Evelyn Mulrooney—her spies were legion. She'd shout all over town about their romance in the most derogatory terms possible, which would be awful, of course, but God only knew what Viv would do to shut that so-and-so down.

I wouldn't feel right describing her as a child completely devoid of conscience, but Viv was impressed rather than appalled by the child psychopath in *The Bad Seed*. I didn't think she'd go as far as trying to drown the Ladies Auxiliary president in Grand Creek or lock her up in the furnace room of the church and set it on fire—little Rhonda Penmark had done versions of both to her enemies—but our girl *was* capable of executing a payback so twisted and heinous that, if caught, she could find herself cooling her heels in the juvenile hall in Port Washington. Frankie and I couldn't let that happen. We couldn't take being apart from one another again. After Aunt Jane May inflicted on us the "severe consequence" of a two-week separation after we'd almost drowned Dutch Van Heusen, the Tree Musketeers swore up and down that we'd run away if she ever tried to pull that on us again.

I yanked Viv down next to me and warned, "You can't tell her what we saw tonight. That could open a huge can of worms."

"Sure, I'll keep my mouth shut," Viv said with a slick grin, "but only if you come spy on her with me."

Frankie lost her cool then and hollered, "Kissin' Norman Wilkes was disgustin', and so is the way ya look at the Jessop boys, and you won't shut up about Uncle Walt and Auntie. I'm so sick of you and your romances I could puke. "

Viv screamed back, "And I'm so sick of—

"Quit it," I hollered. "Do a shoot-out. If you win, Viv, we'll do what you want, but if Frankie wins, you got to swear to stop talkin' about romance for a while, and that includes saying anything to Aunt Jane May about what we saw tonight."

"Fine," the both of them shouted two inches from my face. "Rock, paper, scissors . . . shoot!"

Thank God Viv continued her losing streak.

* * *

The morning after our blowup in the hideout, Viv told us the plan she'd come up with to keep our lack of preparation for the Fourth of July from Aunt Jane May. She peeked out from behind the tree we were hiding behind and said, "She's in the garden, and our bikes are leanin' against the garage, so we'll sneak behind her and ride over to the dime store for supplies. She won't suspect a thing."

We slipped over to our Schwinns all right, and we thought she was too intent on harvesting vegetables to notice us as we wheeled them behind her, but just as we were about to make a clean getaway, she looked over her shoulder and said, "Hold up." She slipped off her gardening gloves and gave us the c'mere finger. "If y'all are intending to ride in the parade on Saturday and win the tickets to the movie theatre the Auxiliary is going to award the winner," she said, pointing to our metal steeds, "you are ill-prepared. Come to think of it, I haven't seen you out here practicing for those egg-and-spoon and sack races like you do every year neither." She withdrew one of her big lace hankies from her red clutch purse and dabbed the sheen off her upper lip. "And ya know what that tends to make me think, girls?"

Viv thought she could charm her out of her surliness by responding like one of our aunt's beloved Shakespeare characters, "Pray tell-eth, what are you forsooth-ing to think?"

"What I'm thinking Vivian Edna, is that the three of you haven't prepared for the big day yet," she replied, not charmed at all, "because you've been too busy doin' things you're not supposed to be doin'."

Viv swore she wouldn't say anything to her about sneaking out of the house the previous evening, but when she grinned, I was sure she was about to throw that remark back in Aunt Jane May's face. Say something like *It takes one to know one* or maybe *The cat's outta the bag-eth!*

Fearing the same, the brains of our operation took charge of the conversation. "We haven't decorated our bikes or practiced for the races yet because we heard they were getting canceled on account of the heat," Frankie lied to Aunt Jane May.

"But we found out last night during kick the can that wasn't true and we're on our way to the five-and-dime to get crepe paper and Kleenex," I said. "When it cools off later, we're gonna give our full attention to—"

"Decoratin' our bikes and making those beautiful tissue flowers you and your sister used to make and—hey!" Viv smacked her forehead like she'd just had the best idea of all time and she needed it to stay put. "You want us to pick anything up for you while we're at the dime store? Since it's a holiday, maybe you'd like to wear different nylons tomorrow?" The gleam in her eye was almost blinding. "A darker shade. With seams?"

I had to work to suppress a moan and Frankie did, too.

"Why, that's a real considerate offer, but I like the nylons I got just fine and . . . oh Lord." Aunt Jane May struck her forehead the same way Viv had. "Did I forget to mention that I ran into Miss Lang this mornin'? She had something very interesting to tell me about you girls."

I felt my heart slip down to my socks at the mention of the vice president of the Ladies Auxiliary, who prided herself on having her finger in every pie in town. Besides doling out character assassinations on gals—mostly Lutherans and their new target, Audrey Cavanaugh, who'd still not answered any of their invitations to tea—she and those other prim and propers got a big charge out of wagging their tongues about the misadventures of children at their daily coffee klatches. Since Ruthie Lang liked to call the girls and me the "Unholy Trinity," I was pretty sure that whatever "interesting" something she'd shared with Aunt Jane May wouldn't include us receiving gold stars for good behavior.

Frankie must've been feeling as wary as I was, because the Roman numeral II had sprung up between her eyes, but Viv was bursting with false pride. She blew on her fingernails, ran them up and down her blouse in that "I'm a big shot" gesture, and said, "I bet when you ran into Ruthie, she told you what a good job we did helpin' out at the paper drive last week."

"You would've lost that bet." Aunt Jane May picked up the pile of radishes laying in front of her and yanked the green tops off. "What *Miss* Lang told me was that she saw you three ridin' your bikes on the county road that runs past Broadhurst yesterday afternoon, when you told me you were at the park."

I was desperate to tell her that we were on the county road for some other reason, but there was nothing else out that way except for the Withers' farm and she wouldn't believe we'd been overtaken by a sudden urge to milk a cow or collect eggs. For a child who put so much stock in hope, I don't know why I tended to slide into despair like it was a pair of worn slippers. Maybe it was because I could always count on Viv never going down without a fight.

"She told you she saw us on the county road yesterday?" she asked Aunt Jane May.

"That's what she said."

"Oh my goodness, that's too bad," Viv said in her most consternated voice. "Next time you see *Miss* Lang, you got to tell her to pay a visit to Doc's office as fast as her shoes can take her."

"And why's that?" Aunt Jane May asked.

"'Cause the poor thing needs her eyes examined for Cadillacs," Viv said. "We weren't anywhere near the county road yesterday, were we, girls."

"No, ma'am, we weren't," Frankie said, and I felt so relieved to say, "Cross my heart and hope to die," and mean it for once. That busybody must've gotten her days mixed up because we'd taken an entirely different route to the mental institution yesterday afternoon.

Aunt Jane May said, "They're called *cataracts*, not *Cadillacs*, Vivian, and I'll be happy to pass that news on to Miss Lang 'cause I go to sleep every single night knowin' the three of you wouldn't dare lie to me." She shook the dirt off her garden gloves and repeated her daily litany. "Keep away from Broadhurst, mind your own businesses, don't visit Mud Town after dark, and"—she paused—"remember what the sheriff told you about keepin' away from the Merchant boy."

She looked like she wanted to say more, but she settled on giving us a worried look and went back to ripping carrots out of the ground like Satan had a hold of the roots and they were engaged in a tug of war for our eternal souls and she was on the losing side.

Chapter Ten

After the three of us swooped onto Honeywell Street, Viv, who never missed watching the boxing matches with Aunt Jane May and Uncle Walt on Friday nights, rang her bike bell, threw her hands into the air, and announced, "The final round goes to the Unholy Trinity!"

Unlike her, I took no pride in sparring with Aunt Jane May. I was wracked with guilt for lying and disobeying her, so as children often do, I came up with an explanation for my deceptiveness that laid the blame elsewhere.

The pull I felt to Broadhurst was so powerful—almost irresistible—and my impressionable mind was so crammed with the Bible stories and legends of saints the nuns and priests taught us at St. Thom's that it was a short leap to hold the Almighty responsible for my disobedience and deceit. It wasn't *my* fault He insisted that good Catholics were supposed to visit the sick, and the Broadhurst patients certainly were. And it wasn't like it was the first time He had chosen someone our age to carry out His will. Take Joan of Arc. I bet she had to tell those she loved a pack of lies and sneak around her small town so she could do what God commanded her to do, too. And since His will overrode all others, including our aunt's, unless the girls and I were willing to spend all eternity in the hellfire for disobeying a direct order from Him, what choice did we have?

When I shared that epiphany with the girls after we rounded the turn on Franklin Street, I thought they'd be impressed as all get out and feel like little saints, too. But Frankie looked at me like I was two beads short of a rosary, and Viv laughed so hard she almost fell off her bike before she said, "You're gonna have to come up with something better than blamin' God for lyin' to Auntie. That sounds a lot like what Wally Hopper told the cops about the Archangel Michael forcing him to strangle the Gimble sisters."

I consoled myself by thinking that at least we hadn't lied to Aunt Jane May about what we were doing *that* afternoon. Frankie had told her we were on our way to pick up supplies to decorate our bikes for the Fourth of July parade, and we were. We just had something else to do first. Red, white, and blue crepe paper spinning around in our spokes and those pretty Kleenex flowers bobbing around on our handlebars would've drawn entirely too much attention on our ride over to Broadhurst.

After the girls and I reached Main Street dressed to its teeth in American flags that hung listlessly from lamp poles above baskets of wilted red, white, and blue carnations, instead of heading straight toward the road that led out of town, Frankie made an abrupt unscheduled stop in front of Whitcomb's Drugstore.

Peering longingly and lovingly into the plate glass window at the packed fountain counter, she announced, "Change of plans." She reluctantly pulled herself away and swung her leg back over her bike seat. "We can watch the patients today for a little while, but instead of visitin' with them, we're gonna come back here so I can get a brown cow, and then we'll head to the five-and-dime to get our decorating supplies."

I wasn't happy about that change in our plans because I wanted to discuss something important with two of my favorite Broadhurst patients that afternoon. But woe be to anyone stupid enough to stand in Frankie's way when she got a hankering for her all-time favorite treat, and it *was* blistering hot and the air felt thick enough to eat with a spoon. Pressing our sweaty cheeks against that cool, yellow Formica counter and watching an army of goose bumps rise on our arms in the newly air-conditioned drugstore as I dug into one of their excellent hot fudge sundaes sounded almost as good as talking to the patients.

For once, Viv was on board with one of Frankie's ideas because it was a two-fer deal for her. She could dig into a banana split, and she'd have the opportunity to get caught up on the latest gossip. If we could find empty twirl seats when we returned from what Frankie decided would be a shorter than usual visit to Broadhurst, the girls and I were bound to get an earful.

The latest sightings and newest embellishments of Audrey Cavanaugh attempting to nab kids in Founder's Woods so she could throw them into her cauldron—always bubbling—would be a hot topic. There'd also be much bragging about vacation exploits, a sort of can-you-top-that? roundtable. When it was our turn, the girls and I would mumble something about catching bloodsuckers at the creek and seeing *I Was a Teenage Were-wolf* at the Rivoli, because we couldn't share how we were spending most of our days and nights. Letting them know about our visits to the mental hospital and Mud Town, and how we were keeping an eye on Aunt Jane May and Uncle Walt and

Evelyn Mulrooney, wasn't a good idea because some of those kids had inherited blabbermouthism from their mothers.

With our new plan for the day set in motion, we rounded the corner of Main and Hadley Streets at top speed, but then Frankie made another out-of-the-blue decision. She slowed down and called over her shoulder to Viv and me, "We better take the shortcut again. Ruthie Lang could still be watching the county road."

True, but taking the shortcut to Broadhurst was not without risk either. The dirt path we'd pick up at the park petered out on the hospital grounds, but we'd have to make it through Founder's Woods first without getting ambushed by that group of teenage bullies who acted like they owned the place.

If they caught us, they might shove us around, give us Indian burns on our wrists, and make us empty our pockets, but they wouldn't do any permanent damage. In a few years, those boys would trade their ducktails in for crew cuts and, same way their fathers had, they'd marry their high school sweethearts in blue suits instead of blue jeans. They'd work the family fields or sell life insurance, get their babies baptized at St. Thomas's, and chuckle about their wayward adolescences over beers at Top's Bar on Saturday nights. All those boys except for one of them, that is. And as we drew closer to the shortcut through the woods that afternoon, I found myself doing what Aunt Jane May had told us to do before we'd left the house that day—"Remember what the sheriff told you about keepin' away from the Merchant boy."

When a tease of an easterly breeze had come up off Lake Michigan a few nights ago, Frankie, Viv, and I were sitting on the front porch of the house trying to catch our fair share of it, when the sheriff's squad car pulled up the driveway. There wasn't much crime in Summit other than occasional drunk-driving or traffic violations, so he'd often stop by when he was on patrol in the evenings to have a slice of warm pie and a glass of cold milk with Aunt Jane May.

Over the years, the girls and I had amassed a treasure trove of talents—lip reading, burping the alphabet, secret hand signals, and producing flatulence under our arms—but above all, we prided ourselves on our ability to pay close attention to details, so we knew right off that the sheriff had not stopped by for a social visit that night. When he came across the lawn toward us, he didn't look like the cock of the walk the way he usually did, and when he set his foot on the bottom step of the porch, he didn't show off his dimples or pull a quarter out from behind one of our ears.

As serious as I'd ever seen him, he said, "Girls, I have something important to talk to you about." He was fidgety and sounded so uncharacteristically ill at ease that I knew at once why he'd come. To put him out of his misery, I almost told him that we'd already heard how Elvin Merchant had attacked Cindy Davenport at the Starlight Drive-In. That he'd ripped her blouse off, pawed at her chest, and thrust his hands up her pleated skirt. When she fought him off, he pushed her out the door of his souped-up hot rod, took off, and left her crying hysterically in the dust.

Mr. Hawthorne, the owner of the Starlight, called the sheriff. When Uncle Walt showed up, he calmed Cindy down and offered to call her parents, but Dr. and Mrs. Davenport were in Chicago at a dental convention, so he ended up taking her home. Because it was late, he told her to get some sleep and come to the station house in the morning so he could take her statement.

She showed up bright and early and sat on the edge of the wooden chair across from the sheriff's desk. Told him she was sorry for wasting his time, but after she thought about it, she realized she'd made too big a deal of what'd happened up at the drive-in. "It was all just a silly misunderstanding," Cindy said with a smile. "High jinks! *Hardy-har-har*."

The sheriff didn't believe her, of course, but he had no choice but to accept her story. Seemed like everyone in town wanted to chalk up the incident to "boys bein' boys," but there were some rumors, of course, about what Elvin Merchant had done to ensure that Cindy would keep her mouth shut.

Supposedly, he'd knocked on the Davenports' front door soon after the sheriff had dropped her off, and Cindy, who thought Elvin had come by to say he was sorry for the way he'd treated her at the drive-in, welcomed him with open arms. And when that handsome boy smiled and told her so sweetly, "I got a little something for you, honey," she thought he was holding apology flowers behind his back, but it was his switch-blade and her pet tabby cat. "Real bad things can happen to pussies that don't keep their mouths shut," Merchant said when he brought the knife up to Queenie's furry throat, which was so god-awful that when we found out later that summer that the rumor was true, nobody could blame the girl for not pressing charges at the time.

Uncle Walt thought we were too young and naive to go into any of the particulars of that incident when he came to talk to us that night, so he kept it simple. He fingered the silver star pinned to his tan shirt pocket—what he did when he wanted to remind us he was speaking to us as the sheriff, not our uncle—and said in his lawman's voice, "The Merchant boy is a rotten apple who didn't fall far from a rotten tree. I want the three of you to keep away from the woods and the service station. That's an order."

Easier said.

The girls and I would wait to mount our bikes until it was too dark to be seen by Aunt Jane May or someone who might snitch us out, but there was only one way to get over to Mud Town from Honeywell Street. We couldn't avoid going past Merchant's Service Station, even if we wanted to. It was next to the railroad tracks that separated white Summit from not-white Summit.

Mr. Merchant would've hung the garage's "CLOSED" sign and taken the proceeds over to Top's Bar hours before we'd reach the station, but no matter what time the girls and I departed from the hideout, there Elvin would be. Leaning back on an orange crate in front of a garage door lit a hazy yellow by a tin overhead light. He would give Viv and me the once-over as we pedaled past, but it was lovely Frankie who grabbed the lion's share of his attention. He'd take a long draw off his Lucky Strike and in its amber glow we'd see the sickly way he grinned at her, and we'd pray our bikes wouldn't get caught up in the tracks and buck us off, and our prayers had always been answered.

Hindsight being what it is, I can see now that Frankie, Viv, and I were on the road to hell paved with good intentions that afternoon, but when we burst out of the trees at the edge of Founder's Woods and onto the sunny grounds of the mental institution unscathed by Merchant or any of his disciples? It felt like a miracle to me, like a parting of the Red Sea, and like God had our backs yet again.

Chapter Eleven

～

After the three of us propped our bikes against the trunk of the Hanging Tree, we got comfortable on our lookout branch. We were up high enough that if you got shoved off by the kid sitting next to you damage could be incurred. Frankie and Viv were giving each other stink eyes on the way ride over, so as a precautionary measure, I planted myself between them to wait for Jimbo and Albie to guide their charges out of the hospital and into the recreation yard after Bigger Dolores fed them lunch in the dining room.

Frankie repeated to me for the fourth time, "Remember, no visiting today. We're headin' over to Whitcomb's soon as—"

"All right already," I said as I focused on the hospital door the patients would be exiting from. I'd be able to see them just fine without the glasses, but I liked looking closely at their faces, not just the big picture. "I *capiche*."

As Dr. Cruikshank had mentioned at the town hall, the top floor of the hospital was reserved for the patients who'd committed monstrous acts and had been judged criminally insane in a court of law. A lock secured their cell doors, the windows were barred, and they weren't allowed out without having their feet and hands shackled. Jimbo told us that Wally Hopper had been

moved into a corner room a few days after the emergency meeting, which was sooner than Dr. Cruikshank had led folks to
believe. The girls and I thought it was pretty sharp of him to slip
the child killer into town while folks still felt their children were
safe, because Evelyn Mulrooney was bound to get them worked
up again. She hadn't succeeded in convincing anyone at the
emergency meeting to close Broadhurst down, so she'd have to
dream up some other way to prove to the sheriff that she was
marriage material, and give the voters another reason to oust
Mayor Kibler and write her name down on a ballot come
September.

The room next door to Hopper's belonged to Douglas Quick,
the man the newspapers had dubbed the "Blackjack Scalper"
because he'd stabbed those gals twenty-one times each, sawed
the hair off their heads, and made wigs for himself.

The final patient on the top floor was the one we'd learned
more about at Earl Spooner's place when I'd first gotten the idea
to visit with the patients the previous summer. Albie had told us
that the man believed that he was a newspaper reporter, but I
could no longer recall his name.

The middle floor was reserved for deeply disturbed but non-
violent patients who were rarely allowed in the yard. Some of
them were schizophrenics, and some of their lives had become
so unbearably painful they'd attempted to end them. A couple
of them had received what Jimbo called "treatments" in the
basement room only Dr. Cruikshank and Nurse Holloway could
open. And Viv. We figured that one of her keys was sure to work
on that door, too. Because Jimbo and Albie would speculate as
often as we did about what went on in that room, if we got an
opportunity to take a peek inside the Chamber of Horrors, I

hoped we could count on them to lend a helping hand—or at least turn a blind eye.

The patients who were the least threatening to society, and themselves, were housed on the ground floor. They were the ones Frankie, Viv, and I were most familiar with, and some we counted as dear friends.

Because we'd not been stopped by Dutch Van Heusen, Elvin Merchant, or any of the other bullies that afternoon, we made such good time through the woods that we arrived before the first-floor patients had been turned out into the recreation yard, and Frankie was not happy. I was afraid she might tell us she didn't want to wait, that we needed to go back to Whitcomb's immediately for her brown cow, but other than shooting a disgruntled look at me, she suffered in silence.

Viv, on the other hand, was passing the time until the patients showed up by torturing us for refusing to spy on Aunt Jane May after we'd heard her leave through the screen door in those high heels the night before.

"First comes love, then comes marriage, then comes Auntie and Uncle Walt with a baby carriage. *Va-va-va . . . voom,*" she was chanting over and over. Frankie and I knew she would pull something like that and had agreed beforehand that we wouldn't rise to the bait, so Viv had to resort to other tactics to extract her pound of flesh. She gnawed on her fingernails that were already bitten to the wick—a habit she knew Frankie and I found revolting—and when we didn't react to that either, she started whining, "What's takin' them so long? I'm hot and hungry, and I'm tired of—"

"And you know what *I'm* tired of?" Frankie jabbed her finger into Viv's chest. "Stop buggin' us or I'm gonna shove you off this branch!"

"Then I'll climb back up and scratch your eyes out!"

Frankie pointed to her nubby fingers and snorted. "With what?"

When they lunged at each other, I stiff-armed them apart and said, "Knock it off! Look! They're comin' out!"

I was thrilled to see one of my favorite patients float out of the hospital first that afternoon. Nowadays, Florence Willoughby would have made a fortune in the stock market or had her own cable show, but in 1960 she was institutionalized after telling her family and friends that she could foretell the future, which was what I needed to talk to her about.

Florence was able to predict all sorts of things—near and far. She knew that an orderly's wife was going to have a baby months before he himself did. The previous summer she'd told us there was going to be a big plane crash in Indiana in March, and there was. And she'd recently told the girls and me something that had tilted my world off its axis: "Dark forces are gathering around the three of you," she said in a hushed voice. "A raven-haired woman will come to protect and guide you, but beware. Evil lurks on the horizon. Take heed, little ones."

Frankie was too logical to believe Florence and called her predictions coincidences, and I think she might've reminded Viv too much of her spooky, superstitious granny, so they made circles around their ears and laughed off the warning Florence had given us. But I didn't. Aunt Jane May telling us to watch out for lurking evil was bad enough, but the both of them? It was eating at me.

I'd always taken a back seat to Frankie's high IQ and Viv's cunning, but I was beginning to think that maybe I wasn't such a dumb chump after all. I seemed to know things they didn't.

Things that didn't rely on brain power or craftiness. I had my mother's light eyes, and I'd been told that my storytelling ability got passed to me from my grandfather Rufus Mathews, who was known to spin such a spellbinding yarn that those who listened appeared enchanted. But I might've inherited something else from that side of my family, too. I was starting to believe that I had been born on the right side of the blanket—the same way Aunt Jane May had. The gift felt like a new friend that would take some time to get to know before I trusted it, but it was speaking to me loud and clear, and I was finding it difficult to ignore. I loved Aunt Jane May, but she wasn't all that approachable. I didn't feel comfortable asking her if what I was experiencing was the same thing she did, but I thought what I'd begun to call the "little voice" might be identical to her ability to know things that she seemed to pluck out of thin air.

"Here comes Roger," Viv said.

Roger Osgood looked like a big cherub. He had a sumptuous head of curly dark blond hair and the longest eyelashes I'd ever seen. Because he spent most of his time in the yard tending the small flower garden he'd been allowed to plant, he made a beeline for it after he left the building. He was always so well-mannered and gentle that when I saw him that afternoon, I wondered for the hundredth time why he'd been committed to Broadhurst. Jimbo acted peculiar whenever Roger's name came up, and would only tell the girls and me, "He's one of those who bats for the other team." We knew there had to be more to Roger's story than an interest in baseball, but whenever we tried to press Jimbo further, he'd get an enigmatic smile on his face that let us know that he'd reached the end of his story, and he'd go into the house for another bottle of beer.

A young woman, Karen Loomis, a slip of a thing, who rocked and sang lullabies to an invisible baby she called Carl, came strolling through the door after Roger.

Frankie's favorite patient, Teddy Ellison, marched out after Karen. All Catholic kids were taught about Father Damien and his colony in Molokai, so before Jimbo explained to me that Teddy was suffering with an obsessive compulsive disorder, I thought he was a leper because his hands bled and were so raw. But other than soaping and rinsing his fingers a ton of times every day, and treating the other patients like they were rooks or knights and the recreation yard was a chess board, his mind was very sharp. Once upon a time, Teddy had been a world-class chess champion, and when Frankie expressed an interest in learning the game, he taught her how on a set she'd lay out on our side of the fence.

Harry Blake was the last to empty into the yard that afternoon. He'd arrived in the fall. The girls and I were back to school by then and didn't spend time with the patients, so we hadn't known him that long. But he was so charismatic that we quickly developed a deep affection for him and felt like we'd known him for years. Viv adored Harry most of all because, just like her, he was green-eyed and able to make just about any cockamamie idea sound plausible.

From her spot next to me on the branch, Viv said, "Holy shit on a shingle." She ripped the binoculars out of my hand. "There's a new patient!"

"What?" I said. "Where?" I hadn't seen anybody in the yard who hadn't been there yesterday and I wanted to get a closer look. "Gimme the binoculars back."

"Get your own."

"Those are my own."

"Tough titty."

Because Broadhurst had been built as a home and not a hospital, space was at a premium, and cures didn't happen overnight. There was little patient turnover, but a lot of turnover in staff, which was why I leapt to the conclusion that instead of getting locked up on the third floor, Wally Hopper must've been accidentally released in the yard by one of the new employees who didn't know the rules yet. Or maybe letting that homicidal maniac mingle with the less disturbed patients was another one of Dr. Cruikshank's innovative treatments that my father thought was the antithesis of "first, do no harm."

Killing children was Hopper's specialty, and the Hanging Tree was just a couple of yards away from the wrought-iron fence that Mr. Willis had pointed out at the emergency meeting was mostly decorative and a piece a cake for Hopper to climb.

I was about to tell the girls to run for their lives, when it occurred to me to ask Viv, "Is this new patient male or female?"

Her answer was a saucy grin.

"Is he . . . ah . . . carrying a pink pillowcase?"

Soon as she sighed, "Only in my dreams," I knew that it couldn't be Hopper. Viv was very hormonally revved up, but she wasn't blind.

Aunt Jane May had used Hopper's picture in the newspaper as a visual aid during one of her "mark my words" lectures about taking rides from strangers. That's how he'd gotten his hands on the young Gimble sisters. He watched them walk home from St. Sebastian School in Milwaukee every day and waited to approach them until the time was ripe. His patience was finally rewarded when a thunderstorm came up out of nowhere one afternoon. He was wearing a Roman collar when he pulled his car up to the curb and told them to get in, and those two little Catholic girls wouldn't think of disobeying a priest. After Hopper asphyxiated them with pink pillowcases at Michael the Archangel's behest, he left their desecrated bodies on the steps of their church.

"Sweet Mother of God and Erzulie, bless their tiny hearts," our Catholic and voodoo-believing aunt told us as she withdrew from the pocket of her apron a St. Christopher medal and the small brown cloth bag that contained herbs, stones, and special charms—her gris-gris. After she set them both atop Hopper's picture in the *Milwaukee Sentinel*, she told us, "You girls ever find yourselves in a position to choose between gettin' struck by lightning or jumpin' into an automobile with a man who looks like something a dog would drag out from under a porch after a flood, I heard electrocution isn't a bad way to go."

With Hopper no longer a concern, I searched the recreation yard further for whomever Viv was seeing. When I still saw no one that fit the bill, that's when it hit me that there *was* no new patient. She knew how excited I'd be, and she dreamed him up to get back at me for refusing to chase after Aunt Jane May when we'd heard her leave the house in those high-heeled shoes with cleats.

Furious at Viv for making me feel like a glass-half-full half-wit again, I delivered a sharp elbow to her ribs and said, "New patient, my foot. I'm not fallin' for your—"

"There *is* someone new," Frankie said, rushing to Viv's defense. "You just didn't see him 'cause he's been playin' peeka-boo from behind Harry Blake's back. Don't take your eyes off him."

As usual, I did what the brains of our operation told me to do, but when a boy who looked to be about our age stepped out from behind Harry Blake, I wished I hadn't.

Afraid the girls would tease me to no end, I'd never told them how I'd lie awake some nights in the hideout, trying to slow my racing heart and thoughts down. Most of the stories that popped into my mind were fun adventures that the girls enjoyed falling asleep to, but sometimes the stories that came to me were dark and confusing and didn't seem so different from some of the bizarre tales the mental patients told us. That, combined with the little voice I was hearing in my head, made me wonder sometimes if my screws were loose, too. The only way I'd found to reassure myself was to run my rosary through my fingers and recite on every bead, "Kids don't go crazy, only grown-ups do . . . Kids don't go crazy, only grown-ups do," and the new patient had just ripped that comforting ritual out from under me.

Viv handed the binoculars back to me and said, "Focus in on his right eye, and while you're at it, see if you see him doing anything else really weird."

Of course, she wasn't asking because she was fascinated by peoples' inner workings, the way I was. Seemed like all Viv had on her mind that summer was boys and she'd been so quick to jump the gun—kissing Norman Wilkes at the Rivoli—that I wouldn't be surprised if she was experiencing love at first sight again. The patient who'd been hiding behind Harry Blake was just her type.

I'd noticed that girls our age tended to be attracted to boys who resembled their fathers, so Viv usually went in for wan, fragile-looking ones. The kind who looked like her undertaking pa, who was so pale that he resembled the deceased at a funeral more than those that filed past the coffin. I wasn't enamored with the opposite sex yet, but every once in a while I did think that tall, sturdy boys, like Doc, were kind of cute. Frankie didn't know what her father looked like, so I thought that's why she thought boys were loud, stank like ditchwater, and were dumb as dirt.

Viv nudged me. "So?"

I'd gotten caught up in rumination and had forgotten what she'd asked me. "So . . . what?"

She let loose one of her long-suffering Irish sighs, then said to me like I was deaf and dumb, "Do you see him"—she pointed at the new patient—"doin' anything else nutty"—she circled her finger around her ear—"besides winking"—she pointed to her right eye that was blinking like the caution light on the edge of town—"and squeezin' the stuffing outta that raggedy bunny?"

The boy didn't appear to be muttering to himself, and he wasn't walking in circles or staring off into space. Not shouting out chess moves or cradling an invisible baby or ranting about brain-sucking space creatures either. But he *was* winking more than normal, and gripping a stuffed, one-eyed bunny to his chest, which seemed like an odd thing for a kid about our age to do, but who was I to throw stones? There were nights I couldn't fall sleep unless I held Jazzie, the rag doll Aunt Jane May had brought on her first trip from Wildwood. Viv would often nod off with the tattered satin of her favorite baby blanket pressed against her freckled cheek. Even our tough cookie, Frankie, still sucked her thumb some nights.

Giving Viv a taste of her own medicine, I said, "No, I don't see him"—I brought my hand up to my eyebrow and did my

impression of an Indian scout searching for a wagon train—
"doin' anything else nutty"—I pantomimed cracking open a
peanut and tossing it in my mouth—"but you can't always judge
a book"—I withdrew one from an imaginary shelf and pointed
to the front of it—"by its cover."

She cocked her head and looked at me like she had no idea
what I was getting at, so I tried a more direct route. "He looks
okay from here, but that doesn't mean anything." You'd run to
the other side of the street if you saw some of the patients heading your way, but most of them looked like any Tom, Dick, or
Harry Blake. It wasn't until you tried to have a conversation
with them that you'd realize how tortured their minds were.
"We need to talk to him to know for sure."

Thinking that Frankie might have additional information, I
asked her, "Did Jimbo say anything to you about a kid gettin'
committed?"

But Viv didn't want a second opinion from romance-hating
Frankie, and she told her so.

"If you're gonna say that Jimbo told you he's got some kind
of incurable craziness, you can sit on a screwdriver and rotate
you . . . you—*goomba*."

Frankie flicked her fingers under her chin and hissed at Viv,
"And you can *baciami il culo*, you stupid Mick."

Suggesting that Viv should kiss her ass in Italian meant that
Viv had no choice but to fire back one of her Celtic curses. More
poetic than scary, the curses amused Frankie, so Viv would get
even hotter under the collar and nothing good ever came of that.

"May the north wind always find your ugly face, Frankenstein," Viv said, and in one smooth move she swung down from
the branch.

Frankie laughed and called down to her, "Where do you think you're goin'?

"Biz said we should go talk to the kid!" Viv said and took off at a gallop.

"Not today!" I yelled as she veered toward the path that'd deliver her to our visiting spot behind the fence. "We're goin' to the drugstore to—"

"I'm gettin' my brown cow!" Frankie shouted.

"You *are* a brown cow!" Viv yelled back.

"We're not comin' after you this time!" Frankie threatened.

"Yeah! Get back here!" I insisted, but only because Frankie expected me to back her up.

I was secretly thrilled that Viv had taken off, because we'd have to go after her, and I'd get the chance to talk to the patients I wanted to.

Tomorrow we'd have to skip our visit to the hospital because we'd be celebrating America's birthday, and I didn't want to put off asking Florence about the dire prediction she'd made. I was tired of staring at every "raven-haired woman" in town, wondering if she was the one who'd "protect and guide" us from the evil that was lurking on the horizon. I'd come up with a likely candidate in Sophia Maniachi, but I wanted to know for sure.

I also had something important to discuss with Harry Blake.

And, truth be told, I wanted to meet the new patient almost as much as Viv did. Sure, he looked about our age, but I was secretly hoping he was an extremely short man like Tiny Tommy, who ran the carousel at the County Fair carnival, or Mr. Ellison, who used a stool to see over the counter of his jewelry store. I hadn't seen any wrinkles on the patient's face or stubble on his chin through the binoculars, but if he introduced himself to us in a deep, husky voice, I'd still be able to chant on my rosary beads, "Kids don't go crazy, only grown-ups do," when the stories that made me feel like I belonged on the other side of the wrought-iron fence drifted into my mind.

I finagled myself off the branch and yelled up to Frankie, "Don't be so mad." I reached for the binoculars she was dangling toward me. "I think wantin' to meet the new patient is kinda like what she did over at the Rivoli when she kissed Norman Wilkes. She can't seem to help herself. Maybe her granny's right. Maybe she really *is* possessed by an evil spirit."

Frankie leapt down and landed beside me. "I don't give a flying Fudgesicle if she is or not. I'm sick and tired of her runnin' us ragged." She took two giant steps toward her bike. "I'm going to Whitcomb's and gettin' my brown cow. She'll come back."

I thought Viv would turn around when she noticed we weren't hot on her trail, too. She talked a good game, but she counted on Frankie and me in a way we didn't count on her. She'd curse and vow the worst kind of vengeance when she caught back up to us, but she'd been behaving so capriciously—what if this time she didn't?

The path Viv had disappeared down encircled the dense woods that were the hunting ground for the bad boys captained by Elvin Merchant. It was him and his second in command, Herman "Dutch" Van Heusen, that I was most anxious about her encountering. But a few of the kids who hung out at Whitcomb's counter had reported seeing the Summit Witch gathering ingredients for her supernatural stew in that neck of the woods, too. If Viv bumped into her, she'd panic and could hyperventilate to the point of passing out.

And even if she did make it safely to our visiting spot, she might do something else we'd all live to regret. She was so eager to meet the new patient that she might get too close to the fence. He might've looked like Casper Milquetoast, but what if he was a pint-sized Dr. Jekyll chomping at the bit to claw his way out of his meek exterior? He could thrust his hands through the black bars and choke Viv, gouge her eyes out, knock her teeth down her throat, or heaven only knows what.

I grabbed Frankie's arm and said, "We gotta go after her. Merchant or the witch or the new patient . . . what if they hurt her?"

"I hope they do!"

"Frankie!"

"Fine!" She dropped her bike in the dust and stuck her fist in my face. "But when we catch up to her, don't you dare stop me from knockin' some sense into her boy-crazy head or you'll be eatin' a knuckle sandwich, too."

She didn't fool me. Her anger was shielding a heart full of worry and hurt feelings. She was far out in front of me when we ran down the path that skirted Founder's Woods, and when we didn't catch up to the girl whose hand she'd reach for in the middle of the night and whose hair she'd ruffle so tenderly, I heard her whimper, "Please, Jesus."

Heaving like race horses going neck and neck, the two of us ran through the pine woods and burst into the clearing next to the wrought-iron fence. I was scared we'd find Viv gasping for breath after a run-in with the Summit Witch or nursing a bruise inflicted by the bad boys or the new patient, but what we found instead stopped Frankie and me in our tracks.

If I hadn't been out of my mind with fear, I would've burst out laughing, because there Viv was in all her glory. Like she was waiting to be discovered by a Hollywood talent scout, she was posed against the fence like a pin-up girl. Smiling like Rita Hayworth.

When she batted her lashes and purred, "What took you so long?" Frankie roared, "Goddamn it all!" and got Viv in a half nelson.

I didn't go easy on her either. I gave her a vicious noogie and called her a brat, and that fight could have gone on longer and would have had we not been interrupted.

"Greetings, Earthlings!" Harry Blake announced from the other side of the fence. "Got cookies?"

Chapter Twelve

Harry Blake's sandy hair was trimmed into a tight crew cut, but the girls and I hardly ever saw it on account of his shiny hats. Some days the tinfoil would be fashioned into a stove-top model like President Lincoln's, or he might show up at the fence wearing a sailor cap shaped like Popeye's. He was also fond of French berets and would sometimes greet us with "*Bonjour!*"—but only if he was feeling jauntier than usual.

That afternoon, Harry was wearing a fedora and he looked like a movie detective on the job. He was a handsome man when he stood still long enough to let you get a look at him. His green eyes darted like minnows in the creek, and his nose looked like it belonged to an English king, except for the bump on the bridge. That always made me wonder if he'd been unable to dodge a punch despite being up on his toes all the time, which, considering his mental state, he sort of had to be.

Shortly after we'd made his acquaintance, I'd asked Jimbo, over a plate of Earl Spooner's excellent onion rings with blue cheese dressing, why Harry Blake believed everyone was out to get him.

"Most folks feel safe in the world most of the time, Bizzy," he explained, "but a paranoid person sees danger everywhere.

Harry can't stop himself from looking over his shoulder and waitin' for the other shoe to drop."

Thinking how awful it must be to not have best friends that you trusted with your life or a safe place to hide out, I dipped a crunchy onion into the creamy dressing and said, "But Harry mostly gets worked up over those space aliens trying to snatch his brain and Bigger's poisonous cooking."

"Yeah," Jimbo said with a sad smile. "Those are his bugaboos."

During one of our visits, Harry had told us that he'd been receiving "extra-strong vibrations" from the outer-space creatures he called the Mondurians and aluminum foil was his only defense. He'd tried to steal some from the hospital kitchen, but Bigger caught him. She told us that if she ever saw him skulking around again, "I'll take my rollin' pin to him."

Unlike her, the girls and I really liked Harry and wanted to do all we could to make him better. We pooled our pennies, bought him his own roll of Reynolds Wrap at the five-and-dime, and kept it hidden in the woods, should he need reinforcements. And after he told us that the hospital food was deadly, Viv started stealing shortbread cookies from Aunt Jane May's jar and passing them to him through the fence.

Believing that Bigger was slipping poison into his food might've been a reaction to her being stingy with tinfoil, but no matter how many times we tried to explain to Harry that she was a dear friend of ours who'd never do something like that, he remained adamant and unconvinced. We probably would've had more success convincing him if we could've told him that we were living proof, but she'd made us swear not to tell anyone that she fed us peanut butter and marshmallow sandwiches. That's how the girls and I knew how the hospital was laid out. On the days her bunions bothered her and Bigger needed help peeling potatoes and such, she'd tell Jimbo and he'd pass it on during our afternoon visit. After the patients headed back inside, we'd climb the part of the wrought-iron fence that ran behind the hospital, and she'd let us into the kitchen. Not through the rear door, mind you, but the *Greer* door.

Bigger started calling it that soon after Mr. Ralph Greer, who'd been institutionalized for what Jimbo called "payin' too much attention to his privates in public," crawled past her and the Wonder Bread delivery man when they were chatting over coffee one afternoon. He hid among the fluffy loaves in the truck parked outside the bay door. Bigger still cracked up over the look the delivery man had on his face when he showed up an hour later and shoved his stowaway back into the kitchen still holding onto his "little dickie sandwich."

Ralph Greer was the man Frankie and I'd smiled about when Doctor Cruikshank had assured everyone at the emergency meeting that none of the patients could escape from Broadhurst. Of course, the psychiatrist didn't mention his escapade to the worked-up crowd that night, but not because he was hiding something. He didn't know what Ralph Greer had done because Bigger never reported it to the head of the hospital. Only an idiot or a Catholic would confess something that'd get her fired and our friend was a smart Baptist who prized her job.

After Harry showed up on the other side of the black fence that afternoon wondering if we had any cookies, I quit giving Viv a noogie for running away from Frankie and me, and said to him, "Hey, there! I got something important that I need to talk to you about."

Aunt Jane May had been giving me a really hard time about the shortbreads disappearing from her jar at a "gluttonous rate." Viv wouldn't listen to me when I told her to quit stealing them, so I came prepared that afternoon to convince Harry once and for all that Bigger wasn't trying to poison him.

I reached into my back pocket and withdrew the speech I'd written the night before. But before I could say word one, Viv passed Harry three cookies through the fence, and like they were the price of admission, he launched into a description of his latest tussle with the Mondurians that I had no problem picturing on the Rivoli's silver screen.

Frankie was held rapt by Harry's recounting of the evil space beings that appeared in his room in the middle of the night with the sole purpose of turning his brain into mush, but I found myself puzzled that afternoon, not for the first time. During most of our visits, Harry acted and sounded as genuinely unbalanced as the other patients, but every so often I'd be reminded of Viv putting on one of her little performances. I never mentioned that observation to the girls because I was sure they'd tease me endlessly for thinking something so whacky, and I couldn't completely blame them. Who in their right mind would pretend to be mentally ill? That alone would make them certifiable.

Viv was nuts about Harry and would usually hang on his every bizarre word, but, like me, she had something else or, I suppose I should say, some*one* else on her mind that afternoon. She was looking past Harry and focusing on a spot mid-yard where Jimbo was talking to the new patient. He was ticking something off on his fingers, probably getting him up to speed on the yard rules, I thought: *"No touching the fence, no picking or eating flowers from Roger's garden, no peeing or spitting—especially on the* *other patients.*" And most importantly, when the school bell affixed to the side of the hospital started clanging, he was to stop whatever he was doing and line up outside the door with the other patients—pronto!

After Jimbo finished reading the new patient the riot act, he did exactly what Viv had been praying he'd do. He patted him on the head and pointed him in our direction. A chunk of my heart was still hoping he was a tiny man, but the closer he got, there was no denying he was a boy about our age. Paler and thinner than he looked from afar, he wore his white-blond hair much longer than any of the boys in our grade, and he didn't move anything like them either. Experiencing growth spurts and not used to the new skin they were in, they were clodhoppers, but as the new patient came across the yard, he moved like he was climbing the steps of a haunted house.

I was surprised to find myself growing more excited to meet him with each hesitant step he took, but *not* surprised that Viv's eagerness had shifted to agitation. Considering how close the kid had stuck to Harry Blake when he'd been released into the yard, I suspected that she was worried Harry's more familiar presence would outshine hers and she never was one for sharing the spotlight.

"And in conclusion," Harry said as he ended that afternoon's story about the outer-space aliens, "I got away from them again last night, but . . ." He looked down at a part of the fence about fifty yards to the right. He'd been stopping there before he came to visit with us to have an animated conversation with no one we could see, so we figured he was trying to convince a Mondurian to go back to their own planet and leave him be. "It's just a matter of time before those slimy devils show up again."

"Sooner than you think," Viv told him in her most ominous-sounding voice. "I saw one of them slinking behind the hospital not more than ten minutes ago."

Up on his toes and all ears, Harry said, "Just the one?"

"That's all I saw, but ya better watch your back," Viv told the man who never needed that reminder. "You should go hunt it down before it turns invisible and jumps into your ear like that one did last week."

Harry tugged his aluminum fedora further down on his forehead and got a battle-worthy look in his eyes. "Don't go anywhere," he told us. "I'll be back for more cookies after I dispose of that outer-space garbage."

Soon as he took off toward the back of the hospital to search for the Mondurian, I wanted to say something to Viv about how mean that was, but I knew she'd just laugh it off because she was in the grip of boy craziness.

Frankie and I had roughed her up pretty good during our scuffle, and in an attempt to make herself more attractive for the new patient, Viv scraped the dusty sweat off her arms, fluffed her pixie cut, and resumed the glamour-puss pose we'd found her making when we burst into the clearing.

"How do I look?" she asked with puckered lips.

"Like a movie star," I hurried to say before Frankie could say, *Like a hussy.*

When patients first approached us, they'd stand back and spend some time looking us up and down, trying to gauge if we were friends or foes, or if we were really there at all. But when the object of Viv's newfound affection finished his journey across the yard, he didn't do that.

He came right up to the fence, threw back his puny shoulders, and said, "Good afternoon. It's a pleasure to make your acquaintance. I'm Ernest Joseph Fontaine, but everyone calls me Ernie. I'll be twelve next month, but I don't need any presents. I love dogs and knitting, I'm a good dancer, and I'm a lot stronger than I look. I can mow a lawn, shovel a sidewalk, and"—*wink* . . . *wink*—"I'm so quiet you won't even know I'm there."

Chapter Thirteen

❧

Sometimes patients with physical manifestations of their illnesses—bleeding hands, shaking, rocking, yelling, or singing softly to an invisible baby—could manage to conceal them long enough to engage in a conversation with us, but you'd still know something was wrong with them. Their words would be non-sensical like Harry Blake's or frantic like chess champion Teddy Ellison's were when he got wound up about rooks and knights, or their mouths would go so dry they'd sound like they'd been lost in the desert for forty days and forty nights.

But the boy standing in front of the fence that afternoon didn't fit that mold.

He did wink an awful lot and sounded stilted and out of place when he'd introduced himself, as if instead of standing in the recreation yard of a mental institution, he was in the front of a classroom reading an essay entitled "My Good Qualities." But he was well-spoken, his mouth didn't go dry, and his sentences made sense—except for that part about loving to knit and dance. Those weren't hobbies any boy I knew would get caught dead doing.

Because he didn't come across like any of the other patients we'd met or I'd read about in Doc's medical books and files, or seen in the movies, I had no way to judge his state of mind. Was he only up to his ankles in lunacy or was he in over his head?

Further intrigued, but anxious to keep Viv safe until I could determine how off-kilter the boy was, I stepped up to the fence, told him our names, and did exactly what I'd been scared she was about to do. I violated one of the rules Albie had made us swear to uphold before he'd given us permission to visit. We were never supposed to discuss a patient's condition with them, but I asked the kid, "What's wrong with you? Other than . . ." I mimicked his winking eye.

He lowered his head, toed the grass with the tip of his sneaker, and replied, "My mom and dad were killed in a car crash two months ago."

Heartbreaking, certainly, but even though it might feel like you've lost your mind after someone you love with your whole heart and soul passes over to the other side, grief was not considered a mental illness. Not unless the boy experienced the kind of profound sadness that'd imprisoned Katherine Broadhurst in a pit of despair. Was that why he'd been committed? Had he grown so desperate to be reunited with his parents that he'd tried to take his own life before the Lord could?

Only, he wouldn't have been allowed out in the yard with the first-floor patients if he'd tried to hang himself or stick his head in a gas oven. He would've been turned out later in the afternoon with the more seriously disturbed second-floorers who'd tried the same.

While I continued puzzling over the boy's condition and Frankie further sulked about being kept from her brown cow, Viv was preparing to use one of the "helpful hints" she insisted on torturing us with after we turned the lights out in the hideout. "Lucky for you two looks aren't everything," she'd say, though on a scale of beauty Frankie was a ten, I was an eight, and she languished around a five. "According to *Ladies Home Journal*, even if you're butt-ugly, you can still get a boy interested in you. Ya just gotta have something in common with them. Biz, you should be on the lookout for one who likes to write stories and talk to mental patients. And hard to believe,"—she flicked Frankie on the leg to get her attention—"but the article said doin' crossword puzzles and thinking a dumb game like chess is fun could even put stars in a boy's eyes."

And I guess Viv thought *death* would do the trick, too, because she aimed her best puppy-in-a-pet-store look at Ernie and said, "I'm so sorry your parents kicked the bucket. My family is in bad shape, too. My ma's got a kind of leprosy and is hangin' by a thread, my father owns a funeral home so he's around tons of dead people all the time, and my granny's knockin' on death's door."

Malarkey.

Her mother had psoriasis caused by the peroxide she used on gals after she convinced them their husbands would appreciate coming home at night to a blond bombshell. Viv's father *did* own the only funeral home in town, but my father was very good at keeping people alive and wasn't supplying Mr. Cleary with a "ton" of customers. And telling the boy that the Grim Reaper was about to pay a visit to her granny? She wished.

I shouldn't have, but I couldn't help but appreciate Viv's galling performance. After an afternoon so fraught with fear and tension, it was a relief to see her doing what she did best, and I elbowed Frankie in get a load of her gesture. Unfortunately, she did not find Viv's attempts to find something in common with the boy funny in the least.

Frankie got a death grip on Viv's shoulders and told her gruffly, "Happy now? We need to get to Whitcomb's. Say goodbye."

Viv squirmed out of her hands and said to Ernie so pleasantly that I thought Frankie might knock her block off, "As you were saying before we were so rudely interrupted, you're an orphan?"

"Yeah, from St. Jude's." *Wink . . . wink.* "In Milwaukee."

Oh, I knew where it was.

St. Thomas's Ladies Auxiliary had decided last Christmas that it'd be in keeping with the season if some kids from the junior choir sang carols to "the poor unfortunates." Frankie and Dell were trimming Jimbo's tree that night, and Viv feigned a stomachache. I didn't want to go without them, but Aunt Jane May pressed a pair of red mittens into my hands and said, "Buchanans put the needs of others before their own. The bus is leaving in fifteen minutes. Don't let the door hit ya in the backside on your way out."

Can't say exactly what part of Milwaukee St. Jude's was in, but the bus pulled up in front of a two-story house that stood out on a block of nicer homes like a poor relation in a family Christmas photo. A snowman with stick arms stood in the front yard, but it had no nose or mouth. And when we came through the door of the orphanage, it wasn't the smell of a pine tree that greeted us, but the stink of ammonia. The orphans appeared well fed but looked love starved, and after we sang the last refrain of "Angels We Have Heard on High," a pigtailed girl put her hand in mine and begged me to adopt her. I threw up twice on the ride back home.

Losing his mother and father and then having to live day in and day out in that rundown house full of other heartbroken kids only to find out that a mental institution was the answer to his prayers is what might've driven the boy standing in front of us crazy. It certainly made me feel sorry for him, but Frankie was having none of it.

"Cry me a river," she said. "What's the *real* reason you're here, Ernest Joseph Fontaine? Did you burn down a building? Drown a cat? Try to strangle one of the nuns at the orphanage with a rosary?

"Cut it out, Frankie!" Viv said. "You're scarin' him!"

"I wouldn't . . . I didn't do anything bad," the boy whimpered, "but I can't tell you why I'm here 'cause I don't know."

"Really?" I said, trying not to sound as enthusiastic as I was feeling. "Do you have amnesia?"

After the girls and I had seen *Blood of Dracula*—a teenager went on a killing spree and couldn't remember a thing—I read up on amnesia in Doc's medical books. Shell-shock, intoxication, hypnosis, and a few sleeping medications could cause the condition. Ernie was too young to enlist in the Army, and his breath smelled like Bigger's tuna noodle casserole, not booze. That left only two other reasons he couldn't remember why he'd been committed.

"Did somebody swing a pocket watch in front of your face and tell you, 'Look into my eyes . . . look into my eyes . . . you're feeling sleepy'?" I asked him.

He shook his head.

"Did you take any medicine that made you feel groggy?"

"No, I didn't mean—I meant . . ." Ernie flapped his arm toward the hospital. "This isn't where they told me they were bringin' me."

"*Who* told you?" Viv asked.

"Them."

Besides being the title of a horror movie about gargantuan alien spiders, Harry Blake often referred to the Mondurians as "them." Is that what was wrong with the boy? Paranoia? Birds of a feather flocked together, so maybe that's why he'd hidden behind Harry when he was first let out of the hospital doors?

Viv must've been thinking along the same lines because she asked Ernie, "Them who?"

"The people who said they wanted to adopt me yesterday." He hugged his one-eyed stuffed bunny closer to his chest, like it needed consoling, too. "When I got called into Sister Clement's office, there was a man with a big moustache, and his wife was wearing perfume that smelled like the kind my mother wore." He took in a shuddering breath. "They told me they lived in the country and they had a dog and mine was killed in the crash with my mom and dad. And then the man asked me if I had any relatives, and when I told 'em no, he smiled at Sister Clement and said, 'He'll do.'" Ernie shrugged the way I did when I didn't want anyone to know how dumb I felt after getting my hopes up too high. "I thought they were taking me home and I don't get many chances 'cause . . ." He pointed to his winking right eye. "I only do it sometimes, but nobody wants a kid that's defective."

He made the orphanage sound like a car dealership where shoppers wouldn't choose a dented model. Since St. Jude was the patron saint of lost causes, that made some sense.

"Then what happened?" I asked him.

"I packed my suitcase and waited for the man and lady to pull up front, the way Sister Clement told me to. We listened to a ball game on the car radio and Hank Aaron hit a home run and then"—he scrunched his face into a remembering look—"we stopped at a drive-in for food. The man ordered me something called a Mars Malt and a Jupiter Burger, and then a girl who looked like she was an alien from outer space brought it out to the car. She had silver antennae bobbing on her head and . . . her skirt looked like it was made out of aluminum foil."

Even though that sounded exactly like something else Harry Blake would say, I knew that Ernie was telling the truth because the bus had driven past the Milky Way drive-in—"Our Food Is Out of This World!"—on the way home from St. Jude's. Powdery snow was whipping across the parking lot that night, so waitresses weren't delivering food to car windows, but through the plate glass window, I could see them dropping orders at tables in their outer-space costumes.

Because Viv had gotten out of that choir trip, I could tell by the crumpled look on her face that she was having second thoughts about Ernie. A boyfriend who was always looking over his shoulder instead of gazing deeply into her eyes, one who would never tenderly utter, "I love you, darling," but would go on and on about aliens from outer space wasn't what she had in mind.

I knew I should tell her what I saw at the Milky Way, but I was still angry at her for running off, so I thought *Who's the dump chump now?* and took great satisfaction in saying to Frankie, loud enough for Viv to hear, of course, "Aluminum foil?" Aliens? Boy, it sure sounds like Harry and Ernie have a *lot* in common."

"It sure does," Frankie said with a sneer. "We should give them some time alone so they can get to know each other better. C'mon, Viv."

Suggesting her Prince Charming was a paranoiac would've been enough to dissuade a child of average gumption, but Viv landed a loogie on my sneaker, shot a withering look at Frankie, and told Ernie with one of those smiles of hers that could charm the pants off anyone, "I bet if you try real hard you can remember why you're here. Jimbo and Albie must've told you."

"Who?" Ernie asked.

"The big brown guys," Frankie said and pointed to where they were riding herd on two patients who were going toe to toe in the middle of the yard.

I'd been so focused on the drama unfolding between Viv and the boy that I hadn't noticed Karen was throwing one of her conniption fits. She was screaming something about her imaginary baby and stabbing her finger at Roger Osgood, who was always asking Karen if he could hold Carl. I guessed that hadn't gone well, but it never did.

When I asked Jimbo why Karen would regularly pick fights with the male patients, he explained, "I think she's actin' out the night she couldn't stop her drunk husband from throwing their baby out a second-story window. Tryin' for a better ending I 'spose."

With their back muscles coiled beneath their sweat-stained white jackets, Jimbo and Albie were cautiously circling Roger and Karen. Nothing had erupted yet, but they had to be extra vigilant when an argument like this broke out in the yard. Rage opened the door to fear, and if the orderlies didn't act fast to resolve the problem, it would spread to the rest of the patients. They'd dart around helter-skelter or bang their heads against the fence or howl. A few might even try to scale the fence, which would leave Jimbo and Albie with no other choice but to pull the handle on the point-of-no-return siren.

In a matter of moments, reinforcements would come barreling out the front doors of the hospital to administer tranquilizing shots or wrap the patients in straitjackets. If the nurses and other orderlies couldn't get close enough to medicate or restrain them, they'd stun them into submission with cattle prods before they could hurt themselves or someone else.

After Ernie finished checking out Jimbo, who'd avoided a disaster by escorting a distraught Roger back to his flower garden, and Albie, who was leading Karen to the opposite end of the yard so she could rock Carl in peace, he turned back to us.

"The biggest guy told me not to spit on anyone and to line up at the door we came out of as soon as I heard the school bell ring," Ernie said. "I don't think he told me why I was here, but maybe he did." When he knocked his knuckles against the side of his head, he loosed a rivulet of tears that came squiggling down his pale cheeks. "I . . . I've been having a hard time thinkin' straight."

"Aw, jeez, please, don't cry," Viv said. "Everything's gonna be okay. I promise. The girls and me are gonna help you out."

I loudly gasped and every muscle in Frankie's body went rigid.

"And then a family in town can adopt you," Viv bubbled on. "We can be your new friends and you can come to our hideout and—hey! You could even get a dog! I love Lassie, don't you?"

Ernie brought his bunny up to his cheek, used it like a hankie, then nodded.

"Well, that's great," Viv exclaimed, "because the Forresters have a collie that looks just like her and she had eight puppies last week, and—"

The *brrrring* of the school bell signaling the end of yard time drowned out the rest of Viv's sales pitch, but Ernie wouldn't have heard her anyway. Per Jimbo's instructions, he had taken off across the yard to line up with the other patients outside the hospital's side door.

Viv cupped her hands around her mouth and shouted at his fleeing back, "See ya tomorrow!"

I wasn't so sure about that.

Frankie looked like she was about to murder Viv and I wouldn't have lifted a finger to stop her.

Chapter Fourteen

What Viv had told Ernie Fontaine was far worse than wanting to spy on Aunt Jane May or kissing Norman Wilkes or any other of the foolishness she'd been doing, so I didn't bother to stop Frankie when she lunged at her and said, "You just promised that kid that we'd help him out without checking with me and Biz! You broke the Good Samaritan rule!"

That might've been forgivable, say, if we'd come up with it a few weeks ago and Viv had forgotten that she'd made a solemn oath to uphold it, but that rule had gone into effect as a result of what'd happened two days after Christmas.

Other kids besides us were willing to brave the bitter cold to try their new ice skates out on Still River that day, but not many. The conditions were barely tolerable when the sun was high, so when the north wind kicked up, clouds rolled in, and flakes began to fly, it was time to head home before frostbite set in.

Frankie, Viv, and I were about to undo our laces when we heard muffled calls for help further downstream. In the dusky light and squalling snow, we could barely make out Dutch Van Heusen shoving the puniest girl in town, Elsie Burke, toward a jagged hole in the ice that had been cordoned off. He was a farm boy, a hay bale–throwing hulk of a kid, but I had broad shoulders, too, and a full head of righteous steam when I blind-sided him. Van Heusen slid a few feet on his stomach before he disappeared into the icy hole he'd been threatening to push little Elsie into. That part of the river wasn't over his head, but it was frigid, and he wasn't getting out of that hole anytime soon. After the girls and I positioned ourselves around it and brought our blades down close to his hands whenever he tried to boost him-self out, a blue-lipped Dutch threatened, "I'm gonna get you for this, ya little sh-sh . . . shits."

We had to wait until after most of the fight had gone out of him before Frankie called the sheriff from the pay phone across the street. When he showed up to pull Van Heusen out, the girls and I expected a round of applause after Elsie corroborated our story, but the little ingrate had taken a powder and left us hold-ing the bag.

Of course, when the sheriff questioned Van Heusen, he denied everything. But he'd been in trouble before for pushing kids around in Founder's Woods and his proclamations of innocence didn't impress the sheriff. After he ushered Van Heusen into his county car and dropped him off at the family farm, he must've called Aunt Jane May, because when the girls and I came through the back door of the house, the two of them were waiting for us in the kitchen, and they didn't look happy.

The sheriff fingered the silver badge on his shirt and said, "What you did today was out of line. Your hearts were in the right places, but it's not your place to punish. That's my job."

"Ditto," said Aunt Jane May. And after the two of them spent a brief time talking about severe consequences and how to "teach us a lesson we'd never forget," she ordered the girls and me to spend the rest of our Christmas vacation apart from one another.

Given Frankie's and Viv's squabbling, that punishment didn't sit too bad with me at first. Day three is when I started to miss them. We stared woefully at one another through our bedroom windows, read each other's lips, counted down the days until we'd be reunited in our foggy breaths, and barely slept or ate. When I didn't think I could bear being apart from them for a minute longer, I went looking for Aunt Jane May and found her in the kitchen, running sink water into a wash bucket. Since I was much better at refereeing than I was at arguing, I told her what I thought Frankie would say if given the chance.

"Keeping the Tree Musketeers apart is cruel and unusual punishment. Have you no mercy?" I said and dropped to my knees on the cold, linoleum floor.

She responded to my pleas by setting the bucket down next to me, handing me a scrub brush, and saying, "Long as you're down there."

But as it turned out, while we were separated, the Tree Musketeers *had* learned a lesson we'd never forget. We learned that we could never, ever endure being separated like that again. And one of the ways we could avoid that severe consequence was if we swore to one another that no matter how dire the circumstances, no matter how desperately someone needed our help—the way Little Elsie had that afternoon on Still River—we would not rush to their aid. Not without having one of our "powwows" first.

It was a sacred ritual we'd performed many times throughout the years whenever any of us had something troubling to discuss or we had an important decision to make. We'd head out to the hideout and light the train lantern. After we set it atop the blood stain that'd been created when we became sisters, we'd gather around it and say, "All for one and one for all," and then whoever called for the powwow would share what was on her mind. After we talked it over, a vote would be taken to decide what to do, and it had to be unanimous.

So when Viv went rogue and promised Ernie Fontaine that we'd "help him out" that afternoon, she'd violated a Tree Musketeer rule, and there was no worse offense in our books.

I felt horribly betrayed, but I'd rarely seen Frankie so bent out of shape. She yanked Viv away from the wrought-iron fence and said, "When you told that kid we'd help him out, ya didn't mean that we'd be nice to him and bring him shortbread cookies, did ya. You meant that we'd help him out of Broadhurst so he could be your boyfriend!"

We expected Viv to deny it and put up her dukes, but she cried, "I'm sorry I didn't call for a powwow. I'm sorry I broke the Good Samaritan rule. I . . . I don't know why, but when I see a cute boy, somethin' just comes over me. I'll take my licks, and I promise that I'll never—" She stopped whimpering, narrowed her eyes, and pointed over our shoulders. "Don't look now, but . . ."

"Are you kiddin' me?" Frankie said, because she couldn't believe Viv had the nerve to use her favorite distraction tactic to keep us from getting more ticked off at her, or that we'd been stupid enough to almost fall for it.

But just as she was about to start ripping into Viv again, a screeching sound punctured the air and the three of us dropped to the ground, the same way we did when the air raid siren went off during the drills at school.

I yelled, "What's happenin'?"

"It's the point-of-no-return siren," Frankie shouted.

I knew that because we'd heard it a couple of times before, but what I didn't understand was why Jimbo or Albie had tripped it. Last time I'd checked, the patients had lined up at the side door of the hospital to go back in after their yard time, just the way they were supposed to.

"Somebody must be tryin' to escape," Viv said. "Look at Albie!"

He was running toward the back of the hospital, frantically gesticulating and shouting something at Jimbo, who was still at his post at the side door with the rest of the patients, who were now keening and rocking and covering the ears.

Moments after Albie disappeared behind the building, Harry Blake came ripping around the opposite end, arms and legs pumping. Usually a man who avoided working up a sweat, I was surprised to see that Albie wasn't more than fifty yards or so behind Harry, who was so quick on his feet.

"Blake!" Albie bellowed as he chased after him through the middle of the yard. "Stay away from that fence!"

The girls and I knew what was about to happen and could barely stand to watch when the front doors of the hospital burst open and members of the staff flooded out in response to the siren. They rushed to help Jimbo round up the patients, who'd scattered like a panicked herd, all of them exhibiting the aberrant behaviors they'd rely on to comfort themselves when pushed beyond their limit.

The only one who didn't look like she'd gone over the edge was Florence. She must've sensed that I'd planned on talking to her about the raven-haired woman she told us would protect and guide us from lurking death, because she was giving me the same intense gaze she had when she'd made that prediction. I couldn't hear her, but I could see her lips moving, and I thought she was saying, "*Help . . . hurry*," before an orderly ran in front of her and slapped a syringe into Albie's hand like they were running a relay and he was passing the baton. When I looked for Florence again, she'd disappeared in the maelstrom.

Feeling more confident now that he was armed with the tranquilizer, Albie further picked up his pace. "I'm warnin' you, Blake!" he bellowed. "Stop or you'll pay the price!"

Frankie and I wrapped our arms around Viv because, even though she'd sent her favorite patient on a wild goose chase for an alien so she wouldn't have to share the spotlight when she talked to Ernie Fontaine, she was whimpering. She cared deeply about Harry. We all did. He was our friend.

Between the siren's wailing and Albie's hollering, Teddy Ellison shouting out chess moves, and Karen screaming about baby Carl, I could barely hear Viv say, "This is all my fault. I shouldn't have sent Harry to look for a Mondurian behind the hospital. When he didn't find it, he thinks it seeped into his ear and burrowed into his brain. He's comin' to ask me to pull it out."

That sounded like something he'd do except he wasn't coming our way. Harry was running toward that section of the fence about fifty yards to our right that he'd been stopping at before he'd come to visit with us. When he reached it, he wrapped his hands around the iron bars and peered through them, like he was searching for something—maybe a way out, maybe a Mondurian. It wasn't until he didn't find what he was looking for that he came charging our way.

Considering how much money Albie owed Chummy Adler, the fear of getting fired for losing control of the yard was a powerful motivator. Despite the heavy blanket of heat and his heft, he was breathing down Harry's neck, just feet away from tackling him to the ground. But what the Almighty wants, the Almighty gets, and I believe it was His foot that tripped Albie that afternoon just as he was about to grab a hold of Harry's shirt.

When he skidded to a stop in front of Frankie, Viv, and me, Harry was shivering and panting and didn't look anything like the man we'd grown so fond of. He looked like a movie mad-man, like someone straight out of *The Snake Pit.*

Fighting an urge to back away from the fence, I dug into Viv's pocket for a shortbread cookie, passed it through the iron bars, and tried to reassure him with a smile. "Everything is going to be all right," I told him, the same way Doc told his patients, even though it wouldn't be.

Albie had already struggled back to his feet and was barrel-ing toward us with a look on his face that was almost as desper-ate as the one Harry had on his when he knocked the cookie out of my hand, grabbed my wrist, and pressed a piece of paper into my palm.

He was hurting me so badly I could hardly say, "Let go of me, Harry. Please. My wrist is gonna snap."

Like he hadn't heard me or couldn't stop himself, he panted, "You've got to help . . . they're going to kill—"

"Gotcha," Albie yelled, and in a practiced move, he wrenched Harry into a chokehold and jabbed the syringe into his backside. In a matter of moments, the powerful tranquilizer hit his blood-stream, his hand melted off my wrist, and he collapsed to the ground at our feet.

"See what ya done?" Albie hollered at us. "I warned ya about upsettin' them, didn't I?" He reached down and slung Harry's unconscious body over his shoulder like he was a sack of nothing special. "With all the talk goin' on 'bout escaped patients, if Blake'd made it over the fence . . ." His eyes brimmed with rage, perspiration was cascading off his contorted face, and his precious conk hairdo was going every which way. "I got a half a mind to call the sheriff and report ya for trespassin', and if I do, ya better not . . ." I could see his wheels turning, straining to piece together the best way to keep himself out of trouble. "If you tell him that I gave ya permission to visit with the patients, I'll deny it and make sure the three of you get blamed." He gave us such a low-down, dirty look that I was grateful for the fence between us. "Now git, goddamn it, and don't come back!"

The girls and I didn't need to be told twice.

Our legs were a blur when we scrambled back through the pine trees and down the dusty path with Harry's desperate request for help and Albie's threats ringing in our ears. When we reached the Hanging Tree, Frankie and I jumped on our bikes, but Viv didn't. She hopped in place, cupped one hand over her crotch and used the other to point at the back of the hospital. "I can't. I gotta pee," she cried. "Really, really bad."

Her bladder wasn't only tiny, it was bashful, so she couldn't find a spot in the woods, the way Frankie and I would. Viv needed a proper bathroom and she wanted to use the one adjacent to the hospital kitchen. I was tempted to let her try. I would have loved to get folded into Bigger's arms and beg her to intercede with Albie, but what if we bumped into him?

He saw himself as a pretty boy, and as soon as he dropped Harry off at the infirmary or dumped him into one of the padded cells to punish him, Albie would want to pull himself together. After he changed into a fresh uniform, he'd take the back stairs down to the kitchen and ask his girlfriend to fix his conk. He'd whine to Bigger about what'd happened in the yard and complain that he could lose his job and it'd be our fault if he did. Albie wasn't family the way Jimbo was. He owed us no loyalty and he had no backbone. After he was squared away and looking sharp again, I wouldn't put it past him to pick up the wall phone in the kitchen and dial up the sheriff, the way he'd threatened he might.

Uncle Walt wouldn't play favorites. He'd do to us what he did to any other kids in Summit who got caught breaking the law. After he hauled us into the station, the whole town would be gossiping about what we'd done. That'd humiliate our families—I couldn't even picture what Aunt Jane May would do to us—but it was Frankie I was most concerned about.

The group of Germans who remained suspicious of her skin tone might dig deeper into the background of the troublemaker who'd broken the law. They'd say and do awful things when they found out the truth. Dell thought so, too. The girls and I had heard the fear cutting through her voice during that back porch meeting when she'd said, "If the truth ever comes out . . . God help us, Jane May." She'd not allow her daughter to be exposed to that hatred. She'd quit her job at the Maniachis, pack their suitcases, and she and Frankie would march over the tracks to Mud Town—or all the way back to Milwaukee.

I clamped down on Viv's shoulders and tried to shake some sense into her. "If we go into the kitchen so you can pee, we could run into Albie and . . ." There was no time to explain the damage that'd be done. "Get on your bike!"

"Albie didn't mean it. He's just mad 'cause he got sweaty and his conk got messed up," Viv said. "He wouldn't dare turn us in to the sheriff."

"Oh yeah, he would," Frankie hollered. "I've seen him pass the buck in Mud Town plenty of times. He'll do whatever he needs to do to keep from gettin' fired 'cause if he doesn't pay off his gambling debts, he could end up—" She ran her finger across her neck in the cutthroat sign.

Those high-tone clothes, his fancy haircut, and the shiny black Chrysler Albie drove didn't come cheap. Everyone knew that he was in over his head with Chummy Adler, who owned a bar in Mud Town called The Top Hat, but whose real business—cards and dice—was done in the back room. To keep him and his new collection goon—Elvin Merchant—at arms' length, I had no problem imagining Albie explaining to Dr. Cruikshank that circumstances beyond his control made him pull the siren: *"Three girls trespassed onto the property. They're the ones who upset Blake and the other patients. It's them that should get the blame—not me."*

I wasn't sure if Albie would sink so low as to reveal our names to the psychiatrist, but he might not have to. He'd told us that afternoon at Earl Spooner's Club that we needed to be careful when we visited the patients because there were "eyes everywhere." I didn't believe him when he told us about those hidden cameras on the property, I thought he was just trying to scare us. But what if he hadn't been lying? Not even Viv could talk us out of the trouble we'd be in if there was proof we'd trespassed on private property. A picture is worth a thousand words.

"Ride!' I shrieked at her.

"I can't! I'll wet my pants!"

"Good!" Frankie said before she pedaled off.

As we watched her disappear down the path and into Founder's Woods, Viv told me the same thing that Frankie had said about her when she'd taken off earlier without us. "She'll come back. She's—"

"Shut up," I yelled. "This is all your . . ."

With one last glance at the recreation yard and the patients getting dragged or carried back into the hospital, and the knowledge that there was a very good chance we'd never get to visit with them again, I wanted to punish Viv for taking that away from me. Tell her that whatever awfulness happened to the patients, us, and the people we cared about was all her fault.

But in all good conscience, I couldn't do that, could I. She might've pulled the trigger that afternoon, but I'd loaded the gun. If I hadn't forced the girls to visit with the patients in the first place, none of what had happened would have.

I lowered my voice and told Viv, "If you get on your bike, I'll forgive you for promising the new patient that we'd help him out, and I'll beg Frankie to forgive you, too."

That did the trick, and thank the saints that it did, because I might be in Viv's shoes soon and need her to repay the favor. I knew what I needed to do, and if the two of them didn't agree with me, I'd end up breaking the Good Samaritan rule, too.

Chapter Fifteen

The girls and I had pedaled about three-quarters of the way back to town on the twisty path through Founder's Woods when I flew over my handlebars. Last thing I heard before I landed in the dirt so hard that all the breath was knocked out of me was Viv shouting, "Frankie! Stop!"

When I came to, the two of them were kneeling next to me. Frankie was patting me lightly on the cheek because Aunt Jane May had told her plenty of times that if she changed her mind about becoming "the next Perry Mason," her unflappability and steady hands would make her a wonderful physician.

"You got knocked out," she said as she inspected me. "Anything broken?"

I wiggled my arms and legs. "Don't think so."

"How many fingers am I holding up?"

After I told her, I asked, "What the heck happened?"

"Stupid boys and their stupid booby traps," Frankie said.

She helped me to my feet and pointed behind me at the length of rope that'd been tautly stretched across the path. It hadn't been there on our ride over to the hospital, so I figured that one of the little cowboys who liked to play shoot 'em up in the woods must've tried to bushwhack a little Indian while we were up there. I felt stupid for not seeing it. No matter how desperately I wanted to get away from Broadhurst, I should've let our lookout and scout lead the way instead of breezing past her when Viv and I caught up to her on the path.

Frankie dusted the dirt off my front side and said, "You sure you're okay? You look a little green around the gills."

"She's fine—let's go," Viv said to Frankie as she picked her bike back up off the path. "You need your treat and I need to pee."

As tempting as a brown cow must've sounded, Frankie was still ticked off at her for running away from us so she could meet Ernie Fontaine and was not one to be won over too easily. "Not so fast," she told Viv. "Biz is lucky she didn't crack her head open and more sharp turns are comin' up. We won't see another trap until it's too late, and we can't risk gettin' hurt in a way that we can't hide from Auntie."

Unless Jane May Mathews, RN, was otherwise occupied, she'd do what she always did when we returned from a day out of her sight. She'd exam us from top to bottom. We'd concealed bruises and sprained ankles from her many times throughout the years, but we'd never be able to hide a broken limb or nose.

"We're walkin' the rest of the way out," Frankie said in a way that let Viv and me know that it was not open to discussion.

Something about being on foot set alarm bells off in my head, but I thought it was a side effect of getting knocked out, so I gave Frankie the okay sign. Viv pranced in place, mumbled something about a bathroom, but she didn't fight Frankie's decision either. She knew she'd irritated her enough for one day.

Despite the pounding in my head, my sweat-soaked blouse, skeeters buzzing around my ears, and the shocking upset that'd happened with Harry Blake and Albie, I told myself to take heart as we made our way down the winding path, because the rest of the afternoon could only go up from there.

Once we got through the woods and emptied into the park, we'd get back on our bikes and pedal over to the drug store. I envisioned Frankie quickly downing at least two brown cows. After Viv availed herself of the facilities and probably scrawled something hateful about Evelyn Mulrooney and her wretched daughter Brenda on the stall that was covered with her previous insults, we'd head straight to the five-and-dime for our decorating supplies. When we returned home, I was counting on the coast being clear. Aunt Jane May had already done her gardening, so she would probably be at Rusty's Market shopping for what she needed to prepare the Buchanans' picnic lunch for the Fourth of July bash. Her absence would give the girls and me the chance to clean ourselves up and get busy winding red, white, and blue crepe paper around our spokes and handlebars. By the time she came home, we'd be making Kleenex flowers, and it'd look like we hadn't lied to her earlier about where we were going that afternoon.

After supper, we'd climb up to the hideout. I'd call for a powwow, then ease into telling the girls why I thought we needed to add a number eight to our summer list: *Make things right.* Hopefully, they'd be on board and we could begin throwing ideas around. If they weren't, I was prepared to go it alone.

Most importantly, we needed to protect Frankie from unwanted attention, so we had to come up with a way to convince Albie not to report us to Uncle Walt for trespassing. I thought we should bribe him, buy his silence with a stack of Superman comic books or pool our pennies and take them to Chummy Adler's bar to knock off some of Albie's debt.

When a Tree Musketeer made a promise, we were bound to honor it, but I had no idea how'd we keep the one Viv had made to "help out" Ernie Fontaine.

Harry Blake was a whole 'nother ball of wax. I didn't know what to make of how he'd acted that afternoon or what he'd meant. Was he talking about the Mondurians when he said, "You've got to help . . . they're going to kill—"?

Considering his place of residence, someone who didn't know him might say that he was experiencing a paranoid delusion, but it didn't seem like that to me. Harry had sounded desperate, but not crazily so when he came running to the fence and pressed the piece of paper into my hand.

We'd been in such a hurry to get away from Albie, and then I'd had that fight with Viv and took a tumble off my bike, so I'd forgotten all about the note. Hoping that it might give me a clue to Harry's behavior, I reached down to dig for it in my shorts pocket, when Frankie stopped without warning on the skinny path. I narrowly missed colliding with Viv, who'd bumped into Frankie hard enough that she lost her footing.

"What the hell, Frankenstein?" Viv said as she fought her way out of the bush she'd tumbled into. "Is there another trap?"

I looked over Frankie's head to see that indeed there was. The worst trap imaginable.

"Good afternoon, ladies," Elvin Merchant said with a lopsided grin. "Fancy meetin' you here."

The boy blocking our way down the path was a real looker. His dark hair was styled in a pompadour and his eyes were the color of the blue stones you'd see in fancy jewelry. His mother, Emmy, was the one who'd taught him his good manners before she went for a walk around the block a few years ago and never came back. Unlike some of the folks in town, I didn't look down on her for disappearing because I'd seen firsthand the damage her husband could do the times she'd show up at our front door late at night asking for Doc. Her husband, Jasper Merchant, would've eventually killed her—of that I was certain. To this day, I wonder if that's exactly what he'd done. That mean son of a bitch was bad enough when he was sober, but when he drank, he would knock his boy around and treat him like hired help, too.

Elvin did most of the work at the family service station and his arm and chest muscles were obvious beneath his stained white T-shirt. He was hovering so close to us that I could smell the beer, sweat, gasoline, and something else that I was unfamiliar with at the time but now know was masculine need.

I tried to tell him to leave us alone, but all that came out was a croaking sound. Viv was in the same boat as me. She looked like a silent movie heroine screaming at a villain. Frankie was cooler under fire because she'd had some experience with this kind of belligerent behavior before. On the nights we'd play ghost in the graveyard in the Mud Town Cemetery, we'd sometimes sleep at Jimbo's house. If in the wee hours he was called over to Earl Spooner's place to give the heave-ho to a man who was too full of booze and himself, Frankie would tag along. She'd watched and learned how to handle a mean drunk.

"Go home and go to bed," she told Merchant.

"Only if you come with me." He grinned at Frankie the sickly way he did when we'd ride past the service station late at night. "I've been waitin' here, so I could show you a good time."

So it hadn't been some little cowboy who'd stretched the rope across the path. Merchant must have seen us riding over to Broadhurst and knew we'd come back this way. The trap was his handiwork, or one of his gang's. I looked around for the other juvenile delinquents, but if they were hiding and waiting their turn to have at us, they were doing a good job. The woods were as still as a tomb, and the only sound to be heard was the whine of mosquitoes and our shortened breath.

Merchant was swaying on his feet, but when he made a move toward Frankie, he might not have been as drunk as I thought he was. When she went to shove him away, he caught her hand mid-flight and did not slur his words when he said throatily, "Don't be like that, honey. I wanna get to know ya better."

Viv finally found her voice and hollered, "Let go of her, ya stinkin' grease monkey!" She drew her leg back, but I got her by the waist and pulled her back. One of her knobby-kneed kicks wouldn't dent the anesthetized state Merchant was in. It'd only make him madder, and I could see the outline of his switchblade in the pocket of his tight blue jeans.

Our only hope was that someone would hear us scream for help, but the mercury had topped ninety degrees five days in a row, the humidity had refused to take a back seat, and what breeze there was served the devil. Kids who'd been playing in the woods earlier in the day were now cooling off at Grand Creek, jumping off the diving boards at the community pool or sucking up phosphates in air-conditioned comfort at Whitcomb's, and we were much too far off the beaten trail for any adult to come running.

"If you hurt her, you won't get away with it like you did Cindy Davenport," I hollered at Elvin. "You'll go to jail this time 'cause I'll—"

"You'll what? Tell your fuckin' uncle?" Beyond caring and seemingly beyond the law, Elvin laughed, got a fistful of Frankie's blouse and tugged her closer, but she didn't go easy. Twisting and slapping at his chest, she was doing her best, but she could not free herself from his drunken desire.

When I heard bushes rustling behind me, I figured one of the other bullies *had* been hiding, and he'd come to join the party. I didn't want it to be Elvin's second-in-command, Dutch Van Heusen, making his way toward us through the brush, but feared that it was. He'd sworn that he'd get back at us for what we'd done to him at Still River and it looked like the time had come for him to make good on that threat.

Merchant was powerful, but it was three against one. Escaping from him might've been doable, but getting away from two almost-men bent on getting what they wanted? That'd be something only a dumb chump would believe. All Frankie, Viv, and I could do at that point was windmill our arms, kick, and pray that we'd land a blow painful enough that the boys would loosen their grip and we could make a run for it.

I couldn't let Van Heusen leave a mark on my face that I couldn't hide from Aunt Jane May. I'd wait until I smelled cow manure and heard him growl, "Gotcha," and after he shoved me to the ground with his filthy, farm-boy mitts, I'd roll up like a slug to minimize the damage.

Tensed and ready for his attack, about the last thing I expected was to feel a small hand placed softly on my shoulder and to hear a gal with the voice of an angel call over my shoulder to Merchant, "Let go of the girl."

I was so grateful that it wasn't Van Heusen that I was about to drop to my knees and cry, "Hallelujah" before I realized how foolish that was. It was kind of the gal to come to our aid but she couldn't back down a boy who was so full of beer and anger and wanting. Elvin Merchant wasn't intimidated by grown men, even ones with guns and badges. He'd never get scared off by a member of the weaker sex.

I didn't turn around to see who our would-be rescuer was right away because not only was I stunned by her sudden appearance, I was feeling bad for her. I was thinking that this was another one of those situations when it didn't pay to be a Good Samaritan and she'd be lucky if he didn't attack her, too, when I saw something suddenly come over Merchant. Not compliance, because he didn't let go of Frankie the way the gal had told him to, but he didn't look so cocky anymore.

And that wasn't my imagination or hope blinding me. Viv saw the hesitation wash across Merchant's face, too. She heaved a sigh of relief, picked up my hand, and the two of us spun around together to thank the gal for interceding, but when we came face to face with her, it wasn't words of gratitude that came tumbling out of our little mouths. Viv groaned, collapsed to the ground, and streams of pee gushed down her legs, and I bent over and dry-heaved because this gal didn't look like anyone's savior.

With the wide, white streak in her raven black hair muddied and her face covered in scratches beneath a blood-streaked dusting of dirt, Audrey Cavanaugh looked like a monster born out of the very bowels of the Earth.

She also had the deadliest-looking knife I'd ever seen in her hand when she brushed past Viv and me and demanded again that Merchant, "Let go of the girl."

Elvin's hand inched toward his back pocket. He was itching to withdraw his switchblade, but the boy was drunk, not blind. His knife would look like a plaything compared to the one Audrey Cavanaugh was holding in her hand. But that wasn't why he finally let go of Frankie. The look on her face did that. I wouldn't describe it as threatening exactly. It was more chilling than that. Chopping Elvin into little pieces would be all in a day's work was what that look said.

That's when it dawned on me that he might not be the only one in danger. A gal who rarely ventured out her front door materializing in the woods at the exact same time the girls and I needed saving? No way, no how was that a coincidence. She must've been tracking us, like we were ingredients for her supernatural stew, and she'd only rescued us because Merchant had been trying to poach Frankie. Once she'd finished hacking him into little pieces, we'd be next.

I opened my mouth to scream, *"Run!"* but the Summit Witch beat me to it. Without taking her eyes off Merchant, she said in a voice that was both motherly and menacing, "Run along now, girls. I'll deal with you later," and for the second time that day we didn't have to be told twice.

Chapter Sixteen

～

Of course, all thoughts of a brown cow had been knocked out of Frankie's head by the time we came flying out of the woods after our encounter with Merchant and the Summit Witch.

As we made the turn down Main Street, it felt like the forces of evil were nipping at our heels. I was pedaling my bike like my life depended on it. Viv was to my right and in the midst of a breathing attack. Frankie was on the other side of her, saying, "Cup your mouth or you're gonna faint!"

Beset by confusion, guilt, and exhaustion, all I could think about was retreating to the security and safety of the hideout. I was sure the girls felt the same way, but when I started to make the wide right turn toward Honeywell Street, Frankie yelled, "Stop!" and pointed over our heads at the sagging white banner strung between two streetlights:

"July 4th, 1960!

Come one, Come all!

Parade, Picnic, Prizes, Pyrotechnics!"

"The five-and-dime is closin' at three today," Frankie hollered at me over Viv's head. "If we don't get those decorating supplies, Auntie's gonna—"

Her voice was drowned out by Viv's raspy breathing and horns honking, but Frankie's face said it all. If Aunt Jane May wasn't at Rusty's Market buying food for the Fourth of July picnic like we hoped she was, she'd be keeping watch for us out the kitchen window.

If the three of us rolled up the driveway without our bike baskets full of decorating supplies, she'd badger us until I, the weakest willed, confessed where we'd been that afternoon. If she didn't cook our gooses beyond recognition and bury them beneath the backyard willow tree then and there, she was bound to dole out severe consequences, and we would have no choice but to run away. Seemed like the County Fair's traveling carnival gave jobs to just about anyone, so we'd sell cotton candy or run a game like Guess Your Weight, and, you know, as the girls and I came blazing down Main Street that afternoon, that sounded like a solid idea. I saw no other way out of the fixes we were in, and it's not like I wasn't trying.

The Rivoli was showing *Psycho*, and as we sped under the marquee, I remembered all the times I thought Harry Blake's Mondurian stories belonged on the silver screen. When we flew past the bakery owned by two of the Germans who might dig up Frankie's roots if we got reported for trespassing, I wished they'd choke to death on their strudel. And as soon as I saw my uncle's county car parked in front of the police station, I thought as angry as he'd be at the girls and me for disregarding his order to keep away from Elvin Merchant, shouldn't we tell him that Audrey Cavanaugh was probably chopping him into little pieces as we spoke?

"Biz!" I heard Frankie hollering at me from a distance. "What the—where ya goin'?"

Consumed by my racing thoughts, I hadn't noticed that the girls had stopped in front of the five-and-dime. In a rush to be reunited with them, I turned my bike too sharply and smashed into a row of folding chairs the town handyman was setting up for the Fourth of July parade.

When Lance Howard heard the ruckus, he swiveled around with a face full of fury, but when he saw it was me, he waved and came trotting to my side like he couldn't believe his good luck. The girls and I always made sure to steer clear of him, so I hadn't seen him up close since he lowered the bar on the Camelot Ferris wheel. He looked and smelled worse than I remembered. The pores in his bulbous nose were potholes, and he stank of cigarettes and sweat.

"You hurt, princess?" he asked.

"Naw," I said as I tried to disentangle my front wheel from a couple of the wooden chairs.

"You sure 'bout that? Looks like you banged your knee." I didn't feel anything, but I must've caught my right kneecap on the edge of one of the chairs, because it had a scratch running across it. "Wouldn't be right if I let ya ride off without checking it out."

When he reached out, I pulled back. "Thanks for the offer, but I'm fine." The Victorian clock that stood outside Armbruster's Jewelry store was telling me that the dime store would close in nine minutes. "I gotta go now. They're waitin' for me." I pointed down the block to Viv and Frankie. "Maybe we can talk more at the picnic tomorrow, Mister Howard."

"Call me Sir Lancelot." He gestured to his pants pocket. "Let me give ya a piece of saltwater taffy before you go and some for your friends, too." I didn't want to take it, but I promised myself I would because he didn't sound the alarm after he spotted us on the catwalk the night of the emergency meeting. "You're the Buchanan kid," he said as he withdrew from his pants pocket three pieces of taffy that had gone warm and soft in their wax wrappings. "Biz, right?"

I wished he didn't know my name, but there was no use denying it. "That's what my friends and family call me. Thanks for the candy, and I'm really sorry about running into the chairs but I—"

"Funny thing is, Biz, I've been hopin' to run into *you*." He gave me a gnawed-on-piece-of-corn-on-the-cob smile. "I seen you girls around the hospital and ya better be more careful." He tipped his head back, scratched at his neck, and left red claw marks. "Somebody sees you talkin' to the patients from that spot in the pines or sneakin' over the fence and goin' through the door into the kitchen . . ." He low-whistled. "Man, that could spell trouble with a capital T."

Albie had warned us when we'd asked for permission to visit with the patients that we had to be careful because "there's eyes everywhere." It made my stomach lurch to think the eyes he'd been warning us about were the bloodshot ones staring down at me. Lance Howard had been watching us? If so, how closely and for how long? When Viv had pulled her "don't look now, but . . ." diversionary tactic during our first overnight in the hideout, she'd told us the handyman was watching us. Frankie and I thought she was just trying to get out of the witch dare, but what if she'd been telling the truth?

Howard slid a Lucky Strike from the pack he kept in his T-shirt sleeve, slipped a Zippo out of his pants pocket, rubbed it across his thigh, and brought the flame to the tip. "You girls ever seen anything that you might call strange going on around the hospital or in the woods?" he said from behind a cloud of smoke.

The patients did strange things all the time, and we'd just seen the Summit Witch threatening Elvin Merchant in the woods with what looked like a pirate sword, but I didn't think that's the sort of thing he meant. I was pretty sure he was talking about what Albie had told us after we'd sworn to uphold his visiting rules on the menu at Earl's: *"There's mysterious goin's-on at the hospital."*

I couldn't tell if Howard was angling for information about what the girls and I might've seen around Broadhurst or whether he was the one acting strange up there and wanted to know if we'd ever seen him doing so, but I told him, "Nope, never seen anything. Gotta go."

I tried to turn my bike in the direction I'd come from, but he set his hands down on my handlebars and locked me in place. "If ya ever do see somethin' strange goin' on, I want you and your little friends to come find me right away," he said like he'd be the trouble with a capital T if we didn't. "Deal?" The bologna sandwich I had for lunch rose into my throat when he held out his hand, but I was too afraid not to shake it.

"Now say it," he demanded.

"Yes."

"Yes, what?

"Yes, Mister How—Sir Lancelot. My friends and I will come find you right away if we see anything strange goin' on at the hospital or in the woods."

He said, "Good girl," and patted my head like a dog he'd just taught to roll over. "One more thing. If you don't want me tellin' Doc Cruikshank about all the times I seen you and your friends talkin' to the patients and sneakin' into the kitchen, next time you're visitin' Dolores, I want you to tell her that if she don't want to lose her job . . . naw, forget that. More flies with sugar." He took a last, wet draw off his cigarette and flicked it into the street. "Just tell that cook I think she's mighty fine and I been cravin' some dark meat."

"Okay."

"Okay, what?"

"I'll tell Bigger that you think she's a mighty fine cook and next time she roasts a turkey, to save you some dark meat."

I had no idea why he burst into a barking laugh that turned into a cough, but when he turned to spit out what he'd brought up, he released my handlebars and I made my getaway.

"Yeah, you do that. And don't forget about our deal," the handyman called after me, still hacking.

I felt like a wounded animal culled from its herd by a hyena and I couldn't wait to be reunited with the girls again, but when I looked down the block, they were no longer in front of the dime store. I didn't think they'd up and leave without me, or the decorating supplies we needed. Well, Viv might if she had one of her flights of fancy, but Frankie knew how vital it was to pick up the crepe paper and Kleenex. We'd face the wrath of Aunt Jane May if we returned home without them.

I put my head down and pedaled toward the five-and-dime, hoping that they'd stepped inside before Mr. Elston could hang the "Closed" sign on the door. But if they had, where were their bikes?

I was scared, and unsure if I should head uptown or downtown to search for them, when Frankie stepped out of one of our better hiding places in town—the passageway between the

Emporium and the Rivoli—and blocked my way. I had to skid to a stop to keep from mowing her down the same way I had the parade chairs.

"Where'd you go?" I yelled. "And where's Viv?"

"She's waitin' for us behind the dime store. We almost got caught by Auntie when she came out of Rusty's Market. I didn't want her to see me lookin' like"—she pointed to her sweat-stained, dusty blouse—"and Viv's shorts have pee all over them, so we ducked inside the passageway."

"You sure she didn't see you?"

"She would've if she looked our way, but she walked right past us. She was juggling an armful of groceries, so if we cut over to Fulton, we should be able to beat her home. But that was ten minutes ago, so we gotta move."

Maybe I was relieved that she hadn't left me, or I was thinking about those Germans and the church busybodies who were gunning for her and how I couldn't let them take her away from us, but I reached out and wrapped my arms around her and squeezed for all I was worth. She didn't really go in for that sort of thing, unless it came from Viv, so it was like hugging one of the pillars outside of the library.

"Ya got it out of your system?" she asked after a bit.

I hadn't, but nodded anyway.

"Then let go of me. Viv's off her leash."

As I followed her back through the passageway I thought I could've stayed in that cool darkness forever, and began to wish that I had when we stepped back out into the pounding sunshine. Viv's blue Schwinn with the bedraggled white streamers, silver bell, and basketful of decorating supplies was in the parking lot behind the five-and-dime, but she was nowhere in sight.

Frankie's brow winkled, but I figured Viv was paying us back for reaming her out pretty much the whole day. She was probably hiding behind one of the cars in the parking lot so she could jump out and scare us worse than we already were.

"Quit screwin' around, Viv," I yelled. "We need to get home."

"For crissakes, what took you so long?" she said as she bounded out the back door of the dime store with a box of aluminum foil in her hand.

I knew who it was for and that it was an apology present. I felt kind of bad then for thinking the worst of her and said, "That's such a nice thing to do for Harry. He'll be so—"

"Can it, ya dumb chump, and get the lead out. We gotta beat Auntie home," she said and took off across the parking lot.

Frankie knocked her kickstand back and asked me, "What'd the handyman want?"

I gave her the telegram version, and when I stuck my hand into my shorts pocket to show her the saltwater taffy, the note Harry Blake had passed me at Broadhurst fluttered to the ground. Viv was on the move, Frankie was dying to go after her, and I didn't want to get caught by Aunt Jane May either, so when a breeze sent the piece of paper sailing across the parking lot, I was tempted to just leave it. Until my little voice told me that was a bad idea.

Frankie nodded at Harry's note and asked, "Did you read it?"

When I shook my head, I thought she was about to tell me good riddance to bad rubbish. Say that the note was probably just more of his ranting about the Mondurians or Bigger's poisoned food and we were in a race to beat Aunt Jane May home and I couldn't waste time chasing after it, but she fixed her wise beige eyes on mine and said, "Hurry," and rocketed after Viv.

After I dropped my bike to the ground, it took me a minute or so to trap the skittering piece of paper beneath my foot. Because I needed to catch up with the girls, I was just going to stuff it back into my pocket. But when I bent down to pick it up, I noticed the mark Harry's fingers had left on my wrist and remembered the desperation in his voice and I couldn't stop myself from reading what he'd broken every rule in the Broadhurst book to press into my hand: *Tell Audrey Cavanaugh they're going to kill Leo.*

Chapter Seventeen

I told myself to remember Mrs. Keller in my prayers that night because if she hadn't called to Aunt Jane May from her front porch and offered her a glass of iced tea, Frankie, Viv, and I wouldn't have had enough time to clean ourselves up before she returned home with the armful of groceries from Rusty's Market.

I showed Harry's note to the girls right off, of course. Frankie seemed unimpressed. Viv had barely recovered from coming face to face with the Summit Witch, and she started breathing weird when she saw what Harry wanted us to do, but we couldn't discuss our encounter with her, or anything else that'd happened in the woods that afternoon. Aunt Jane May would've heard us through the open kitchen window. I guarantee you, though, that when the girls and I were weaving the crepe paper through our bike spokes and pinning carnation flowers to our handles in the backyard, we were all thinking the same thing: *For cryin' out loud, what happened to the good old days of getting the wits scared out of us by movie monsters instead of real ones?*

By the time we'd finished, the three of us had managed to deck out our bikes so they'd look like they belonged in the parade—in the *way* back. Aunt Jane May harrumphed after she inspected them and was suspicious about how little effort we'd put into a task we'd always taken enormous pride in.

"Soon as you're done eating, let's have a little chat, shall we?" she said when she brought our hot dogs and chips out to the screened porch.

Her idea of a little chat was giving us a lengthy third degree, and the girls and I had made other plans. We'd not had a moment alone since we'd come home, so right after dessert we planned to retreat to the hideout. After we talked about what'd happened that afternoon at Broadhurst and in the woods afterward, I planned to tell them that I wanted to add *Make things right* to our summer list, and I hoped they'd see things my way.

But best laid plans and all that.

I'd been one hell of a day, and after we licked our bowls of strawberry ice cream clean we conked out on the wicker sofa. Aunt Jane May must've been dead on her feet, too, because the next time we heard from her was when she came out to the porch the following morning to beat a serving spoon against a pot and yell, "Up and at 'em, girls! *Tempus fugit!* The parade starts in a half hour."

*   *   *

The heat that rose in shimmering waves off Main Street made the shops look like mirages. The modern new electronic sign the Summit Savings and Loan had attached to the side of their building to give the bank an inferiority complex informed us that it was 9:10 in the morning and eighty-seven degrees, but failed to mention that it was so humid that it felt like we were riding our bikes underwater.

When the parade finished the route on Main Street and dragged itself over to Grand Park on its last legs, it was time for the bike judging and races. The Tree Musketeers' decorating efforts garnered no special attention. And Viv and I didn't even finish the three-legged race. She kept whining about how sweaty I was, so I fell on top of her just to shut her up. The only ribbon we'd have to hang in the hideout by the end of the day was the blue Frankie won in the egg and spoon race, which was nothing to brag about either. The other two entrants were Cathy Dineen, who was blind, and Norman "Norma" Wilkes, who wanted to beat Frankie so bad for giving him that nickname, but had yet to be fitted with his special shoe that corrected his shorter by two inches left leg. It was just pitiful to watch him hopping after her like that.

After the races concluded, Mayor Bud Kibler awarded the ribbons. He was a real sweetheart who practiced the Golden Rule—he was particularly admired in Mud Town—but he'd just turned eighty-three, and as much as the girls and I hated to admit it, Evelyn Mulrooney was right. He was often forgetful and sometimes confused.

Bud's hair looked like he'd got it caught in a box fan and his shirt was inside out, but it was so good to hear him say, "Why, hello there, small fries." He congratulated Frankie on a job well done and told Viv, "Nice try." To me, he said, "What's this?" He pointed at my shorts pocket and plucked out Harry's note that must've worked its way out when Viv and I were rolling around on the ground after the three-legged race. If he read it, we'd be in big trouble. How would I explain: *Tell Audrey Cavanaugh they're going to kill Leo?*

"Excuse me, Mayor, but Biz needs that back," Viv stepped up and said. "It's a clue in a detective game we're playin'."

"*Clue?* That's a great game! Can I play?" Bud said and tucked the note in the back pocket of his shiny brown pants.

Viv held out her hand and said, "Sorry, sir—maybe next time."

"Ahoy there, Mayor. I've been looking all over for you," the owner of the Rivoli and picnic organizer, Mr. Willis, shouted as he came bustling our way. "Hello, girls. Happy Fourth. Where've you been? I've missed seeing you at the matinees." He put his arm around Bud and began walking him away. "We need to get you to the stage. You have to make that special announcement before everyone starts unpacking their baskets."

What Harry had asked us to do wasn't complicated, so the girls and I didn't need the note to refer to. But I was planning to give it to Audrey Cavanaugh. Viv had my back once, but I didn't expect her to try and save the day again. She was jealous that Harry had given me the note instead of her, so I was surprised when she said "Be right back," and trotted off. I figured she'd pester the mayor for the note until he lost whatever brains cells he had left and forked it over, but not more than a minute later she came running back to us.

Frankie jeered at her and said, "What happened? Bud wouldn't fall for your blarney? Maybe his arteries haven't gone as hard as we think they have."

"Shut up, Frankenstein." Viv shoved her aside and laid into me. "Harry should've given me the note 'cause I woulda taken much better care of it than you have. You shouldn'ta brought it with you today. You know what a big crush the mayor has on Auntie. What if when he goes over to visit with her, he shows her the note?" She let me imagine what a disaster that'd be before she grinned and opened up her hand to reveal the piece of paper Bud

Kibler had taken from my shorts. "I snitched it out of his back pocket. Finders keepers, losers weepers," Viv said as she jammed Harry's note so deeply into her pocket that I, or anyone else, would need a crowbar to remove it.

I was going to protest and demand a rock, paper, scissors shoot-out, but then the mayor's voice reverberated out of the speakers that'd been set up around the park. "Good morning, neighbors!" He waited for a minute until the crowd piped down. "Doc Buchanan has recommended that we postpone our picnic and return to the park when it's cooler. And kids, I've opened up the pool for you. See you all back here at six sharp."

* * *

Rinsing off the heat of the day in that cool pool sounded awfully good and the girls and I, as well as most every kid in town, took the mayor up on his offer. After we all went home to pick up our bathing suits, we spent the rest of the afternoon doing cannonballs off the diving boards and daring each other to hold our breath underwater the longest. Brenda Mulrooney was a horrible swimmer—couldn't even dog paddle—so she won that dare. But only because Viv surreptitiously pushed her into the deep end. Frankie and I knew it was wrong, of course, but watching that junior so-and-so sputter and flail until Tommy Boyd quit drooling over the teenage girls long enough to leap from his lifeguard chair was the most fun the three of us had had in weeks. And it wasn't like Brenda didn't deserve a comeuppance after accusing Aunt Jane May of performing unnatural acts with Uncle Walt.

"That brat should thank me," Viv said after she shoved Brenda in. "Tommy givin' her artificial respiration will probably be the only time she's gonna get a boy to put his lips on hers."

When St. Thomas's bells pealed six to let us know that it was time to enjoy the postponed picnics our families had waiting for us, sunburned and water-logged, we trooped back to Grand Park. We'd worked up quite the appetite and made a beeline to the dedicated Buchanan table that sat in a prime spot in the shade next to the creek. Aunt Jane May was waiting for us, but Doc and the sheriff would eat later. They needed to be available to our neighbors, who would thank them for being such good stewards of the town, the way they did every Fourth of July.

"How was swimming?" our aunt asked as she passed out the paper plates.

"Fun, especially when," Viv suppressed a smile, "I mean, *until* poor Brenda Mulrooney almost drowned."

After we answered Aunt Jane May's questions about Brenda's near-death experience Frankie, Viv, and I scarfed down the fried chicken, potato salad with deviled eggs, and biscuits she'd prepared to show off her Southern roots. For dessert, the best baker in town handed us slices of her award-winning apple pie with Dixie cups of vanilla ice cream—now melted—that the chamber of commerce had passed out.

When we wanted to take another bite but knew we had to save room for more, we thanked her and wiggled off the picnic table bench. "See you later!" I said.

"Oh, you can count on that." Aunt Jane May's lips were set in a cunning smile. "I got a little something special in store for you three that, mark my words, you'll never see coming."

That sounded pretty ominous, like she'd heard about what had happened at Broadhurst and couldn't wait to lay into us, so we sped off across the park to eat ourselves silly and try not to think of it as our last meal before Aunt Jane May cooked our gooses.

Every year on America's birthday, the families in town celebrated what a melting pot we lived in by showing off their old-country food. The girls and I would always make our way around the spreads that'd been laid out on blankets or tables and then decide what we'd like to sample. Previous Fourths, we'd enjoyed the Vander Veens' herring swimming in sour cream and onions and the Holzhauers' sauerkraut and kielbasa, but we spit Mrs. McAllister's haggis into the bushes and said a prayer for Scotland. Irish food was never high on our list either, especially Mrs. Cleary's.

As we neared her family's blanket, Viv waved at them but said out of the side of her mouth, "Keep movin'. My ma is good at one thing and it ain't cookin'. And quit lookin' at Granny, Biz,"—Esmeralda Cleary was eyeing us like we were a coven on our way to sample the heart of a virgin—"or she's gonna come after me with that bottle of holy water and start shoutin' about me being possessed."

But we wouldn't think of missing the abundant feast Frankie's adopted family would set out every year. Uncle Sally, who was wearing a knit white shirt that showed off his muscles and accentuated his tan, exuded graciousness when we arrived at the Maniachis' table. His twin sister, Sophia, was wearing a red, white, and blue dress, but not in her wheelchair. Her brother must've set her and her useless legs down next to him so she'd feel more normal.

I felt peeved at God whenever I'd see them sitting next to each other like that. Giving Sophia a damaged spine should've been enough of a cross to bear without making her look like her brother in a dress and a long black wig. She was identical to Sally in other ways, too. Just like him, she always made the girls and me feel like she'd been counting the minutes until she could spend time with us again. Not in so many words, of course. Sally was very outgoing, but Sophia let her beneficent smile—the one that reminded me of the Madonna statue at St. Thomas's—do most of her talking. I, of course, no longer thought she was the raven-haired woman Florence had predicted would keep us safe from lurking evil—Audrey Cavanaugh had done that—but it could've been Sophia. She had sharp knives and a lot of guts, too.

"*Mangia, bambinas, mangia,*" Uncle Sally said jovially as he passed around pasta salad, plates of salami and crackers, and slices of Sophia's remarkable pizza pie. After the girls and I helped ourselves to some of each, the corners of his eyes drew down, and he grew more serious. "You haven't been around much lately, girls. You keeping your noses clean?"

I couldn't tell if he was upset because we'd hardly spent any time with him, or if he asked us if we were keeping our noses clean because he knew that we were in trouble up to our necks. Could someone have seen us and spilled the beans? Told him what'd happened at Broadhurst and in the woods yesterday?

Next to the Buchanans, the Maniachis were the wealthiest family in town. Albie might've come knocking at their front door to promise Sally that he wouldn't turn Frankie in for trespassing if he could see his way to gracing his palm with some Benjamins. That sounded like something he'd do to keep Chummy Adler and his new goon, Elvin Merchant, off his back. Lance Howard seemed to know an awful lot about how the girls and I spent our time, too. Maybe he told Uncle Sally that we visited with the patients and snuck into the hospital kitchen, because those carnies were always happy to separate folks from their money. Or it might not be either one of them, and someone unknown had been watching us.

I was trying to figure out how to reply to Uncle Sally's question when Viv said to him, "We were just talkin' today about how much we missed Aunt Sophia's cooking and helping you out in the garden, and we're plannin' to come around a lot more often. Could you pass me more of the tomatoes, please? They're the best ever."

She knew he was a sucker for compliments about his green thumb and that'd put a big smile on his face and he'd get busy forking the juicy beefsteaks onto her plate instead of pursuing further if we were keeping our noses clean.

I could've kissed Viv for coming up with that because I was so overwhelmed by all the hot water we were in that if Uncle Sally had pushed a little harder, I was pretty sure I would've broken down and told him everything. Considering that he let Dell raise Frankie in his house, I might've even begged him to take in another kid—the winking patient Viv'd promised we'd "help out." If he agreed, that'd take care of at least one of our problems. But no matter how beleaguered I was feeling, I would never have confessed to Sally what was weighing most heavily on my heart that night. He might try to stop us from fulfilling what Harry had asked us to do, what I now felt obligated to do. More than anything, I hoped the other two Tree Musketeers would agree to take the note to Audrey Cavanaugh's house with me—but it wasn't looking good.

Frankie shrugged when I showed her what Harry had written, because she'd heard one too many stories about brain-sucking Mondurians and Bigger's poisoned food to take it seriously.

Viv was still on the fence. Seemed like she was willing to give Harry the benefit of the doubt, but she also dreaded another confrontation with the Summit Witch.

I, on the other hand, believed with my whole heart and soul that someone named Leo *was* about to get killed. With one small reservation. Harry had no contact with the outside world, so Leo had to either work at Broadhurst or he was a patient, but no one there went by that name.

There was a man named Leonard on the second floor of the hospital, who Jimbo told us was another one of those patients, like Roger Osgood, who batted for the other team. And Leona was one of the washerwomen. One of them might be who Harry Blake meant, but I didn't think so. The note specifically said "Leo," and it hadn't been composed by a confused mind. It was well thought out and looked like it'd been written by Sister Raphael, our penmanship teacher.

Leo . . . Leo . . . Leo. The more I repeated it, the more it began to ring a bell. *Where? When? Who had told us something about someone named Leo?* I wondered, and lo and behold, ask and ye shall receive. A picture began to form in my head of the afternoon that we'd asked Albie and Jimbo for visitation rights at Earl Spooner's place.

When I'd voiced my concern that one of the patients might report us to the hospital higher-ups, Albie belly-laughed and said, "You don't got to worry about them none, sugar. Nobody believes a word they say." Then he mentioned something about patients believing that they were the king of England or "Marie Annette." I was positive he said that because I thought it was so typical of him not to know it was Marie Antoinette and he should stop reading so many comic books and borrow one of Jimbo's history books. He'd also mentioned a third-floor patient who thought he was a reporter. Like Clark Kent. I wouldn't stake my life on it, but I was also pretty sure Albie told us that patient insisted his name was Leo, even though he had a different name on his chart. Didn't Albie also say something about that patient offering cash to one of the guards if he'd call his boss at the newspaper where he worked? Or did Albie tell us the patient on the third floor believed that he delivered newspapers for the *Daily Planet* and called himself Clark or Kent?

I'd been focused on getting permission to visit with the patients that afternoon, so much of what else we talked about was fuzzy, like scenery you see out a car window when you're speeding to someplace important. What I needed to confirm my recollection of the conversation were answers straight from the horse's mouth. Only I couldn't approach Albie, not until we knew that he'd forgiven us for making him pull the point-of-no-return siren. Jimbo could give me a second opinion, too, but he was working the night shift at the hospital, along with Albie and the rest of the skeleton crew who wouldn't get to watch the fireworks at the park that night.

Viv had only been interested in "the mysterious goin's-on" and the "private things" that'd been mentioned that afternoon, so she wouldn't be of much help. Frankie would recall a lot more because an elephant would feel absentminded around her. But asking them to tell me what they remembered could be more trouble than it was worth. Chances were, they'd start squabbling about what was and what wasn't said, but it was a gamble I had to take.

I couldn't ask them in front of the Maniachis, of course, so I leaned into Frankie and whispered behind my hand, "I need to talk to the two of you. *Now.*"

I jumped to my feet and thanked Sophia for the delicious food and the pleasure of her company, but I did not want to interrupt Uncle Sally, who was busy passing out slices of his sister's specialty to our neighbors and serenading them with "When the moon hits your eye like a big pizza pie, that's *amore.*"

Frankie knew that I wouldn't have shortened our time with the Maniachis unless what I had to say wasn't extremely important and private, so she jumped up and told Sophia, "*Grazie mille.* The pasta was *multo bene.*"

Sophia stiffened and said to Frankie, "Where are you going? When will you be back? Sally and I have something important to talk to you about."

Afraid that "something important" was that Sally had found out what the girls and I had been up to, a chill walked down my spine. Frankie must've been worried, too. There was wariness in her voice when she answered Sophia. "Sorry, but we promised Dell and Bigger Dolores that we'd come by to see them before it got dark."

So she and I were ready-Freddy, but Viv was so immersed in her food that I had to tug on the back of her blouse and tell her, "We gotta go."

"But I'm not finished," she whined.

Frankie picked a piece of salami off Viv's plate, stuffed it into her T-shirt pocket, and told Sophia, "Please tell Sally that I'll come find you after the fireworks. We can talk then. *Buena sera.*"

Sophia did not grace us with her Madonna smile and wish us a good night back. She got a pained look on her face and said something urgent-sounding in Italian to her brother. Maybe something to let him know that we were leaving and he should stop us, but by the time her words reached Sally's ears, the girls and I had already shouted, *"Arrivederci!"* and disappeared into the heart of the crowd.

Chapter Eighteen

As she had every Fourth of July since she and Frankie had moved to town, Dell set up her picnic with the other Mud Towners alongside Founder's Woods because no one had yet challenged the unspoken rule in Summit: you colored people stay on your side and we'll stay on ours—unless you've come to do yard work, clean house, or haul away junk. Frankie, Viv, and I ignored that rule, of course, and few folks dared to look down their noses at us when we crossed that invisible barrier. I was a Buchanan, after all.

Mud Towners seemed to enjoy the Fourth even more than Summit proper did, and as we made our way toward the shore of brown folks having a good time on our journey toward Dell, I asked Frankie and Viv if they remembered hearing the name Leo on the afternoon we'd spent in the back booth at Earl's. As predicted, Viv remembered her cherry pie and the "mysterious goin's-on" and "private things," and not much else. But when Frankie got done rifling through her memory, she said, "Yeah. Albie said that there was a patient on the third floor whose name is John Johnson, but he calls himself Leo. But that doesn't mean he's the same Leo that Harry was talking about in the note."

In the past, I'd always paid close attention to whatever the brains of our operation told me and abided by her decision, but that had begun to change. Mostly. I was still having a very hard time believing that a nothin'-special kid like me might've inherited what Aunt Jane May called "the gift," what other people called "intuition" or "being tuned into God's wavelength," and I called my "little voice." But when I took a chance and began to listen to it—it hadn't let me down. And it was telling me that I'd been right all those times that I'd thought Harry Blake had been putting on a performance worthy of the silver screen, but that he was speaking the truth now about someone named Leo being in mortal danger.

Problem was, I had no idea how to explain to the girls this undeniable feeling of certainty that ran through me like a river. If I told them, *"I'm hearing a little voice in my head that's telling me we got to take Harry's note to Audrey Cavanaugh or this Leo person could die"* they'd think I lost all my marbles, too. I had to convince them somehow, but I had to pick my words carefully, that much I knew.

I waited until Frankie finished her logical argument to tell her, "Yeah. You're probably right. Harry's just makin' the whole thing up. But I think we should give the note to Audrey Cavanaugh tonight anyway. Ya know, just in case somebody named Leo does turn up dead. That way, our consciences will be clean. What do ya think, Viv?"

The Summit Witch had saved us from Elvin Merchant, but one good deed would probably not be enough to erase Viv's fear of her. I anticipated that she might go as white as Irish linen and break into a wheeze, so I was pretty shocked when she said, "Okay. I feel really cruddy for tellin' Harry there was a

Mondurian behind the hospital that might go invisible and seep into his ear. When he came runnin' to me to pull it out, Albie thought he was tryin' to escape, so it's all my fault that he got in trouble."

It was a rare show of conscience for Viv, and I was so relieved that she agreed to deliver the note, that I almost told her that she didn't have to feel guilty anymore because I thought Harry was just pretending to be mentally ill and didn't really believe in brain-sucking aliens.

I was also tempted to tell the both of them that I didn't think that the Summit Witch popping up in the woods after Albie had told us to "git" was a coincidence. True, I thought at the time that she saw us as ingredients for her supernatural stew. But now I thought she knew Harry and had seen what'd happened at Broadhurst that afternoon, and she followed us into Founder's Woods to find out what he had said to us at the fence—not to eat us—before Merchant balled everything up.

Of course, I wasn't a hundred percent positive about all that. What my little voice had been whispering to me might've felt as sure and true as the Ten Commandments, but what if it let me down, the same way hope was always doing?

More than anything, I wished I could bounce my suspicions off Frankie and Viv, but while my love for them was unconditional and forever—it was not blind. I knew who my blood sisters were, same way they thought they knew my every nook and cranny.

Frankie would ask me *why* I thought Harry was pretending to be mentally ill and *how* a man confined to a hospital that didn't allow visitors and a gal like Audrey Cavanaugh, who barely left her house, could know each other. If I told her, *"I just got this feeling deep inside me"* or *"This little voice told me,"* she'd roll her eyes and treat me like a lost cause. And Viv would laugh, throw a loogie at me, and say something horribly derogatory. Something like, *"Is this like the time you thought for sure that Mister Baglavich was a Russian spy because he has an accent and a two-way radio in his basement? Or maybe it's like the time you were so positive that Mister Paulson was a werewolf until you found out from Doc's files that he was so hairy because he had something wrong with his glands? Is thinkin' Harry's only pretendin' to be nuts and that he's in cahoots with a witch like that, Biz? Huh . . . huh?"*

You know, it wasn't anything like those times, but without some kind of proof to back me up, I'd have such a hard time convincing the girls of what I believed that I decided to keep my mouth shut until further notice.

I dialed back into their conversation about what Harry was counting on us to do just as Viv said, "Okay, Frankenstein. But Biz can do it, and you and me'll wait around the corner, okay?"

When Frankie nodded and turned to me, I could tell she didn't think that delivering the note was worth the sweat we'd break, that she was only agreeing to because Viv thought we should. "That plan good with you?" she asked me.

I told her that it was, so barring something else monstrous coming out of the woodwork to throw us off track, it looked like Audrey Cavanaugh would receive a visit from the Tree Musketeers right after the fireworks.

When the girls and I reached the invisible line that separated the Mud Towners from Summit proper as distinctly as the railroad tracks did, Frankie asked me, "Ya see Dell?"

She had better eyesight than me, but I had those five inches on her. When I got up on my toes, I spotted her mother right off. It made me sad that Frankie could never call Dell "mom" in public because if anyone should hear her she would no longer be considered "that Italian family's orphaned relative." That would be what Uncle Sally called, "*il bacio della morte*"—the kiss of death.

Dell had staked out a spot near the stage where the mayor would soon give his tedious speech about the founding fathers of our country and the founding father of Summit, my great-great-grandfather, Percival Buchanan. Around the time we lost the will to live, he would wrap things up, and we'd stand and sing "The Star-Spangled Banner"—or as Viv called it, "The Star-*Mangled* Banner"—and the whole town would ooh and ahh over the fireworks.

Dell was sitting on an ice chest and fanning herself in the prettiest ruby dress. The kind she'd usually wear beneath her white choir robe at Emmanuel Baptist on Sundays to really show off her skin tone.

Bigger Dolores was sitting next to her in a metal kitchen chair. She kept her hair in a net at work, but that night it looked like she'd just walked out of Violet Penny's home salon. She was wearing her Sunday best, too. I hadn't seen her out of her kitchen uniform in a while and she looked almost glamorous and . . . for God's sakes. If Viv was in the little girls' room when God was passing out patience and big bladders, then I must've been in there the day He was passing out brains, because how dumb could I be?

Bigger!

She could confirm if there was a patient who called himself Leo on the third floor. While she assembled their trays of food, she liked to chat with an orderly, Mitch Washington, who slid the meals through the slots in the bottom of the doors of the criminally insane patients. Mitch was bound to have mentioned someone who thought he was a newspaper reporter to Bigger because they were good friends who liked to shoot the bull.

"Dell is sittin' with Bigger close to the stage, which is gonna work out great," I told the girls as we drew closer to them. "We can visit with them a little and then I'm gonna ask Bigger what she knows about a patient named Leo so we can get this settled once and for all."

Viv stopped and pointed across the crowd. "What the heck is goin' on over there?"

To the side of the stage, it looked like Aunt Jane May was going toe to toe with the president of the Ladies Auxiliary, who seemed fired up, too. I'd expect that kind of behavior from Evelyn Mulrooney, who knew no bounds and loved to shoot off her mouth, but participating in a screaming match was very out of character for a lady from the South and a member of the Buchanan family, especially at a social gathering.

There were too many babies crying and cherry bombs going off and radios playing for the girls and me to get even a hint of what the two of them were squaring off over, but, thanks to our years of practice, that wouldn't be a problem. We could read their lips.

"Holy hell," Viv said. "Auntie just told that so-and-so that she's got a big gut. No, wait. She called her a bigot!"

Frankie said, "And now Mulrooney is yellin' about jungle music and saying—"

"Blackball . . . blackball," I said.

"What ya wanna bet that's why Auntie didn't come have that little chat with us last night?" Viv said. "She must've snuck over to Mud Town to meet the sheriff at Earl's Club again. Those religious gals must've seen them when they were parading past the back door with those 'Get out of town' signs, and now Mulrooney is gonna kick Auntie out of the Auxiliary and . . . aw, shit."

It didn't feel so good to be right sometimes.

Frankie said, "Looks like Mister Willis and Reverend Archie are breaking them up."

Separating hotheads is the kind of thing the sheriff would usually be in charge of, but I saw him and Doc leave the park together in a hurry shortly after we left the Maniachis' table. I thought they must've been rushing to the site of a car accident, which was not surprising. The juvenile delinquents celebrated the holiday by drinking too much beer and racing for pink slips on that straight stretch of Highway C every Fourth of July. Last year, Buzz Arnold's Chevy skidded off the road and he broke both of his legs, and I hoped it was Elvin Merchant who'd wrecked this summer. If he was recovering from his injuries, he wouldn't be able to watch us ride over to Mud Town with that sickly grin on his face, or come after Frankie again in the woods.

When the sheriff rushed out of the park with Doc, he must've left picnic organizer, Mr. Willis, in charge of keeping the peace, because he said something to Mulrooney, who gave one last furious look at Aunt Jane May and then stomped off. The man who inspired confidence on the Mud Town side of the line was Reverend Archie. He put his arm around Aunt Jane May and guided her to the back of the stage, which would be a good place for her to cool down.

Viv didn't say anything else about the sheriff and our aunt having being seen over at Earl's Club. She was beyond gloating.

I could tell by the look in her eye that she was busy planning a hideous revenge for Evelyn Mulrooney, when she began to spread bad gossip about them.

Frankie thought that's what she was doing, too, because she told Viv, "I know what you're thinking, and you're jumpin' the gun again. Auntie could've said something else besides 'bigot,' and Mulrooney coulda said 'baseball' instead of 'blackball.' And they might not have been fighting about her getting seen with Uncle Walt at Earl's either."

I nodded and said to Viv, "Remember what happened after we read Mrs. Chastain's lips?"

We couldn't sit down for a week after we'd called the sheriff at the station and told him that he should arrest Mrs. Chastain because we'd just seen her ask Rusty to *kill* her husband, when what she'd really told the owner of the market in the checkout line was "Could you *bill* my husband?"

Viv rubbed her backside and said, "Yeah, maybe we should just go ask Auntie what she and Mulrooney were yellin' about."

"Good idea," Frankie said, "if you want your head bit off." Aunt Jane May didn't lose her temper often, but when she did, you did not want to be the one standing next to her. "On second thought, maybe you *should* run over there and ask her, numnuts."

Those were fighting words, so to defuse the situation I jumped in and told the kid with a sweet tooth a mile wide, "You know what you need, Viv? You need pie. Let's go get a slice of Bigger's lemon meringue."

It'd always been her favorite and she perked right up. "First one there gets the biggest piece!" she said and turned to trot off.

Frankie reeled her back and said, "I'll *give* you the biggest piece if you promise to keep your mouth shut about what we think we saw Auntie and Mulrooney say to each other. I don't want you to upset my mom before I talk to her. She's been arguing with Uncle Sally and Aunt Sophia about something all week and I need to know what before I go lookin' for them after the fireworks, so I'm not caught off guard."

When Viv chuckled and said, "I promise I'll only open up my pie hole to stick Bigger's lemon meringue in it," I thought she better keep that promise because Frankie might shove it down her throat if she didn't.

Chapter Nineteen

When we arrived at the spot where Bigger had set her kitchen chair, she was wrapping up a conversation with Sissy Leonard, who assisted Reverend Archie with the choir at Emmanuel Baptist, so I wouldn't have to wait long to ask her about Leo, and Viv could get her pie.

Dell was sitting on a blanket, looking gorgeous. She was shades darker than her daughter, and her hair was curly, more like Jimbo's, but Frankie had inherited her stunning beige eyes and pretty, full lips. Seeing them together, I thought, not for the first time, that if those nosy Germans and church gals paid as much attention to the details as the girls and I did, they'd no longer be entertaining any doubts about Frankie's heritage. It was as plain as the noses on their faces.

Frankie was primed to ask her mom what she and Uncle Sally and Sophia had been fighting about, but Dell didn't give her the chance. "Seeing you three together always fills my heart with hope," she said when we came to her side. "Sure wish Jimbo could be here. He's been looking forward to spending tonight with you and is so disappointed that he has to watch the fireworks at the hospital."

"Ditto for Albie," Bigger said when she said came to join us. She made a funny *oomph* sound when she eased into the kitchen chair that struggled to contain all of her. "He sure could use some good food and relaxation after the awful day he had yesterday." She gave the girls and me the evil eye. "Don't know if you heard, Dell, but Albie had to pull the siren because one of the patients almost escaped."

When Frankie uttered, "That's too bad," she wasn't sympathizing with Albie, but with us. As we'd feared, Bigger Dolores's boyfriend had told her what we'd done, and it looked like she was about to share that with Dell.

"Yeah, Jimbo mentioned something about that in passing," Dell said. "What happened?"

"Honey, that's a story I'd be more than happy to tell ya, but I'm so parched my tongue is swelling," Bigger said. "Would you mind fetchin' me one of those colas they're giving away at the refreshment stand? My bunions are botherin' me somethin' fierce."

"Now? Not sure there's enough time." Dell glanced down at the gold watch the Maniachis had given her for her thirty-fourth birthday last year. "Can't it wait until after—" She looked up at the girls and me, then popped up off her blanket. "Be right back."

As she walked off, I was struck yet again by how lovely she was. Slim, but with muscular legs, a nice-sized bosom that held itself high, and hips that swayed just the right amount. Why she'd not found a nice man in Mud Town to have and to hold until death did them part was beyond me, but I wondered if Frankie had inherited her dislike of romance from her.

Now that we had Bigger alone, I was going to ask her about Leo, and was even considering showing her the note Harry had given me, but she turned on us. "You three stepped in it now," she huffed. "Albie spent most of last night swearin' to go to the sheriff to report you for trespassin'." She shook her finger in Frankie's face. "You know how scared Dell is of folks findin' out who you are. Some of them already look at ya like you're one of us. You bring attention to yourself . . . what in God's name were you thinkin'? You wanna stop livin' in that nice house with those people who love you? Quit going to the school you do? I thought you was so smart."

Frankie could've stuck up for herself, told Bigger what happened at Broadhurst wasn't her fault, that it was Viv who'd started the ball rolling when she flipped for Ernie Fontaine, but she'd never do something like that. "I'm sorry" is what she told Bigger.

I said, "It's not like we meant to cause—"

"What you *meant* to do don't mean nothin', little girl," Bigger said with a dismissive wave. "Even if you don't mean to run someone over with a truck, they still dead, ain't they? If it weren't for me talkin' Albie out of it, you'd be answerin' to the sheriff."

I loved Bigger, but I thought she vastly overestimated her powers of persuasion and her boyfriend's mettle. Albie might not have reported us the night before, but he was slippery and two-faced. If a time came when he needed to save his hide, he'd make us his scapegoats.

"Y'all are lucky as the devil that Cruikshank and Holloway are out of town and don't know about you gettin' the patients all worked up yesterday," Bigger added with an *mmm . . . mmm . . . mmm*. "Albie would've turned you in to Walt for sure if he got called up to the office, and there wouldn'ta been a thing I could do to stop him. He's scared of losing that job on account of owin' Chummy. He's way over his head this time."

Wanting to do my part to calm her down and smooth things over, I told Bigger something that I thought she might like to hear. Everyone likes flattery, even if it comes from someone who is on the iffy side. "Lance Howard told me to tell you that he thinks you're a mighty fine cook and he's been craving some of your dark meat."

"Oh, he did, did he?" When Bigger looked over at Howard, who was adjusting the musical instruments on the stage, her body rippled like the creek did after I tossed in a big rock. "When I told Albie that man had been starin' at me and showin' up in the kitchen for no reason, he laughed and told me he sure 'nuff had a reason. Then he suggested I be more friendlier to the handyman on account of him havin' Cruikshank's ear." She shook her head in disgust. "You know that I been puttin' up with a lot from Albie for a long time, girls, but after the coarse words he had to say about you three yesterday and him suggestin' that I should cozy up to that man . . . those straws broke my back. I can't tell Albie just yet or he might go runnin' to the sheriff and report what you done, but I decided that I'm through with him for good, and I already got someone else in mind to take his place." She gave us a shy smile. "I'm thinkin' that me and Jimbo would make a fine couple, don't you?" She knew the answer to that question because we'd been trying to convince her ever since she took up with Albie to show him the door and give sainted Jimbo a chance. She looked back up at the stage at Lance Howard. "Dark meat . . . *pfft*. Over my dead body."

I didn't know how to tell her that she'd need to reconsider that decision because if she didn't give Howard what he wanted, he was going to tell Dr. Cruikshank that she was letting us come help her in the kitchen, so I didn't say anything. But since he'd been eyeing us the whole time he was setting up the microphone for the mayor's yearly speech, I felt sure that he'd hunt me down later to ask when he could expect his dark meat turkey and quiz me some more about the "strange" stuff he was interested in learning more about when he cornered me on Main Street.

I thought it might be smart to throw Lance Howard a bone to get him off my back, so I asked Bigger something I was surprised I'd never thought of asking her before. "You ever seen anything strange goin' on around the hospital and the woods, the way Jimbo and Albie have?"

When Bigger looked off into the distance toward Broadhurst and fingered the cross around her neck, Viv took that as a big fat yes. "You know something don't you. Tell us," she begged, "but before ya do, can I please have a huge slice of your pie?"

Bigger should've been feeling proud of the dessert she lifted out of her ice chest. The meringue was high and fluffy and the lemon a rich, deep yellow. But after she sliced off a piece for Viv with the big knife she used in the Broadhurst kitchen that looked a lot like the one Audrey Cavanaugh owned, she sunk into herself.

"Ya mean have I seen anything strange besides patients disappearin' into thin air, lights in the woods, and that room in the basement you call the Chamber of Horrors?" When we nodded, she looked left and right, the same way Harry Blake always did before he told us something. "Ain't told no one about this and not sure I should be tellin' you, but feels like if I don't tell somebody soon I could burst." Seemed for a moment like she was having second thoughts, but she decided to go ahead anyway. "You remember the day you first heard those drillin' sounds comin' up through the kitchen registers?"

That'd been some time ago, and we'd heard that noise off and on since then, but we knew who was making it and he *was* strange, so I guessed that's why she was bringing it up.

"When you asked me what that racket was, I told you that it was just the handyman working a repair on the furnace or messin' around with something else in the basement," Bigger said. "But two nights ago, I heard that drillin' sound again. I had to stay late and deliver the dinner trays to the third floor 'cause Mitch took off time to help his wife with their colicky new baby. When the elevator came up from the basement and stopped on the main floor, I thought the handyman had come to pester me some more. But when the door slid open it was . . ."

"It's okay," I said because her face had clouded. "You can tell us. Who was in the elevator?"

Bigger's voice cracked when she said, "It was Holloway and poor Roger Osgood."

Just like us and Jimbo, Bigger cared about the patients, and Roger Osgood, who tended his flower garden, yearned to rock invisible baby Carl, and liked to bat for the other team, was her favorite. But she despised the head nurse of the hospital, thought Holloway treated the patients meanly and spoke to the staff like they were nothing more than servants there to do her bidding.

"Roger looked so helpless lyin' on that gurney," Bigger said, choked up. "He was unconscious, with a big bandage upside his head. One of the corners had slipped off, and when Holloway saw me lookin', she rushed to stick it back up. She told me that he had an accident but that Doctor Cruikshank had seen to it and that I should take next week off with pay."

Viv scratched her head and gave voice to the same thing I was wondering. "So what's so strange about that?"

"'Cause Holloway was bein' nice to you, for a change?" Frankie guessed.

"Nice? That gal don't have a nice bone in her body," Bigger spat out. "That was just her way of tellin' me to forget what I saw on Roger's head, and that ain't never gonna happen."

Imagining all sorts of dreadful things, I said, "What was under the bandage?"

"Yeah, what did ya see?" Viv said.

Bigger's eyes had gone shiny, but there was fierceness in them, too, so I reached over and patted her hand until she said, "What I saw was a hole in that poor man's head about the size of a quarter. Not just any hole, mind you. The kind of perfect hole a drill bit makes."

It took me a minute to piece together what she was saying and if it was what I thought it was, it was so bizarre that I believed Bigger might be having a heat stroke. I was about to ask her if she felt lightheaded or clammy, but decided to seek a different kind of clarification instead.

"Are you tellin' us that when you heard the drilling sound comin' up from the basement a couple of nights ago that you think someone was down there putting a hole in Roger Osgood's head?"

A gob of pie came sailing out of Viv's mouth when she guffawed and said, "You're such a dumb chump."

Bigger shot her a look and said, "I know what I heard and I know what I saw, and ya know what I think? I think you girls came up with a real good name for that secret room 'cause there's something real horrible goin' on down in that basement."

Frankie digested what she said and asked, "But why would Lance Howard drill a hole in Roger's head? Couldn't he get fired for doin' something like that?"

"The handyman ain't the only one knows how to work a drill," Bigger said. "I think it was Cruikshank that put that hole in Roger's head." She really was fond of him and looked like she was about to cry. "Why'd he want to do that to a man who never hurt another soul in his life? Ain't he supposed to be fixin' holes in patients' heads, not makin' new ones?"

Of course, the girls and I were completely taken aback. What she had told us was not only shocking, it was highly unbelievable. I probably would've put it down to an overheated brain or working such a long shift at the hospital that her eyes played tricks on her the night she saw Roger and Nurse Holloway in the elevator, if I didn't have a second opinion.

Shortly after the heat wave had descended on us, my bedroom had felt so swampish that I'd come downstairs to stick my head in the refrigerator for a breath of air. That's when I'd heard Doc telling Aunt Jane May in the kitchen, "Arthur Cruikshank calls his treatments innovative, but to my way of thinking, some of them do not adhere to the Hippocratic oath." At the time I thought he might be referring to the cattle prods and straitjackets, the hot baths and powerful drugs that were forced on the patients, but what if he'd been talking about them getting holes drilled in their heads? I couldn't believe that if he knew that was happening in the Chamber of Horrors that he'd allow that to go on.

"I've learned to ignore the bad things I've seen at the hospital over the years, but when Reverend Archie preached this morning about the Bible tellin' us that we're our brothers' keepers, I took that as a sign from God and made up my mind to do something," Bigger said. "There's only a few workin' tonight, so after the fireworks I'm goin' over to the hospital and look in that secret room for some proof that Cruikshank is doin' what I think he's doin'."

"But how you gonna get in?" Frankie said. "Jimbo told us nobody's got a key 'cept for Cruikshank and Holloway."

Bigger hadn't thought her plan all the way through and she looked crestfallen, but Viv could help her out with that. "And me. I got a key," she said and withdrew from her shorts pocket the ring of three the town locksmith had made for her. "They haven't let us down yet." She got down on her knees in front of Bigger. "Can we come with you? Please? I'll peel extra potatoes this week."

Bigger thought about that for what seemed like an awfully long time, then said, "I'd ask ya for those keys, sugar, and make Jimbo or Albie go down there with me tonight, but those third-floor patients are too dangerous to leave unattended. The only other ones working tonight are lazy Eddie King on the second floor, some new nurse watchin' the patients on the first floor, and Cruikshank and Holloway ain't been around in days, so nobody is gonna stop us from takin' a quick look in that room."

"But, what about the hidden cameras?" I said. "Won't they see us?"

"Hidden cameras?" Bigger turned to me. "I don't know nothin' about that."

Just as I thought, Albie must've made that up to scare the girls and me into being more careful when he gave us permission to visit with the patients.

"Truth is, I wouldn't mind the company, and it'd be good to have you girls as witnesses," Bigger said with a little shiver. "But you got to give me your word that if we find something that proves I'm right, we'll go and tell Doc. He'll know what to do."

I liked her idea about trying to get into the Chamber of Horrors, but I'd already decided that what she had told us was too preposterous. Her eyes must've played a trick on her, or she'd imagined what she'd seen that night in the elevator. Or maybe she hated Holloway so much that she made the story up to try and get the head nurse in trouble. But what finally convinced me that Bigger was mistaken about what was under the bandage on Roger Osgood's head was her mention of Doc. He would've noticed a drill hole in a patient's head during an examination, and no way on earth would he let Cruikshank get away with that.

But judging by the thrill running across Frankie's face and Viv bubbling to Bigger, "We promise to tell Doc if we find something" it looked like the two of them couldn't wait to cross off number one on our list: *Visit Broadhurst and try to sneak inside the Chamber of Horrors.*

Although I didn't share their enthusiasm, I certainly understood it. That basement room had always been forbidden fruit and now it was low hanging. "Count me in," I ended up saying, but mostly because I couldn't let the other Tree Musketeers go up there without me.

Bigger said, "All right, then. Meet me up there after the fireworks. I'll leave the Greer door open for ya and be waitin' in the kitchen." She looked over our heads and stiffened. "Here comes Dell back with my cola. Don't you dare say a thing to her 'bout none of this. She has enough troubles on her mind."

Our socks had been knocked so far off by what Bigger had told us that I'd forgotten to ask her about Leo, but if we were going up to the hospital later that night, we'd probably see Albie and Jimbo, and I could ask them. If we played our cards right, maybe they'd even let me talk to the patient I believed was Leo. If he confirmed what I thought he would, that'd mean that Harry was as sane as the girls and me, which, to my way of thinking, also meant the note he'd passed me was true. I wasn't sure if I should tell Leo that somebody wanted to kill him, though. I'd have to think about that.

Dell handed Bigger D her cola and said, "Drink fast. It's time."

"For what?" Viv asked around a mouthful of meringue.

Dell winked and said, "You'll see."

"But I got somethin' I need to talk to you about," Frankie said to her mom.

"Hold that thought," Dell said as she helped Bigger up from her chair. "Be back soon."

The park was teaming with people, and worried that we'd be overheard, we didn't dare discuss what Bigger had told us. But Viv, who had the talent of knowing when others were acting as naughty as her, did say after Bigger and Dell rushed off, "Those two are up to no good. Something's fishy."

There was some commotion up on the stage then, lights popped on, and Mayor Kibler appeared in front of the micro-phone. He looked even more disheveled than he had when he had plucked Harry's note out of my pocket earlier, but proud and thrilled to be there. "Hello again!" he said. "I know how much you're all looking forward to my yearly speech about our founding fathers, and I hate to disappoint you, but I have a little surprise for you this evening."

Frankie leaned over to me and asked, "Can you see if his barn door is zipped?"

"He's probably gonna say something really weird and Mulrooney will use it to prove how addled he is," Viv moaned.

"Please welcome to the stage the Emmanuel Baptist Church Choir, the Earl Spooner Five, and Miss Jane May Mathews!" the mayor said, confirming Viv's worse fear. He might as well have called Mulrooney up to the stage and handed her the key to his office in the town hall.

But then the stage lights went off, and there was some rustling and murmuring and footsteps, and when the lights came back on—boy oh boy. Aunt Jane May hadn't been kidding when she'd promised us earlier that she had something special in store for us that we'd never see coming.

She was standing in front of the Emmanuel Baptist Choir, who were not in their usual white choir robes. The gals were wearing the kind of pretty dresses Dell and Bigger had on, and the men were in pressed white shirts and black pants. Aunt Jane May wasn't as done up as the rest of them, but she looked like a force to be reckoned with in a modest navy-blue dress and matching high heels that I knew had cleats. The girls and I had heard them on the cobblestones when she snuck out of the house that night, humming something low and bluesy. I couldn't put my finger on the tune at the time because it was out of context, but with the park awash in red, white, and blue, and Old Glory waving, I realized what it was and couldn't wait to hear her belt it out. I also knew that not everyone in the park that night would feel the same way.

The crowd made a collective gasp then went mute at the sight on the stage. I could almost hear them wondering what the hell was going on when Aunt Jane May nodded at the musicians and broke into the opening bars of her favorite patriotic song, "God Bless America."

We liked to do things the way we always had in Summit, but to many of our neighbors' credit, they allowed her creamy alto voice, the choir's uplifting backup vocals, and the band's soulful rendition of the song win them over. Many of them got to their feet or cheered them on from their lawn chairs, but there were exceptions. Most notably—those Germans who didn't like Mud Towners.

I thought black and white folks coming together to perform at one of the biggest town gatherings of the year, one that Mulrooney had probably known nothing about, was probably what she and Aunt Jane May had been fighting over earlier, which meant that our lip reading had been right on the money.

Aunt Jane May would be blackballed from the Auxiliary for bucking Mulrooney's desire to close Earl's Club down, and Frankie and I were never prouder. Viv was too, of course, but she took learning why we'd been forbidden to ride over to Mud Town and Earl's place after the sun set pretty hard. The star of that night's performance must've been rehearsing with the band and the choir at the club, so the man she'd been sneaking out to meet late at night wasn't Uncle Walt, but preacher and choir director Reverend Archie. Viv did take some comfort in knowing that she'd been at least partially right because our aunt's so-called mystery man was tall, *very* dark, and handsome. But they could not be trotting hotly together. That sort of mixing might go on in a big city like Milwaukee, the way it had with Frankie's mother and white father, but it would never cut the mustard in Summit. And besides, the reverend had been trotting hotly with his lovely wife, Letitia, for over thirty years, and they had a family of seven to prove it.

Funny thing was, I almost felt sorry for Evelyn Mulrooney that night. She had no choice but to plaster a smile across her face when so many in town showed their appreciation as Aunt Jane May hit the last note. That the band accompanying her was the one that performed "jungle music" at the club that so-and-so and her cohorts had been angling to shut down, and that the choir standing behind our aunt was Baptist, not Catholic, had to have added salt to Mulrooney's wounds.

But, you know, watching just about everyone in town breaking tradition to enjoy folks from both sides of the tracks making beautiful music together on the birthday of the land of the free and the home of the brave, I couldn't help but feel that I was witnessing a small miracle. I even dared to hope that things might be different around here from now on after the performers filed down from the stage, because the girls and I had to stand in a long line to wait our turn to heap praise upon them.

Mayor Kibler finally broke things up when he announced into the microphone, "Happy you enjoyed that wonderful performance, but Jim Winner needs to get home so he can wake up early to milk." That wasn't him getting confused again. Mr. Winner was the man who was in charge of organizing the pièce de résistance of the Fourth of July every year. "It's time for the fireworks!"

Frankie, Viv, and I raced across the park toward Grand Creek and, along with the other kids that could elbow their way in, we sat on the bank and dangled our feet into the water and watched the explosions paint the sky about our heads. Mr. Winner had pulled out all the stops to give us the best show ever, and the finale truly was grand.

Soon as the last big bang sounded, like we always had, the girls and I dove into the creek, clothes and all. Frankie was a mediocre swimmer, and Viv was nothing to write home about, so they popped to the surface right away, but I'd always felt at home in the water, and flipped onto my back. I was relishing the night's patriotic performance, thinking about the strange story that Bigger had told us, and searching the night sky for my favorite constellation—I thought of the stars on Orion's belt as the sky's version of the Tree Musketeers—when the park's powerful pole lights came on and all but obliterated my view.

Because those lights were only used when the men in town played baseball, I thought that some of them had decided to cap off the evening's festivities by having a few more beers and enjoying America's favorite pastime, until the sheriff's voice came booming out of the loud speakers to inform me otherwise.

"Attention, everyone," he said. "Three patients have escaped from the mental hospital, and one of them is a known murderer. Go home, lock your doors, and keep watch out of your windows. You see anything suspicious, call the station immediately!"

Chapter Twenty

After the sheriff hustled the girls and me and Aunt Jane May down the street and into the county car, we cruised past neighbor upon neighbor scurrying down the sidewalk like characters in a horror movie fleeing monsters that'd descended on their quiet, little town.

"Don't worry, girls," the sheriff said. "Like I just got done telling Eddie King at the hospital, every law enforcement officer in the county has been told to report for a search. We'll round those escaped patients up and bring them back to him in no time."

He sounded so confident, but he had to have been castigating himself for not stepping on his soap box more often to pontificate about the need to shut Broadhurst down. Maybe if he had, those he'd pledged to protect and serve wouldn't be in danger of losing their lives when a "known murderer" struck again.

That wouldn't happen, of course, because the sheriff had been horribly misinformed. My heart went out to him, and I very much wanted to reach over the car seat, stroke the curls rubbing against his uniform collar, and tell him that he could stop working himself into a lather. When Bigger had told the girls and me her drilling story, she mentioned that Eddie King was in charge of the *second-floor patients* that night and those poor souls weren't capable of killing anyone. Not even themselves. And there was no need for a search party because they wouldn't get far. The schizophrenic and suicidal patients were so heavily medicated that they moved slower than zombies.

But I couldn't tell him that, could I. Frankie understood the need for caution as well.

When we drove under a streetlight, I saw her give Viv the "zip your lips" sign and then point to me. She wanted me to do the talking because she didn't trust Viv any more than I did. The escape was prime gossip. In her enthusiasm to learn more, she could accidentally blurt something out that the girls and I weren't supposed to know about the patients and the inner workings of the hospital. The sheriff would be furious, and Aunt Jane May would be apoplectic. She would inflict the severe consequences so fast it'd make our heads spin. The girls and I would have to run away and we couldn't that night. People were counting on us.

After we swung by Audrey Cavanaugh's house and I gave her Harry's note, we planned to ride over to Broadhurst. We'd meet up with Bigger in the kitchen, then go down to the basement and use Viv's key on the Chamber of Horrors door. I highly doubted it, but if we found a bloody drill or any other evidence of wrongdoing, as promised, we'd tell Doc. He'd do the right thing. Unlike Cruikshank, he respected the oath he'd taken: *First, do no harm.*

The escape wouldn't alter our plans, but as our designated mouthpiece, my job was to get all the information I could from the sheriff. Since it was important not to seem too eager or give anything away—that'd make him suspicious—when he pulled onto our cobblestone driveway I asked him as casually as I could, "So who escaped?"

When he looked to Aunt Jane May for permission to answer, I thought she'd puff up and go prickly, but she told him, "Go ahead. They're going to find out soon enough. But let's get in the house first."

She must've had the jitters before her performance at the park, because she'd forgotten to switch the globe light on above the back door. The night was still and dark, and there were leafy bushes to hide in alongside the house. Even though I knew we weren't in any danger, I couldn't blame her for worrying that one of the patients would jump out at us. I startled even harder than she did when the county car's radio suddenly crackled to life.

"Sheriff? You there?" came out of the tinny speaker.

He grabbed the handheld microphone off the hook on the dashboard and said into it, "What's going on, George?"

"Ted Withers just called the station. He heard his dogs barking and when he went to investigate, he saw someone disappearing behind his barn. The back boundary of his place borders the highway, so it looks like the patients are making a run for it. I'm waiting for the rest of the county deputies to check in, but this is our town, and on your say-so, me and Joe and Willie are going over to the Withers' place and start searching for them."

Frankie, Viv, and I shot confused looks at each other because the second-floor patients mustering up enough energy to shuffle out of their rooms and make it across the county road to the Withers' farm was out of the question. Ted Withers must have been blind drunk.

But clearly relieved that the escapees weren't anywhere near Summit proper, the sheriff brought his shoulders down from where they'd been parked around his ears and told his deputy, "Roger that, George. I'll be out there shortly. Remember, one of those patients is criminally insane. Keep your weapons drawn, and shoot if you have to."

After he replaced the handheld, the sheriff cocked his head toward our aunt, showed her his dimples, and said, "See, Janie? There's nothing for you and the girls to be concerned about."

We weren't, but she asked him to go into the house first anyway, and after she flicked on the lights in the kitchen, her finger was trembling when she shook it at us. "Ya see now why I've been telling you girls to stay away from that hospital?" It was the kind of thing I'd expect her to say, but she wasn't really thinking straight. When Frankie, Viv, and I sat down at the kitchen table in the same clothes we were wearing when we jumped into the creek after the fireworks, she didn't say anything about us catching our death of cold. Instead, she went to the study, brought back Doc's whiskey, and proceeded to pour Uncle Walt a glass.

"I'm on a duty," he reminded her as he pulled a chair out from the pine table. "You all right? You don't look too good."

After Aunt Jane May sat down and wiped her brow with one of her big lace hankies, she said to him softly, "I'd feel a whole lot better if before you go out to the Withers' you'd tell me what went on at the hospital tonight. I don't want to have to spend the whole night frettin' about you." She looked at Frankie, Viv, and me, turned a color of pink that I'd never seen before, then took a sip of the whiskey she'd poured—and that was a first, too.

The sheriff needed to join his deputies out at the Withers' farm, I figured he'd shoot down Aunt Jane May's request for more information about the escape, but he nodded and took a seat next to her. "I don't have time to go into it all, so in a nutshell, Eddie King called the station tonight a little after eight. Joe had a hard time understanding most of what he said except that he needed Doc and me to get out to the hospital immediately. Three patients escaped, the lights were out, and he didn't know what to do because Cruikshank and Holloway were out of town."

So that's where the Buchanan brothers were going in a big rush earlier—not to respond to an accident one of the juvenile delinquents had out on Highway C.

"Eddie was waiting for us when we pulled up in front of the hospital," the sheriff said, "but he wasn't making much sense. We had to wait until whatever drug Doc gave him to calm down took effect before he could tell us more. According to him, everyone working that night had planned on watching the fireworks together from a third-floor window. When it started to get dark, he went to fetch the nurse who was watching the patients on the first floor, because she was new and didn't know her way around. But when he got down there, she was nowhere to be found. Eddie thought she must've gone up to the third floor without him. When he got up there, he saw that the locked door on the criminal ward was open, so he called out. When no one answered, he figured they'd already gone to the other side of the building to get the best view of the fireworks. But on his way to join them, he noticed that one of the cell doors was wide open."

Because the sheriff was hearing the call of duty, he was machine-gun talking. I thought I must've misheard him, or maybe he'd misunderstood what Eddie King had told him.

"Excuse me," I said, "but you just said . . . did Eddie tell you that one of the patients on the third-floor escaped?" I couldn't give away too much, so I added, "We heard that's where they keep the criminals."

Frankie nodded and said, "You sure Eddie wasn't mixed-up because of the shot Doc gave him?"

When the sheriff shook his head and said, "I saw the empty cell myself," I almost fell out of my chair, and so did the girls, because that changed everything.

I was running through my mind the men confined to the top floor—the Blackjack Scalper, Wally Hopper, and the one that I thought was Leo—when Viv squeaked out, "It wasn't the child killer, was it?"

"Eddie works part-time and never on the third floor, so the only thing he knew was that whoever broke out of that cell was a murderer," the sheriff said. "He was scared to death and ran back down to the first floor to call the station and get a cattle prod from where they're kept. That's when he noticed that a couple of the room doors down there were open, too."

"Why didn't you just ask Jimbo or Albie who escaped?" Frankie asked him. "They know every patient and—"

"What about that new nurse?" I asked, cutting her off because I wanted to hear as much of the story as I could before the sheriff took off for the Withers' farm and he kept checking his watch. "Where was she the whole time?"

The sheriff stood and said, "I found her locked in a supply closet. She was bordering on hysteria and we couldn't get much out of her other than it was her first night on the job and someone snuck up behind her, took her keys, and shoved her in. She thought it was a woman, but it happened so fast she couldn't be sure."

"So if Eddie didn't know and the nurse was incapacitated, how did you find out who escaped?" Aunt Jane May asked.

"Doc checked the files in the office. The cell on the third floor belongs to a patient by the name of John Johnson," the sheriff replied as he edged toward the screen door. "But he couldn't recall ever treating him, and there wasn't anything else of use in his file, so all we know about him at this point is that he's as dangerous as they come."

Except that he wasn't.

Albie had told us that afternoon at Earl's that John Johnson was the name on the file of the man on the third floor who insisted his name was Leo. That's how Frankie had remembered it, too, when I asked her earlier at the park.

That was a big load off my mind, because I would have been worried to death if Uncle Walt was hunting down Wally Hopper or the Blackjack Scalper in the woods at the Withers' place. But Harry Blake wouldn't have pleaded through the wrought-iron fence, "You gotta help . . ." or passed me a note that said, "They're going to kill Leo" if he was a criminally insane monster. Nothing and no one could convince me that our dear friend, who told us stories about the Mondurians and loved Aunt Jane May's shortbread cookies and fashioned cute hats out of tinfoil, would ask us to help a dangerous killer, and I wasn't alone in that belief. My little voice was backing me up.

I asked the sheriff, "Who escaped with John Johnson?"

"Harold Blake and Ernest Fontaine."

That's what I thought he'd say. It only made sense that Harry, who'd been so worried about harm coming to Leo, would be at his side. I had no idea why they'd bring along Ernie, but I was grateful they had. He seemed like a nice, sad kid, and now we no longer had to honor Viv's promise to help him out. Or deliver the note to Audrey Cavanaugh.

"Eddie told us that Blake isn't violent, and Ernest Fontaine is just a boy," the sheriff said, "but we have to find John Johnson before he kills again."

"You didn't leave the rest of the patients unattended when you came back to town, did you?" Jane May Mathews, RN, asked him.

"Eddie was woozy from the shot Doc gave him, so he said he'd call the usual third-floor guard"—he reached into his uniform pocket, pulled out a little red book, and flipped over a few pages—"Mitch Washington, and stick around until he showed up. The nurse agreed to stay, too, but only after I told her that I'd send some deputies out there to search the hospital and the grounds."

"But why can't Jimbo and Albie watch the patients?" Frankie asked him.

The sheriff had big things on his mind and was already halfway through the screen door when he answered, "Because Albie didn't show up for his shift tonight, and Jimbo is on his way to the hospital."

"What happened to Jimbo?" Frankie, Viv, and I cried.

Judging by the stricken look on the sheriff's face, he hadn't meant to tell us that. He looked sheepishly at Aunt Jane May and said, "I gotta go. Can you explain?"

She nodded. "Be careful, and call me as soon as you catch them." When the door slammed shut behind him, she put her arm around Frankie and said, "Jimbo got hurt tonight, honey."

Near tears, Frankie asked, "He's not gonna die, is he?"

"Oh gosh, no. He was knocked out, is all. The sheriff thinks it might've happened during the escape. Doc called an ambulance and rode with Jimbo to the hospital in Port Washington.

Dell and Sally are on their way, too. They'll make sure he gets the best of care."

Frankie said, "I wanna be there! You gotta take me!"

"Us, too!" Viv and I said.

"He can't have visitors right now," Aunt Jane May said. "He's still unconscious, but Doc'll call soon as he comes to, and when he does, I'll come straight out to the hideout to give you the good news." She pushed her chair out from the table and stood. "Now, I want you girls to get out of those wet clothes and say some prayers for Jimbo's speedy recovery, and I'll be out shortly with pie and root beer."

She knew that if we couldn't be by Jimbo's side, we needed to be in our home away from home. And she wasn't afraid that a lunatic madman would climb the wooden steps and murder us in our sleep because the sheriff had told us the escaped patients had been seen way out on the county road at Ted Withers' farm. But unbeknownst to all of us, they weren't the only ones on the loose. Before that night was over, the lurking evil the girls and I had been warned about would step out of the shadows and introduce itself.

Chapter
Twenty-One

As my blood sisters and I made our way across the backyard grass, we were holding hands and reassuring one another that our beloved Jimbo would be fine.

"He's gonna be okay . . . he's gonna be okay," Frankie was telling herself.

"He'll be up and at 'em in no time," I said. "I promise."

"Don't worry, Frankenstein," Viv said. "Doc won't let anything bad happen to him."

Around the time the late train came rumbling down the tracks, we'd grown accustomed to it cooling down some, but that night it seemed to grow warmer with every step we took. I didn't take heed of that harbinger at the time, but looking back at it now, I know that what Aunt Jane May had warned us about at the beginning of that hot summer was true. Satan had fled hell so fast and left the door open behind him because he knew when there were young souls available for the picking, and that was the night he was coming to get ours.

The town had fallen into a scared silence beneath a moonless sky, and the air was so hot and thick that it dampened the crickets and frogs and the other night sounds to near nothing as well. Or maybe those creatures of God were sensing that evil was on the prowl and they didn't want to give their hiding places away. Had the girls and I known what was about to happen, we would've followed their lead, but as we climbed the wooden steps that night, what was on our young minds was Jimbo lying in that hospital bed, the escaped patients, and the bizarre story Bigger had told us at the park.

The least of my worries was Jimbo because I didn't think that the person who'd hit him on the head meant to inflict any real damage. Soon as the sheriff mentioned that the new nurse at Broadhurst thought a woman might've taken her keys and shoved her into the supply closet, I suspected it was the same woman who'd set her hand on my back when she'd come to save us from Elvin Merchant in the woods. But it wasn't until he confirmed that it was Leo and Harry Blake who'd escaped that I became positive that none other than Audrey Cavanaugh had given Jimbo a love tap on his noggin so he couldn't stop her from setting Leo free. Only God knew where Albie was, but it crossed my mind that he hadn't shown up for his shift because Elvin Merchant, acting as Chummy Adler's goon, might've put him out of commission, too.

After Frankie, Viv, and I peeled off our wet clothes, we changed into the black shorts and tops we kept for emergencies and when we wanted to sneak around town at night. It was dark as pitch beyond the hideout walls, but if we decided to do what I thought we should, our flashlights would help show us the way.

I couldn't put off telling the girls any longer, so I screwed up my courage and said, "You can stop worrying about Jimbo because he's gonna be fine, and I need to tell you how I know that, and a lot of other stuff, too. I'm calling for a powwow."

I lit and lifted the train lantern off its hook, set it down on the blood stain in the middle of the hideout floor, and the girls and I sat Indian style around it. Sometimes I'd imagine it was the olden days and the lantern was a campfire during powwows, but when we gathered around it that night and said, "All for one and one for all," it felt like a beacon of truth.

I'd spent a lot of time thinking about this moment, and was feeling both eager and anxious to get everything I'd been keeping to myself off my chest. I'd decided not to mention the part my little voice played in what I was about to tell them, because they'd probably rib me or rub my nose in it. It was important to draw them in, not push them away, so I planned to appeal to their individual ways of feeling and thinking, and hope that I could make them see things my way.

After I made sure they both knew the patient named John Johnson was really Leo, I took in a deep breath and directed my first effort at Viv. I looked over the lantern at her and said, "You don't have to feel bad anymore for telling Harry to go look for a Mondurian behind the hospital 'cause I don't think he really believes in them. I think he's just been *acting* crazy." I reminded myself to speak faster than normal because patience wasn't Viv's strongest suit. "And when he stopped all those times at the fence down from us and we thought he was beggin' a Mondurian not to suck his brain out? I think he was talking to a real person. And when he ran away from Albie in the recreation yard yesterday, I think he was trying to reach that person so he could tell them that Leo's life was in danger. But they musta got scared off by the point-of-no-return siren or something so Harry came to us instead. We weren't his first choice. We were his last resort."

Viv's mouth had dropped open mid-telling, but there was something in her eyes that made me think I'd gotten at least halfway through to her. "I really wanna believe you so I don't have to feel guilty anymore," she said, "but . . ."

I knew what she was about to say, so I made an "X" over my heart and said, "On my honor as a Tree Musketeer, I swear I'm not being a dumb chump. I truly believe that everything I told you is God's honest truth."

"And I truly believe you're full of bull," Frankie said, which pretty much summed up how I thought she'd react to an idea presented by the weakest link of our triumvirate, who wasn't known for coming up with a lot of bright ideas. "You would've told us sooner if you were thinking that . . . and what proof do you have?"

"I didn't tell you sooner 'cause I thought you wouldn't believe me, and you don't," I replied, feeling proud of myself for not backing down. "And I might not have any proof to back me up, but you don't have any proof that I'm wrong either."

"You mean besides the fact that Harry is a patient in a mental institution?" Frankie scoffed. "Looks like we got a stalemate."

Afraid she was going to ask for a rock, paper, scissors shoot-out, I appealed to her better nature. "Could you at least listen to why I think Harry's been puttin' on a performance and why he got himself committed to Broadhurst?"

Frankie crossed her arms over her chest and said snotty, "Go ahead. I'm all ears."

I'd thought up a lot of possible reasons why Harry might've done what he'd done, but this one hit closest to home. "Put yourself in his shoes. What would make *you* pretend you were crazy and get yourself locked up in a mental institution? Would you do it to help Viv or me? Dell? Sally and Sophia? Auntie? Jimbo?"

Of course she would.

There wasn't a force in heaven, on Earth, or in the brimstone below that could keep us from doing battle for one another and those we loved.

"I think Leo must be someone who really matters to Harry," I told Frankie. "Like they're best friends or maybe they're related. Like us."

When she didn't get off her high horse, Viv nudged her in the ribs and said, "Quit being so stubborn, Frankenstein. Ya don't gotta admit Biz is right, but you *do* gotta admit that she could be."

Frankie couldn't deny that anything was possible, even me being one step ahead of her, so she told me, "Fine. I'll give ya the benefit of the doubt—until I can prove you're wrong."

Once we were sort of on the same page, Viv, who was always interested in who was saying what to whom, scooted closer to me and asked, "So who do you think Harry was secretly talking to in the bushes?"

Not in the mood to sugar-coat it, I flat-out told her, "Audrey Cavanaugh."

She gasped, of course, but Frankie pulled a face and asked me, "How come?"

"'Cause when she rescued us from Elvin Merchant, she had the same bloody scratches on her face that we get sometimes when we gotta claw our way through the pines to get up to the fence," I explained. "I think that when the siren went off that day, she ducked out of sight in the bushes but stayed close enough that she heard Harry ask for our help. That's why she followed us into Founder's Woods. She thought he might've told us something else, or maybe she knew about the note, but then Merchant got in the way. I also think she helped Leo, Harry, and Ernie to escape. That's how I know that Jimbo is going to be okay. I don't think she hit him on the head too hard—just enough so he couldn't stop her."

I was hoping that Frankie would be at least a little impressed by my reasoning, but all she said was, "But *why* would she do that?"

Sick of her cross-examining me, I saw red and fired back, "I don't have all the answers, okay? I told ya what I know so far and nothin' you say is gonna change my mind. You and Viv aren't the only ones who can figure stuff out. I know things, too, because"—I stopped myself from telling her about the gift I thought I'd inherited from Aunt Jane May, because she'd probably use it as ammunition against me. I reached for the "Keep Out" sign instead, but Viv grabbed it off the hook before I could and stuck it behind her back.

"Forget it," she said. "I know you're mad, but we gotta stick together."

She was right, of course.

I told Frankie that I was sorry and she apologized, too, and revealed why she was being such a drip and more of a doubting Thomas than usual. She was out of her mind with worry. "You really think Jimbo's gonna be okay?" she asked me.

"I don't think," I said with a smile. "I *know*. And instead of just sittin' around here waitin' for Doc to call and tell us that he's fine, I figure we should do something that we can tell him about when we visit him in the hospital. Something that'd make him proud."

"Like what?" Viv asked.

I was almost positive that if we trooped down to the hospital basement and Viv used one of her keys on the Chamber of Horrors lock that we wouldn't find any evidence of what Bigger thought was going on in there, but it seemed important to at least try to be our brothers' keepers. I also had a more selfish reason for wanting to ride up to the hospital that night. It was a long shot, sure, but if it turned out that Bigger was right, it occurred to me that when we hurried home to tell my father, he would be so proud I'd helped expose that awfulness that we'd talk until the sun came up. And he wouldn't let Aunt Jane May punish us for what we'd done, nor would he allow her to cook our gooses for lying to her about how we'd been spending our time. He might even forget for a little while that when I came into this world I killed the love of his life.

"I think we need to go up to the hospital and meet Bigger the way we told her we would," I told the girls. "Jimbo has been nuts about her for so long that I bet he ends up marrying her, so she's almost part of our family. And the both of them care about the patients as much as we do and . . . and what if Cruikshank really *is* drilling holes in their heads?"

Frankie looked excited to break into the Chamber of Horrors when we were at the park and she still did. Viv had seemed jazzed, too, so I was shocked when she said, "Not sure that's such a good idea anymore."

"How come?" Frankie asked.

"Well, we wouldn't have a problem gettin' past the new nurse because she doesn't know the hospital like we do," Viv explained. "And knowin' Eddie King, he probably went home to sleep off that shot Doc gave him, instead of sticking around. But he told the sheriff that he'd call Mitch Washington to come watch the third-floor patients, and he's got a lot on the ball."

"But we're not going to the third floor; we're going to the basement," I said. "And if Mitch did happen to see us, he wouldn't stop us or report us. He's a good friend of Bigger's."

Viv thought that over, then said, "Yeah, okay, but what about the deputies the sheriff told the new nurse that he was going to send up there to look around the hospital and the grounds?"

I'd forgotten about them, so I didn't have an answer for her, but logical Frankie did. "He told the nurse that before Ted Withers called the station house and said he saw someone at his place, so I bet the sheriff stopped by the hospital and told those deputies to go over there instead. I'm with Biz. I vote we go."

I looked over at Viv. "You in?"

When she nodded and gave me one of those wide smiles that moviegoers would flock to see in the not too distant future, I jumped to my feet and grabbed our flashlights off the shelf.

"We better hurry," I said, "or Bigger will think we're not comin'."

We kissed the crucifix for good luck and were about to crawl out of the hideout when the telephone trilled from an open window of the house. We'd not expected to hear anything about Jimbo's condition for hours, so it probably wasn't Doc on the other end of the line. But who else would call this late at night? The sheriff? Was he calling to let us know that he'd caught the escaped prisoners? I hoped not.

Whoever it was, Aunt Jane May didn't speak to them for long, because the phone rang again, and a few minutes later she came through the screen door and shouted, "Girls!"

We poked our heads through the window to see her coming across the backyard in a hurry. When she reached the bottom of the hideout steps, Viv thumbed her flashlight on and shined it down on our aunt, who had a smile on her face and a wicker basket hanging from her arm.

"I come bearing gifts!" she said. "That was Doc on the phone. Jimbo is comin' around a lot sooner than he thought he would. Doc wants to stay up there until he has some head X-rays in the morning, but it looks like he'll be right as rain in no time."

I sort of wanted to tell Frankie *I told you so*, but gloating was more up Viv's alley, so all three of us let out yips of relief and did the little bunny hop dance we did when things went our way.

"And that other call you heard was from Mister Ellsworth," Aunt Jane May said. "Betsy's gone into labor and the baby's comin' soon. Since Doc's not here, I need to run over there to deliver it. Shouldn't take me long. That's a well-traveled road and that baby is bound to slide out without much fuss." She placed the pie and root beer she'd brought into the bucket affixed to the tree. "After all that's happened, I don't have to tell you to stay put tonight, do I?"

"No siree, Bob. We're half-asleep already," Viv told her. "About to say our prayers."

Our aunt didn't completely believe that, of course, but with a baby on the way, there was no time for an interrogation—only a warning. "I'll be back to check on you sooner than you think," she said and bustled back to the house to grab her nursing supplies.

Our woody car was in for repairs, the sheriff had driven the county car to the Withers' farm, and Doc had ridden in the ambulance to the hospital in Port Washington, so Aunt Jane May would have to walk the five blocks to the Ellsworths' house. But she had a big, determined stride and she'd made it sound like that baby would come squirting out in nothing flat. If we wanted to get to Broadhurst and back home before she did, we needed to be quick about it.

Because we'd left Grand Park in such a panic, there'd been no time to grab our bikes, but they'd be waiting for us not far from the entrance to the shortcut to Broadhurst. It was the handyman's job to switch the big lights off at night, but the sheriff must've instructed him to keep them on after he told everyone to go home and lock their doors. We could see them uplighting the trees over there. They were powerful enough to illuminate the path through Founder's Woods for at least part of the ride over, and the flashlights tied to our bike handlebars would do the rest. But first, we had to get over to the park without getting seen.

We couldn't take our usual way, because our neighbors, who were following the sheriff's orders and keeping watch for the escaped patients, might see us out their windows. They'd call the house and when Aunt Jane May didn't pick up, they'd start their phone chain and would eventually track her down. She'd rush home from the Ellsworths' house, find the hideout empty, and call the station. The deputy would radio the sheriff, who'd come looking for us, with his siren blaring.

As we ran across the backyard, I asked Frankie, "How we gonna get over to the—?"

"Follow me," she said.

Chapter
Twenty-Two

ꝫ

I'd be lying if I told you that it was an easy go through the woods that night.

The powerful park lights illuminated the shortcut, but they also lengthened our shadows. Night animals used to having the woods to themselves scurried to safety in the underbrush—some faster than others. When I went to swat away the mosquitoes swarming around my face, I barely missed running over a possum's tail, and Viv yelped something about bats.

Once we exceeded the park lights' reach, my eyes had trouble adjusting to the darkness, the same way they did at the Rivoli when I'd come in from the sunshine to see a matinee. I reached to switch my flashlight on, but I hadn't taped it securely enough to my handlebars. It fell off near where Elvin Merchant had waylaid us, and I was too scared to stop and pick it up.

The trip through the woods wasn't only disconcerting and creepy, it had taken far longer than I had anticipated. I couldn't wait to empty onto the Broadhurst property, but when we did, everything looked so different in that moonless night that the girls and I had a hard time getting our bearings. We had difficulty finding the Hanging Tree, and by the time we did, I began to wonder if Aunt Jane May had already delivered the Ellsworth baby. I was tempted to play it safe and call the whole thing off. Except I didn't want to let Frankie and Viv down, to be the weakest link again, and I wanted to make Jimbo proud. I told myself that I'd feel better once I saw the hospital, but when it came into sight, I'd eat those words.

If someone unfamiliar with Broadhurst should stumble on it during an afternoon drive, they'd think it was one of the loveliest mansions they'd ever laid eyes on, but in the dead of night? If it didn't look like a haunted house designed by Hollywood to give kids nightmares, I didn't know what did. The sheriff had told us the lights were out, but there was an eerie, pale flickering in the windows, which didn't do much to shed light on anything, including the scary thoughts I was having.

Frankie's and Viv's flashlights helped, but we mostly had to feel our way along the wrought-iron fence to the back of the hospital. When we finally reached the spot that we'd climb over when we'd come to help Bigger in the kitchen, my hands were so sweaty with heat and fear that I had a hard time following the girls over. When, after much finagling, I dropped down next to them on the other side, Viv pointed to the half-open Greer door and said, "Who wants to go first?"

I only said, "Me," because I was sure that Frankie or Viv would fight me for the honor. But they must've been having second thoughts, too, because they seemed more than happy to let me lead the way.

When I reached the top of the stairs, I pushed at the door Bigger had left open for us with my fingertips, and stuck my head inside.

It was one thing to think breaking into the Chambers of Horrors was a great idea when we were in the safety of the hideout, but after that spooky trip through the woods, the ominous feel of the familiar kitchen, and the flickering overhead lights casting shadows every which way, I was shaking harder in my boots.

A grown-up who loved us would've been a sight for sore eyes right about then, and I called out, "Bigger? You here?" When there was no response, I said over my shoulder to the girls, "She musta changed her mind. We should leave and come back when—"

"Or she got sick of waitin' and went down to the basement without us," Viv said as she shoved me over the threshold.

I landed in the kitchen between two doors. The one to the basement was closed, but the door that led up to the patients' rooms was wide open, and I stepped back from it as fast as I could.

The kitchen had been equipped for commercial use after Mr. Broadhurst turned his home into a mental hospital. There was the shiny steel prep table that the girls and I helped Bigger chop vegetables on when her bunions were bothering her. The modern cooler, stocked with farm-fresh vegetables and meats, was where Albie told us he and she liked to play a little ball during their lunch hour, before Nurse Holloway caught them. An extra-large refrigerator that contained mostly drinks sat against one wall, and an eight-burner stove on another. In an attempt to make it feel less institutional, Bigger had embroidered towels that she kept in a drawer next to the double sink. Canned goods and sundries were stacked in a butler's pantry next to the staircase that I found myself standing at the bottom of that night.

Originally designed to allow staff to see to the needs of the Broadhurst family, the staircase was now used by nurses and orderlies when they came to pick up trays of food for ailing patients, or when they themselves needed to use the bathroom adjacent to the kitchen the way Viv so often had to. But the handyman used the staircase, too, when he made repairs in the rooms. Even under the best of circumstances, the staircase gave me the creeps because it always smelled like stale food, the green walls were cracked and the paint was peeling, and the only source of light was a single bare bulb in the high ceiling. I also hated that the steps were spiraled, so you couldn't see who was coming down them until they were practically on top of you.

That night, I thought I'd heard something, but I was so wound up that I wasn't sure if I was imagining it, so when Viv came through the Greer door after me, I put my finger up to my lips, nodded at the staircase, and whispered, "Ya hear that?"

Frankie came up behind Viv and said, "What?"

"I think somebody's comin' down," I said. "From the third floor."

We stuck our heads in, listened for a second, and nodded.

"It might be Bigger, but maybe the sheriff didn't tell the deputies he sent over here to go to the Withers' farm to look for Leo, Harry, and Ernie, like I thought he would," Frankie whispered. "Quick. Hide in the cooler."

She grabbed Viv and turned around so fast that she knocked me sideways. I was still scrambling to get my balance when someone appeared at the bottom of the stairs, took the scene in, and said, "Why, hello there, small fries. What are you doin' here?"

Only one person ever called us that, and Frankie spun around and said, "Mayor?"

To explain our presence, Viv was quick to say, "We're still playin' that detective game we told you about at the park. What are *you* doin' here?"

Bud Kibler's hair was mussed, his shirt untucked, and he seemed more confused than usual when he replied, "I came to speak to the sheriff about the escaped patients, but . . ." He swayed and even under the kitchen's cruddy overhead lights, I could see the blood drain from his face. "There's nobody here except for the orderly on the third floor. Poor guy had accidentally locked himself in, so I let him out with the keys I found on the floor."

Eddie King had told the sheriff that he'd call Mitch Washington to come watch the third-floor patients, but accidentally locking himself in a cell didn't sound like something Mitch would do. He had worked at Broadhurst longer than anyone else, and I couldn't picture him making a bonehead move like that. But he did have a colicky new baby, so he'd probably not slept very much for the past few weeks. He must've gone into one of the empty cells to take a nap and the door swung shut behind him.

Frankie was thinking that, too, because she asked the mayor, "Mitch Washington locked himself in a cell?" like she couldn't believe it.

"I don't think he told me his name." Mayor Bud rubbed his hand against the back of his head and winced. "It's really dark up there and I must've tripped on something. I got an awful bump and . . . do you know the way out?"

When his knees buckled, I got him by the elbow. "You need to sit down, sir. Viv, grab a stool."

She set her flashlight down on the prep table and pulled out one of the tall, wooden ones we'd sit on when we came to help Bigger. I was discombobulated when we arrived and hadn't noticed that the ice chest she'd had at the park was sitting in the middle of the table, until the flashlight shined on it. So Viv was probably right. Bigger must've gotten tired of waiting and gone down to the Chamber of Horrors without us. It was on the opposite end of the basement, so she wouldn't have heard us in the kitchen.

I lowered my hands into the ice chest, lifted out the lemon meringue pie, carefully pulled out the sharp knife she'd used at the park to cut it with, and scooped up a handful of watery ice. "I'll get something to wrap this in so you can hold it on your bump," I told the mayor. "Then one of us can go find our friend Bigger. She can take you home."

I took a few steps toward the drawer next to the sink that Bigger kept her embroidered dish towels in, before I slipped on something and had to reach out for the sharp edge of the prep table to keep myself from sliding into the splits. I thought some of the melted ice must've leaked out of the chest, but when I grabbed Viv's flashlight off the table and aimed it at the floor, I could see that's not what I'd stepped in. It was blood, and it was leaking from a head that was poking out from the other side of the steel table. When I took a tiny step forward, moved the flashlight across the body, and saw who it was, I screamed, "Bigger!"

Confusion registered on the girls' faces because they couldn't see what I was seeing, but Frankie rushed to my side. When she saw Bigger, she said, "Sweet Jesus," and bent down next to her. "She's still breathing but that gash above her eye is really deep, and she's lost a lot of blood.

"We need to call an ambulance," I said.

Frankie straightened up and made a move for the wall phone, but a man emerged from the darkened hallway that led to the hospital reception area and stood in her way. "Good evening," he said.

"Thank goodness, you're still here," the mayor said. "A lady has been seriously injured, and we need your help." He seemed to know the man, but didn't realize who he was. "Girls, this is the orderly I was telling you about. The one who got accidentally locked in a cell."

But he wasn't an orderly, and he hadn't gotten himself accidentally locked in a cell. He'd been put there after he was judged to be criminally insane. Our kind, addled mayor had been tricked into freeing the most dangerous patient at Broadhurst—Wally Hopper.

Aunt Jane May had told us that morning at the breakfast table that the child killer looked like something a cat dragged out from under the porch after a flood, and he did. But what the newspaper photo had failed to capture was his powerful stature. He was tall—taller than Doc—and his upper body was so disproportionately muscled and his arms so freakishly long that he looked like he'd stepped out of a monster movie.

"It's a pleasure to finally meet you girls," Wally Hopper said, but he was looking directly at me when he added, "I've enjoyed watching you from my window."

I thought about how he'd watched the Gimble sisters, too, before he'd strangled them and left their defiled bodies in front of St. Sebastian's church. Because he was pretending to be a priest that rainy afternoon, I thought that's why the little Catholic sisters had gotten into his car, but it might've been his hypnotic voice and warm smile that had convinced them. I was thinking that I might've done whatever he told me, too, when Frankie shouted, "Run!"

Hopper was blocking her way, so she tried to push him, but she was no match for him.

One of his long arms shot out and grabbed Frankie by the shoulder, and when he threw her against the cupboard next to the sink the kitchen filled with the sound of her cracking bones before she slid down to the floor and went still.

When Viv screamed, Hopper reached across the prep table and hit her across the face so hard that she flew backward and landed in front of the Greer door in an unmoving heap.

Obviously confused, the mayor yelled at Hopper, "What are you doing? Stop!" because he still didn't understand what was happening until I told him, "He lied to you. He's not an orderly. He's the child killer!"

When Hopper came at me, I went to snatch Bigger's knife off the steel table to fend him off, but Mayor Kibler beat me to it. He picked it up and staggered toward the killer, who easily ripped the knife out of his elderly hand and slid it between his ribs.

After Bud collapsed to the kitchen floor next to Bigger, the only ones left standing were Hopper and me and he seemed very pleased about that.

"You are such a beautiful child," he said, "and I thank the Lord and the Archangel for giving you to me." He was about ten feet away, but I could smell the stink coming off him when he opened his arms. "Come."

I was paralyzed with fear and when I didn't do as he'd asked, he cooed, "Are you playing hard to get?" He giggled. "How fun."

I knew that behind the windows to his soul there would be nothing but a bottomless blackness that wanted to swallow me up, so I closed my eyes and didn't see the mayor pull Bigger's knife from his side and plunge into the child killer's calf. It wasn't until Hopper yowled in pain that I saw what Bud Kibler had done in an attempt to save me.

Viv was sprawled out in front of the Greer door, and I didn't think I could make it past Hopper and reach the front door of the hospital, but there was one other way out. The basement door was right behind me, and when Hopper turned to pull the knife out of his leg, I took a few steps backward and slipped through it.

The girls and I had gone down the narrow steps during our quests to get inside the Chamber of Horrors and to fetch supplies for Bigger many times. I was familiar with how the basement was laid out, but it wouldn't be easy to make my way through the maze of darkened rooms. There were a couple of wall lights, but like the ones upstairs, they were dim and wavering. But if I could feel my way along the bumpy walls and reach another set of steps at the opposite end of the basement—the ones that led up to the cellar door—I could run for help through the woods or head across the county highway to the Withers' farm. Uncle Walt and almost every deputy in the county were over there searching for the escaped patients.

I had a head start, but it didn't take long for Hopper to realize I'd made a break for it. I heard him pound across the kitchen floor toward the basement door, but I'd already made it to the bottom of the steps and stumbled down one of the hallways when he came limping down after me.

"Come out, come out, wherever you are, pussycat," he sang out.

My heart was drumming so loud that I could barely hear myself think as I felt my way toward the cellar steps. I thought I knew where I was, but it was dark and disorienting and I made a wrong turn and dead-ended into a wall. When I felt my way back to where I'd gone wrong, I could vaguely make out the cellar steps in front of me. I was just moments away from freedom when I stumbled into a gurney. I made a grab for it, missed, and it clattered across the concrete floor and bounced to a stop against the Chamber of Horrors door. Light was coming out from the bottom, and when I heard someone grunt, I hollered, "Help!" but couldn't risk slowing down.

The sound of my voice and the racket of the gurney made it easier for Hopper to home in on me. He wasn't enjoying the chase anymore and was shouting vile curses as he came thundering my way. But the cellar steps stood just beyond the Chamber of Horrors and soon I'd be home free. It wasn't until I reached the bottom of them that I remembered how heavy the thick, wooden door that led outside was—even Bigger struggled with it—but any second, Hopper would be on top of me and cut off all other avenues of escape. If I failed to open the door I'd be trapped, but when I looked up the steps . . . I saw a slice of sky and stars peeking through the door.

Sobbing in relief, I took the steps two at a time, but when I reached the top, I could see more clearly how small the opening was. I wasn't sure I could make it through, but after some wiggling and pushing I popped out into the warm night air and belly-flopped onto the grass behind the hospital.

I didn't know how close Hopper was because I'd been judging his proximity by the sound of his rage echoing off the basement walls, but I was thinking that I'd outsmarted him and that he wouldn't get to do to me what he'd done to the Gimble sisters, when he shoved the cellar door open behind me and yelled, "There you are, ya little bitch."

I tried to crawl away, but he got me by my right ankle and yanked me back down the stairs. After I hit the basement floor, he straddled me, tried to pin me down, but I was slippery with sweat and fear and squirmed out of his reach. I aimed a kick at his bleeding leg and I must've connected. When he bellowed and recoiled in pain, I got to my feet, struggled back up the steps, and burst through the cellar door.

My lungs and legs were on fire and I was heaving for breath. If I could make it to the front of the hospital, I could disappear into the woods or veer across the county highway, but I knew I wouldn't get that chance when an enraged roar came from behind me.

When I looked over my shoulder and saw Hopper charging out of the darkness toward me like a wild animal hunting prey, I wanted to collapse onto the grass and give up, and maybe I would have. I was scared in a way I had never been before and had nothing left to draw on, but the girls needed help, Bigger and the mayor, too, and I believe it was my love and concern for them that drove me toward what could be their saving grace.

I wasn't sure I could reach it before Hopper pounced on me, but I half-ran, half-stumbled toward the front door of the hospital, felt around in the bushes, and when I found what I was looking for, I pulled down the handle on the gray box.

The screech of the point-of-no-return siren piercing the night air was deafening, but it didn't slow Hopper down. He sprang at me, wrapped his hands around my throat, lifted me until I saw the black evil in his eyes and the smile on his face before he said in that warm voice of his, "Some girls like being swept off their feet," and began strangling the life out of me.

When all of the air had left my lungs and a velvety darkness came closing in, the fear left me. In its place came thoughts of a reunion with my mother, and how much I would miss Aunt Jane May and Doc and Uncle Walt, but most of all my precious and dearly loved blood sisters. Then there were miles of stars and from far away, so far away, I thought I heard shouting and gunfire. I was hoping someone had come to save me, but as I fell into the final nothingness, I was pretty sure that was just me being a dumb chump one last time.

Chapter
Twenty-Three

As you might expect, Jane May Mathews, RN, wouldn't let the girls and me out of her sight the entire time we were in the Port Washington Hospital. After she received the approval of Dell and Viv's parents to oversee our care, she was everywhere. Demanding to know the doctors' treatment plans, examining our stitches and assorted bruises, and yes, cross-examining us and promising that as soon as we got better she was going to cook our gooses beyond recognition and bury us beneath the willow tree out back.

Frankie had been hurt the worst. When Hopper had thrown her against the cupboard in the Broadhurst kitchen, her femur cracked in two. She had to have surgery, and afterward—traction and a cast.

When Hopper smacked Viv in the face, she got two black eyes and a broken nose. Probably sensing how important Viv's profile would be to her someday, gifted Aunt Jane May made sure a specialist was called in from Milwaukee so she wouldn't have an unattractive bump in the posters that years from now would adorn the lobby of the Rivoli and movie theatres across the world.

I came away with the least amount of damage. But only if you didn't count my crushed windpipe, dislocated shoulder, and the rainbow of bruises I received when Hopper dragged me down the cellar steps and dropped me on the front stoop of the hospital.

Thankfully, the sheriff had not told the two deputies he'd initially sent to Broadhurst to search for the escaped patients to head over to the Withers' farm, the way Frankie thought he would. They were in the woods when they heard the point-of-no-return siren and they came running with their weapons drawn. They had to shoot the child killer seven times before he crashed down next to me like a diseased oak.

In a ceremony in front of the court house, Deputies Jack Halston and Rob Brody received commendations from Governor Gaylord Nelson for rescuing me, and catching Albie in the act. He confessed that in order to pay back the money he owed Chummy Adler, he'd agreed to haul away evidence of the surgeries Dr. Cruikshank was performing against patients' will in the Chamber of Horrors. That's why that gurney was down there and the heavy cellar door open the night Hopper almost killed me. The girls and I never did like Albie, but we were grateful to him and his gambling ways because if hadn't been in the basement that night, I wouldn't have survived to tell this tale.

Viv and I could have gone home from the hospital sooner, but Frankie had to stay for the rest of July and some of August. Because we couldn't bear to be separated from her, Doc got special permission for us to sleep in cots on either side of her bed. During the day, Viv would run over to Whitcomb's Drugstore, belly up to the fountain counter, and give the other kids in town a progress report while she waited for the soda jerk to make a brown cow to go. My job was to keep the brains of our operation's mind engaged. I wrote and read stories to her about a girl lawyer who was even slicker than Perry Mason and I let her teach me how to play chess.

Aunt Jane May had decided it was important that we concentrate on healing, so the girls and I were kept sequestered and only heard dribs and drabs at first about what'd happened at Broadhurst. It wasn't until the sheriff paid a visit that we got a few more of our questions answered.

He pulled a feather bouquet out from behind his back, gave Frankie and me boxes of Good and Plenty, and handed a sleeve of chocolate mint Girl Scout cookies to Viv. But after he fingered the star on his chest and slid the red notebook from his back pocket, he was all business.

"First things first," the sheriff said. "Do you know how Hopper got out of his cell?"

The girls and I had talked about whether or not we should tell the truth, and we'd decided that it didn't really matter how the child killer got out. We didn't want anyone to think ill of Mayor Bud Kibler, so Viv shrugged and answered the sheriff, "Nope. No clue."

I asked him, "Is Eddie King all right? The new nurse? Mitch Washington? The mayor told us that he couldn't find anyone when he came looking for you to talk about the escaped patients. Did Hopper get them?"

"They're all fine," the sheriff said. "The new nurse—her name is Dinah Harold, by the way—told us that she and Eddie were too scared to stay at the hospital and took off shortly after

Doc and I did that night. Eddie couldn't remember if he called Mitch Washington to come watch the third-floor patients, but when I spoke to Mitch, he told me he hadn't.

Frankie asked, "Did you catch Cruikshank and Nurse Holloway? Are they in jail?"

The sheriff shook his head. "The surgeries Cruikshank was performing weren't against the law, but kidnapping and transporting people across state lines is a federal crime, so the FBI was called in. Agents found them at O'Hare Airport, about to board a plane to Mexico, with suitcases that contained nearly a quarter of a million dollars."

"What about the patients?" I asked. "What's gonna happen to them?"

"The hospital has been closed down, and they've been relocated to other facilities," he said. "Not sure what the future will hold."

Considering how he felt about Broadhurst, I thought he'd be pleased, but he didn't seem so. When I pictured my favorite patient, Florence, and how she predicted that our lives were in danger, and how much Frankie would miss playing chess with Teddy Ellison, and I thought about poor Karen and her invisible baby and gentle gardener Roger Osgood, I wondered if our uncle had learned more about them during his investigation and was as touched by their plight as the girls and I had always been.

As you can imagine, what had happened at Broadhurst was big news. Reporters from all the major newspapers in the country descended on Summit, eager for scoops about the three eleven-year-old girls who had inadvertently ended up exposing what Dr. Arthur Cruikshank had done. At first, Aunt Jane May allowed the reporters to ask us questions and take our pictures to their hearts' content, but when they started showing up all hours of the day and night, she decided that enough was enough.

I couldn't blame the reporters for being persistent, really, because they had to compete against the stirring firsthand accounts of a reporter from the *Chicago Tribune* by the name of Leo Cavanaugh. Frankie, Viv, and I begged to read his articles, but Aunt Jane May rather we didn't.

"That man is too good a writer," she told us as she fluffed Frankie's pillows. "I could barely breathe when I read about the atrocities goin' on beneath our noses, and it about broke my heart when I did. I've clipped Mister Cavanaugh's articles from the paper and put them aside with the others. You can look them over after you come home."

But she did allow Leo to interview us on the telephone, and after one of our conversations, he promised that he and his brother, Harry, who wasn't mentally ill, and his mother, Audrey, who had engineered her sons' escape from the hospital, would come visit us when we were up and running again. The girls and I looked forward to seeing Harry and meeting Leo face-to-face, and their mother. We decided to stop calling her the Summit Witch because, well, she wasn't. But Frankie told Viv that when she moaned in the woods on the day Audrey Cavanaugh saved us from Elvin Merchant that counted as fulfilling the witch dare she'd thrown at her during our first overnight, so all was copacetic in that department. I'd say that Viv was still not enamored with the idea of sitting around our pine kitchen table with Leo's and Harry's mom, but she was anxious to learn what fate had befallen winking, dog-loving knitter Ernie Fontaine, who Leo told us would also be coming along for the ride.

While much of what happened was kept from us in those early days, the girls and I did manage to get our hands on a

Milwaukee Journal someone had left in the hospital cafeteria. Our pictures were on the front page, and I was hailed as a hometown hero. "If Elizabeth Buchanan hadn't been brave enough to elude Hopper and pull the alarm that alerted the Grand County deputies, three more lives would have ended that night," the reporter wrote, but I didn't feel brave. The girls and I wouldn't have been anywhere near Broadhurst the night we almost lost our lives if I hadn't convinced them to visit with the patients in the first place, and I thought it might take a good long time to forgive myself, if ever.

In my book, the real hero was Mayor Bud Kibler. Sad to say, the man the girls and I had been so very fond of—the one who'd called us "small fries" and dressed up as a vampire and handed out all-day suckers on Halloween—died that night from the knife wound Hopper had inflicted on him. Frankie, Viv, and I weren't in any shape to attend his viewing at the Cleary Funeral Home, but when Viv's parents came to visit, her ma told us, "I fixed Bud's hair just so and dressed him in a new blue suit. He looked as distinguished as Ike Eisenhower." And Mr. Cleary said, "Bud's visitation was the largest we've ever had. Wished you could've seen it, girls. The line went out the door."

Thankfully, Hopper's attack on Bigger Dolores in the Broadhurst kitchen looked much worse than it was. The stitches over her right eye and her concussion didn't keep her and many other Mud Towners from attending Bud Kibler's funeral mass at St. Thomas's.

"After Doc got up and spoke about what a good and fair man the mayor was, and how he stuck my knife into Hopper's leg and that gave you a chance to escape, Bizzy, I'll tell ya, there wasn't a dry eye left in them pews," Bigger said during the first of her many visits. "And when your father told them that a statue of the mayor would be erected in front of City Hall, the whole church rose to their feet. Even that Mulrooney gal got off her rear end and was bawlin' into her hankie.".

If Viv could've hawked a loogie on the hospital floor she would have, because she didn't believe Evelyn Mulrooney was mourning Bud at his funeral. "Those were probably tears of joy and that so-and-so was usin' that hankie to cover her gloating mug," she said, because his death meant that after the September election, we'd probably all be calling her mayor.

Of course, we tried to pry more information about what'd happened at Broadhurst out of Bigger during her visits, but she said, "Jane May made me swear to keep my mouth shut, and if you think I wouldn't mind gettin' on her bad side, you'd be wronger than a chicken with teeth." But she kept our spirits us in other way during her visits. She brought us good things to eat from her brother Earl's place, told us how much in love she and Jimbo were, and reminded us that the Grand County Fair was right around the corner. I couldn't remember anymore why she was the one who always took the girls and me to the fairgrounds every summer, but that's the way it'd always been.

"I heard from a friend of mine that the traveling carnival has a new tent show with oddities of all kinds," she told us as she slid chiffon pie onto plates, "so I'm gonna need ya to get better real quick."

Of course, with all the attention the girls and I were getting, I figured it was just a matter of time before we would be separated for good. I worried that when the Maniachis were interviewed by the ace reporters from the fancy newspapers, one of them would question the lie that Sally, Sophia, and all of us who loved Frankie had been telling everyone since she and Dell moved in next door to me nine years ago. I thought if the truth came out, that would change everything, and how right I was.

* * *

A few nights before Frankie was to be released, she was reading *Black Beauty*, and Viv and I were curled up at the foot of her bed playing cat's cradle under the watchful eye of Aunt Jane May. She was sitting in a chair near the window knitting, what I assumed to be a baby blanket for the Ellsworth baby she'd delivered, when Sophia, Dell, Uncle Sally, and Jimbo unexpectedly showed up.

Frankie's family had been by many times, bringing Sophia's pizza pie and flowers from Sally's garden and a Whitman's Sampler box, but they'd never come together or that late.

Aunt Jane May always said, "Bad news travels in the dark," and I feared it'd arrived in our hospital room that night. I thought they'd come to tell us that one of the reporters *had* dug too deeply into Frankie's roots, and as soon as she was released from the hospital, she and Dell would be moving to Jimbo's house in Mud Town or, even worse, all the way back to Milwaukee.

Wanting to be as far away as possible from that bad news, I collapsed the cat cradle string and told Sophia Maniachi, "Viv and I will get out of your hair."

When I started to get off the bed, Sophia wheeled her chair closer and said, "No. You must stay, *cara*. What we have come to say concerns you and Vivian, too." She gave me one of her Holy Mother smiles. *"Tutti per uno, uno per tutti."*

After Dell greeted her best friend, Aunt Jane May, over in the corner, she said something complimentary about the baby blanket she was working on, then came to sit next to her daughter on the bed.

Dell had charcoal circles under her eyes, faded lipstick on her lower lip, and a sleeveless white dress that didn't fit her quite right—too tight. She usually took great pride in her appearance, so that put me even more on edge.

"Honey," Dell said to Frankie, "we've come to tell you . . ." is all she managed to get out before she broke into tears.

Uncle Sally's blue shirt was open at the neck and the bedside lamp caught his gold crucifix when he put his arm around his housekeeper's heaving shoulders and picked up where she'd left off.

"Frankie, dear," he said, "your mother and I need to tell you something that we've put off for—"

"Save your breath," the brains of our operation told him very matter-of-factly from her propped up pillows. "I already know you're my father."

Viv popped up at her feet and squealed, "He's *what*?"

Dell gasped at what Frankie had said and asked her, "How did you find out?"

"I thought you mighta fallen in love 'cause I've seen you holding hands when you thought I wasn't around. And the way he looks at you sometimes . . . it's like watching one of those dumb romance movies Viv drags us to," Frankie told her mom. "But it wasn't until right before the Fourth that I found out he was my father. When you asked me to get you your red belt, I couldn't find it where it usually was, so I reached to the top shelf in your closet and started feeling around. I knocked down a

shoe box and the letters ya wrote to each another spilled out."
Because Frankie looked like she might throw up, I thought the
letters must've been sealed with kisses.

"Why didn't you say something?" Sophia asked.

"And how come you didn't tell Biz and me?" Viv said,
outraged.

Frankie said, "I was waitin' for the right time. "

"But you're supposed to tell us everything right away and—
ouch! What was that for?" Viv said when I pinched her leg to
shut her up.

Sophia reached for Frankie's hand and said, "Now that you
know why Sally and I have always loved you as our own, it's
important that you understand why we've kept it a secret all
these years."

That was Sally's cue. "When your mother and I fell in love,
my father refused to bless our union. He's a very powerful man,
and our family has certain business interests that must be kept
private. I was expected to marry an Italian girl."

"Mister Maniachi threatened to disown Sally and, right or
wrong, family is important," Dell explained to Frankie. "I
couldn't bear to cause him that kind of pain, so I broke off our
engagement and didn't tell him when I found out a few months
later that I was having you."

"I tried many, many times to contact her," Sally said, "but
she refused to take my calls and wouldn't answer the door when
I came to visit. I eventually gave up after Jimbo made it abun-
dantly clear that I better not come again."

Jimbo, who was hovering near Aunt Jane May, said sheepishly, "I roughed him up some and threatened worse if he kept
bothering Dell."

Barely able to contain herself, Viv asked, "Then what happened? I mean, how did you all end up in Summit?"

"Sophia and I had visited when we were children and had fond memories," Sally answered. "After she told me that moving out of Milwaukee and putting some distance between our family and Dell might help heal my broken heart, this is the first place we thought of."

"But out of sight, out of mind doesn't always work out the way you think it will," Dell told Frankie. "I never stopped loving him, and when he started writing to me and we began talkin' again, one thing led to another. When I got up the nerve to tell him about you"—she looked up at Sally with such tenderness—"he drove down in the middle of the night, and we were married at the courthouse soon after."

Sally dug into his brown pants pocket, brought Dell's hand up to his lips, slipped the prettiest gold band onto the fourth finger of her left hand, and said, "'Til death do us part."

I figured that keeping their marriage a secret is what Dell must've meant that night the girls and I overheard her and her best friend talking during one of their late-night back-porch meetings. "If the truth ever comes out . . . God help us, Jane May." It also crossed my mind that when our aunt told her about how the gossips in town had been saying that Sally and Sophia had moved to Summit because they were part of a crime family, they might've been right. Of course, Sophia hadn't been shot and crippled during a bank robbery, but gossip can be like that. A seed of truth can grow into a noxious weed if you throw enough fertilizer on it.

When Dell leaned over and placed her newly ringed hand on Frankie's cheek, she looked like she was on the brink of tears again. "I'm sorry for keeping this from you as long as I have," she said. "Sophia and Sally wanted me to tell you sooner, but I was frightened about the trouble that'd cause on both sides of the tracks. No one likes to see a colored girl and a white man fall in love. I thought when the gossip started that we'd have to move and . . . I couldn't stand the thought of leavin' Jimbo and Jane May behind and breakin' you girls up." The tears she'd been trying to hold back spilled onto her cheeks. "Do you think you can forgive me, baby?"

Frankie was a very tough nut to crack and not prone to waterworks, but when she nodded and told her mother, her father, and her Aunt Sophia, *"Ti amo,"* it came from the bottom of her heart.

Viv started bawling, though, and said, "This is better than any damn romance movie I've ever seen!"

"Language!" Aunt Jane May scolded from over in the corner, but I could tell she shared the sentiment. I'd always thought she was too long in the tooth to crave attention from a man, but something in her face that night made me wonder if she yearned to lie in bed at night with a man's arms around her, too.

"Now that you know that Dell and Sally have been living as husband and wife for many years, the temptation is for them to go on as they have been and not rock the boat," Sophia told Frankie. "But the baby changes everything."

Viv's head jerked up. "Who's havin' a baby?"

Dell moved her hand down to the dress that fit too snugly across her tummy. "In five months."

"There will be no more hiding!" Sophia said with such fervor that for a minute I thought she'd get right up out of that wheelchair. "There will be another wedding. Jimbo will be the best man, Jane May the maid of honor. I will cook, and you, *bambinas*, will be flower girls, *capiche?*"

"And anyone in this town who doesn't like it can *baciami il culo*," Sally said fiercely.

Wished it did, but love didn't conquer all. We all knew the difficulties they'd face, but the feeling in that hospital room that night? It was the same feeling I'd had on the Fourth of July when Aunt Jane May stood in front of the Emanuel Baptist choir and sang her heart out.

Most everyone in town cheered them on that night, and while I wished they'd do the same for Dell and Sally, I knew many our neighbors would turn their backs on them. Singing together was one thing, but it would take time, I thought—years and years, maybe—before people on both sides of the tracks would learn to keep their big fat mouths shut about a white man and a black woman making a different kind of beautiful music together.

But, you know, I recall feeling a little hopeful that day would come as Frankie, Viv, and I drifted off to sleep that night, entwined in one another's arms. We had black and white blood running in our veins, and if the three of us could get along, hell, anybody could.

Chapter
Twenty-Four

∾

After Frankie was released from the hospital, she had a cast on her leg, so we had to take it easy the first weeks of August. The heat had shown no interest in relinquishing its hold, so we mostly hung out at Whitcomb's air-conditioned fountain counter, where, as you can imagine, we were the toast of the town.

We also didn't miss seeing the Saturday afternoon showings of *13 Ghosts* and *Battle in Outer Space* at the Rivoli. After we paid our quarters at the box office and Mr. Willis told us, "Nice to see you up and about again, girls," he handed each of us something called a "supernatural viewer" and told us to wear it during *13 Ghosts*.

Now, that sounded like a pretty cool idea that I was sure would take our minds off all the real-life horror we were trying to forget, until we discovered that the ghosts in the movie were haunting a mansion that bore an uncanny resemblance to Broadhurst. And, of course, the girls and I were reminded of the Mondurians during the second feature, but the real horrifying cherry on top? Margaret Hamilton, the actress who played the

Wicked Witch of the West in *The Wizard of Oz*, portrayed a creepy housekeeper in *Battle in Outer Space*. I expected the worst the second she came on the screen and was so proud of Viv when she retained her composure. I didn't realize she hadn't recognized her until the man named Buck asked the housekeeper, "You really are a witch, aren't you?" and she popped out of her seat and ran out of the theatre like she was getting chased by flying monkeys.

*   *   *

Aunt Jane May did not bury us beneath the willow out back, but to make amends for prevaricating to her and disobeying every rule she'd laid down for us that summer, the girls and I were doing all we could to lighten her load. We weeded her vegetable garden, dusted her knickknacks, and beat the rugs. We also washed the bowls and cleaned the kitchen after she baked pies and shortbread cookies. She'd waited until the last minute to take them out of the oven, so they'd be as fresh as they could be when she entered them in the yearly baking competition that'd be held the following day. That was an easy penance because we shared her excitement.

The Tree Musketeers hit the hay early that night and were up and at 'em before the sun so we could make that day last as long as possible. The first thing I did after we rolled off our cotton sleeping mats was to cross out number six, *The County Fair and Carnival* on our summer adventure list. Because when Bigger came by later that afternoon, we'd head up to the fair grounds and stay until they closed the gates for the night.

After that, we ate our breakfast while Aunt Jane May gave us one of her "mark my words" lectures, took baths—left a ring about an inch thick—dressed in clean clothes, and brushed our hair until it shone. We had out-of-town visitors coming in a couple of hours and we wanted to look our best.

As Leo Cavanaugh had promised during one of the phone interviews he conducted with us while we were still in the hospital, he was driving up from Chicago that morning with his brother, our friend and former patient at Broadhurst, Harry Blake, their mother, and Ernie Fontaine, to talk to us in person. We had so many questions that I suggested we write them down during breakfast. Frankie wanted to, but Viv was too keyed up to contribute anything even halfway reasonable. She was out of her gourd with excitement to see Ernie again, but still a little nervous about spending time with the gal formerly known as the "Summit Witch."

Truer to her word than the girls and I had been that summer, after breakfast Aunt Jane May slid across the pine table the newspaper articles that she'd clipped out of the newspapers for us.

"I don't want you three to badger them half to death after they get here," she lectured. "These articles should answer many of your questions, but some of what you're gonna read . . ." She withdrew one of her big lace hankies from her red clutch purse and fanned her face. "I've not yet discussed the birds and the bees with you, but I guess you're old enough now to learn about . . . there are things of a delicate nature in some of the stories that you might find confusing. When you come across something you don't understand, come down and ask me before our guests arrive. I don't want you to bring something up during our visit that might cause embarrassment."

"Things of a delicate nature" were her watered-down words for sexual matters, so the girls and I scooped the articles up off the table, rushed straight out to the hideout, divvied them up, and read aloud anything new that we learned.

After I skimmed through one of the stories, I told the girls, "Bigger was right when she told us that Doctor Cruikshank was putting holes in the patients' heads in the Chambers of Horrors, but it's not called drilling. It's called *trepanning*. This reporter says it's been done for centuries to the mentally ill or people who were thought to be possessed by evil spirits"—Viv gasped and was probably hoping that Granny Cleary didn't read that particular article—"or didn't fit into society."

"Yeah, and the *Chicago Sun Times* says that Doctor Cruikshank got paid a lot of money to do that to homosexuals," Frankie said.

I put the article I was reading down and asked her, "What are homosexuals?"

"Jimbo told me they're the patients who like to bat for the other team."

I still didn't get it, so Viv said, "I heard Missus Klein tell Missus Patowski at the beauty parlor that homos—that's their nickname—aren't interested in the opposite sex."

Since Frankie and I weren't interested in the opposite sex either, I said, "So we're homos and you're not?"

"You can only be a homo if you're a guy," Viv said. "Lloyd told me that Liberace is one and Mister Yellen the florist is, too."

Her brother Lloyd was an idiot, so that was a little hard to swallow, but if Viv had heard right at the beauty parlor, I suspected that Mr. Yellen wasn't the only homo around here. We had a whole town full of them. The Men's Club at church, the Elks, the police force, the baseball teams, and just about every other important organization in town didn't want anything to do with the opposite sex.

I went back to pouring over another news clipping, then sat up and said, "This one explains how Ernie ended up at the hospital." I had to stop and take a spoonful of honey from the little pot Aunt Jane May gave me, because my throat still hurt where Hopper had crushed it. *"'Medical files law enforcement officials found hidden in the psychiatrist's office revealed that after multiple failed attempts to convert adult homosexuals, Doctor Cruikshank decided that he might have more success drilling into immature brains. He instructed his wife, Nurse Ruth Holloway, to—'"*

"They were married?" Viv exclaimed.

"That's what it says," I replied and went back to quoting the article. *"'He instructed his wife, Nurse Ruth Holloway, to phone orphanages and describe the traits that her husband believed were early indications of homosexuality—sensitivity, avoidance of sports, a soft speaking voice, and a wan physical appearance. She struck pay dirt at St. Jude's in Milwaukee when the director of the orphanage, Sister Clement, suggested they come meet a young boy by the name of Ernest Fontaine.'"*

I remembered how Ernie described the husband and wife he'd thought had come to adopt him. The lady was wearing a flowery dress—Holloway had worn the same to the emergency town hall meeting—and the man had a bushy mustache just like Cruikshank's.

"The article goes on to say that Sister Clement had no idea the doctor and his wife were ill-intentioned," I said. "She thought it was admirable that they showed interest in a boy with an abnormal personality and a birth defect."

Viv blanched and said, "You don't think . . . Ernie's not a homo, is he?"

I shook my head. "I think Sister Clement was talkin' about how he likes to knit and dance and all the winking he did."

Frankie could've contradicted me and said something very nasty because Ernie was still a very touchy subject for her, but she picked up one of the articles from the pile in front of her, cleared her throat, and said, "Leo wrote this one. '*I first discovered what was going on at Broadhurst Mental Institution after my friend, Roger Osgood, disappeared.*'"

When Viv read in another clipping that it was the cook at the hospital, Dolores Spooner, who lead Walter Buchanan, the sheriff of Grand County, to the basement room where the surgeries had been performed, we couldn't believe that Bigger hadn't bragged about that to us.

"Listen to this," I said. "*After town employee and groundskeeper at Broadhurst Mental Institution Lance Howard was arrested for the part he played, he told the police that kidnapping homosexuals and burying their bodies if the surgeries failed was part of his job. The remains of eight men were dug up in the woods that surround the facility after Howard was persuaded to tell the FBI where to look.*"

I felt sick to my stomach to learn that Albie hadn't been lying about patients disappearing and seeing lights in the woods during some of his night shifts.

Viv said, "Let me see that," and ripped the clipping out of my hands. "'*I didn't know it was against the law,' Lance Howard told the police after they arrested him. 'I was just following orders.*'"

Doc had been quoted in a couple of the articles, too. When When Mr. Jack Wilkes of the *Summit Courier* asked him if he was aware of what had been going on at Broadhurst, my father answered, "*I didn't know about the deaths or the illegal manner in which Doctor Cruikshank was securing patients to experiment on, but yes, I was aware that he was performing trepanations.*"

I didn't read that article out loud because Mr. Wilkes had to have been mistaken. If my father knew that Cruikshank had been doing those hideous surgeries at Broadhurst, he would've done everything he could to stop him. *First, . . . do no harm.*

Outraged, I shoved that clipping into my shorts' pocket, then jumped up and told the girls, "I gotta go do something. Be right back."

I was going to ride straight over to the newspaper office and demand that Mr. Wilkes print an apology to the most highly regarded man in town in tomorrow's paper, but then Aunt Jane May shouted out a kitchen window, "Girls. Come down now. Our guests have arrived and they don't have all day."

Chapter
Twenty-Five

~

Leo was already seated at the pine table, but he got up and stood next to his brother, Harry, when the girls and I came banging through the screen door. Audrey Cavanaugh and Ernie Fontaine—and his stuffed bunny that was no longer missing his right eye—were sitting next to one another on the opposite side of the table.

Viv squealed when she saw her favorite Broadhurst patient, smiled broadly at his brother, and waved at Ernie, who waved back just as enthusiastically. She was not as overjoyed to see Audrey Cavanaugh, but at least she didn't start breathing weird.

Harry was wearing a pair of tan slacks and a pale green shirt and looked quite a lot better than he had when we last saw him crumpled up on the ground in the hospital's recreation yard. "Ernie you already know," he said to the girls and me when we took our seats, "but I'd like to properly introduce you to my mother and brother."

Audrey Cavanaugh's black hair with the white streak down the middle had been pulled into a neat bun at her neck. Dressed in a yellow blouse with a bow and a pleated skirt, she looked much more like one of the do-gooders in town than a practitioner of the dark arts.

"It's nice to meet you girls under more pleasant circumstances," she said in the voice of the angel I'd heard the afternoon she'd rescued us from Elvin Merchant. "I believe your uncle has already told you that I filed a formal complaint against the boy who accosted you in the woods that afternoon."

He had.

And after Cindy Davenport heard the sheriff had arrested Elvin Merchant for grabbing Frankie, she went over to the police station and admitted to him that it hadn't been "high jinks" when Merchant ripped her blouse off and put his hands up her skirt at the Starlight Drive-In. She also told him how later that night he'd come to her house and threatened to cut her pussycat's throat and hers, too, if she didn't keep her mouth shut. Hopefully, the time Merchant would spend in the juvenile detention center in Port Washington would rehabilitate him, but nobody really believed that. Like the sheriff said, "The boy is rotten to the core."

Audrey Cavanaugh's sons looked nothing alike, but we already knew that from seeing Leo's picture under his byline in the *Chicago Tribune*. Unlike his sandy-haired, emerald-eyed, burly brother, Leo was slight of build, with hair the color of soot, and he was blue-eyed like his mother, too. His tortoiseshell glasses also made him appear more studious and thoughtful than Harry, who still had the energy of a rabbit eluding a hound, so that hadn't been part of his act.

Leo smiled at us and said, "You're quite the celebrities, you know."

Aunt Jane May harrumphed because her breakfast lecture that morning had warned of the dangers of growing conceited from all the attention we'd been getting. "Can I get anybody anything?" she asked. "Lemonade? Coffee?"

When Viv said, "Harry would like some shortbread cookies," we all got a good laugh, and that broke the ice.

Even though the girls and I had already learned some of what we'd hear that morning in the kitchen, we were still riveted by what Leo had to say. He wasn't as good a storyteller as Jimbo, but he was pretty darn close.

"I first learned about the procedures Doctor Cruikshank was performing after my best friend, Roger Osgood, disappeared," Leo told us. "He and I talked almost every day, so when he didn't return my calls, I got worried. After I called the bookstore he worked at and some of our friends and came up empty-handed, I paid his parents a visit. They told me Roger was fine, that he was on a religious retreat, but when I pressed them for details, they broke down and told me the whole story. Of course, I was horrified by what they'd done, but I've known Bill and Mary Osgood my whole life and knew they'd acted out of love."

"They sure have a funny way of showin' it," Frankie said.

Leo paused, then explained, "You have to understand that the Osgoods are devout Catholics. They'd been taught that homosexuality . . ." He caught himself up short and turned to Aunt Jane May.

"Do you know what that means, girls?" she asked.

We thought we did, and after we nodded, Leo went on to say, "Bill and Mary believed that Roger was committing a grievous sin and feared for his immortal soul. When a member of their parish told them her son had suffered from the same affliction and had been cured by a miraculous surgery performed by a doctor in Wisconsin, they thought their prayers had been answered."

Harry interjected, "Leo found out later that the woman who put the Osgoods in touch with Cruikshank was the mother of Broadhurst patient Stanley Larson." The girls and I knew who he was. Jimbo had told us that Mr. Larson had to wear diapers and babbled like a baby. "His brain had been irreparably damaged during a trepanation," Harry went on, "but apparently his mother believed saving her son's soul was more important than preserving his sanity."

"When the Osgoods asked Roger to have the surgery, he refused, so they took matters into their own hands," Leo said. "They contacted Doctor Cruikshank, who told them that as soon as they sent him his fee and signed a confidentiality agreement, he would make all the arrangements. Roger disappeared a few days after Bill and Mary fulfilled their end of the bargain.

"I told them that afternoon that I knew that their hearts were in the right place, but what they'd done was wrong and against the law," Leo continued. "I had no proof that Roger had been kidnapped and I begged them to go to the police with me, but they were scared. Not for themselves, but because they thought he wouldn't get the surgery if they broke the confidentiality agreement."

Leo thanked Aunt Jane May when she set a cup of coffee down in front of him, and after he took a quick sip, he said, "I left the Osgoods' house that day knowing that it was up to me to rescue Roger and I had to act fast. As soon as I got back to my apartment, I called Doctor Cruikshank and told him the *Tribune* was interested in doing an article about the fine work he was doing at Broadhurst, and he agreed to meet with me the following day.

"I kept the interview simple, flattered him, and afterward, I asked if I could take a look around. I was hoping to find Roger and get him out of there, but Cruikshank cited the importance of patient confidentiality, told me that he looked forward to reading the article, and called Lance Howard to escort me out. Howard recognized me immediately and exploded. He told Cruikshank that he'd seen Roger and me together at the bookstore and a coffee shop when he was looking for an opportunity to grab him, and that I'd come to the hospital to get the goods on them. He coldcocked me, and when I woke up, I was in the cell on the third floor."

Leo looked a little wobbly, so his mom patted his hand and said, "Anytime you want to stop is fine."

"I should've tried harder to get through to the Osgoods. If I had, he might still be alive," he said, because Roger's body was one of the ones that'd been dug up in the woods by the FBI.

"You can't keep blaming yourself. You did your best," his mother said and looked over at her other son. "You better take it from here."

Harry placed his hand on Leo's shoulder and said, "I hate to think what would have happened if he hadn't told me what he'd learned from the Osgoods, and what he intended to do about it, on our drive to the train station the next morning. I tried to talk him out of it, pointed out that he was dealing with a man who'd participated in a kidnapping and done God only knows what else. He called me a worrywart, reminded me what a seasoned reporter he was, and told me that he and Roger would meet me later for dinner. I was on pins and needles all day, and when I didn't hear from him by six, I was sure that Cruikshank had seen through his cover story, panicked, and done something to silence him. I called the hospital and asked to speak to the doctor, told him I was with the *Trib* as well, and asked if he'd had an appointment with a reporter by the name of Leo Cavanaugh earlier that day. He told me he had, but that the reporter never showed up, and he hadn't heard from him. He suggested that Leo might've had some car trouble on his way up, but, of course, I knew he hadn't.

"I called the police and told them that my brother was missing, that he hadn't returned from a trip to Wisconsin," Harry said. "They told me to contact the authorities up here. I spoke to one of the deputies at the Summit Police Station, but he stopped me mid-explanation and told me to get in touch with the Chicago police."

"We were getting the runaround," Audrey Cavanaugh said, "so I called Leo's editor at the paper, Sam Eubanks. After I explained what'd happened and how worried Harry and I were, he told me he'd do some digging and get back to me. When he did, he told me that Doctor Cruikshank had a sterling reputation and was highly respected in the medical community. Then he reminded me that Leo was on a two-week vacation and must be painting the town red, and reassured me that as soon as he sobered up, we'd hear from him."

When Mrs. Cavanaugh cupped her hands over her eyes, I thought remembering the fear and frustration she'd felt when she'd reached that dead end had brought some tears. Aunt Jane May must've thought so, too, because she handed her a big white lace hankies out of her red clutch purse.

After Harry checked to see if his mom was okay, he told us, "I had no idea what to do at that point, so I decided to follow

Leo's lead. I knew I needed to get into the hospital to look for him, the same way he had Roger, but I'm not a reporter, I'm an actor. So I decided to feign mental illness to see if I could get admitted to Broadhurst as a patient. I'd played a mentally ill character in a play a few months earlier, so I drove up here that night and recreated that role. I made a hat out of aluminum foil and began shouting about brain-sucking aliens in that bar on Main Street, and someone called the sheriff. He thought I'd escaped from the hospital, so he threw me in the back of his car and drove me out there. Cruikshank tried to explain that I wasn't one of his patients and that he'd never seen me before, but the sheriff was furious, called him a liar, threatened that he'd be back to make sure that I was being watched more closely, and drove off.

"Cruikshank told Holloway to put me in a room on the second floor until he could examine me. A few days later, he deemed me harmless enough to move me down to the first floor, and I was allowed to spend time in the recreation yard. Leo wasn't out there, of course, but Roger was. I don't think he'd had the surgery yet, but he was so heavily medicated that he didn't even recognize me."

Audrey Cavanaugh set Aunt Jane May's hankie down and took back over. "Harry and I should've done more research before he decided to get himself committed. We assumed that the hospital was a minimal security facility. Much like Leo had when he came up here to save Roger, we hoped that Harry would find Leo and waltz out with him. Of course, that wasn't the case, and as soon as I found out I wouldn't be able to speak to or visit with him because contact with the outside world was forbidden, I closed up my house and bought the Jenkins' place. I wasn't sure how I could save my boys because confronting

Cruikshank would be pointless at best, and at worst, I could be locked up, too. It wasn't until I learned that some of the patients were allowed time in a recreation area that I began to think there might be another way to free Harry and Leo. I bought a map and explored Founder's Woods, and much like you girls did, I found a way through the pine trees to the fence. I was thrilled to see Harry in the yard, but I couldn't get his attention, and when there was a cold snap a few days later, the yard was closed for the winter."

How awful that must've been for her and how she must've yearned for the spring, the whole time not knowing if and when she'd be reunited with her boys. "Why didn't you go to my father or the sheriff and tell them your story?" I asked her. "They would've helped you."

"I almost did," she said, "but I was afraid they might think I'd lost mind when I told them that a world-renowned psychiatrist and pillar of the community was kidnapping men to perform brain surgeries on them against their will, and had imprisoned both of my sons as well."

She had a point.

"When I was allowed out in the yard again in March and noticed Mom hiding in the bushes outside the fence, I told her that she'd done the right thing," Harry added. "Doc treated the wounds of some of the patients who'd had the surgeries, and he'd never sounded the alarm. And when she told me the sheriff was his brother, I didn't think either one of them could be trusted. It wasn't until everything came out that we learned that your father had known about the trepanations, but not that they were being performed against patients' will, and the sheriff had no idea what'd been going on."

So maybe the article Mr. Wilkes had written in the *Summit Courier* hadn't been wrong.

It was still hard very hard for me to believe that Doc knew what Cruikshank was doing to the patients, but he must've had a really good reason for not stopping him, and as soon as I could, I'd ask him what it was.

Frankie asked Leo, rather indelicately, I thought, "How come Cruikshank didn't just kill you instead of keepin' you locked up all those months?"

"Because the doctor sees himself as a savior, not a murderer," he replied. "He visited me many times to discuss what he calls his contribution to society. He believes that homosexuality isn't just illegal, but that it goes against the laws of God and nature, and that it's his moral responsibility to convert homosexuals into normal men with his treatments. He thought the public wouldn't understand that, as with all medical breakthroughs, there were bound to be complications and loss of life. He wanted to wait until he'd perfected his technique before he shared his story with the world, and he promised me first crack at it. I told him time after time that I understood and admired his work, and if he'd release me, I wouldn't write the story until he gave me permission to, but he's a brilliant man and a highly trained psychiatrist. He knew I was lying. He also had to be aware that instructing Lance Howard to kidnap Roger and transport him across the state line to perform a trepanation, even in the name of science and God, was illegal. As was secretly burying patients who'd died as a result of the surgeries. Desperate people do desperate things, but I never thought Doctor Cruikshank would kill me to protect his secrets. But after he fled, I'm certain that I was a loose end that Lance Howard intended to dispose of on the night of the Fourth." Leo removed his tortoise-shell glasses and massaged the bridge of his nose. "There are still many questions that I need answers to, and I've asked to interview Doctor Cruikshank in the Cook County Jail, but he refuses to speak to me."

He was looking a little peaked, and when he excused himself to use the bathroom, I asked Harry, "After you got committed, when did you find out that he was okay and locked up on the third floor?"

"When I heard Albie laughing about the patient up there who thought he was a reporter like Clark Kent, I knew Leo was still alive. But after I heard the stories about patients that'd mysteriously disappeared, I began to wonder for how long," Harry said. "Holloway told the staff the missing patients had been transferred in the middle of the night and would shut them down if they asked questions. I didn't know then that was a sick joke. That Holloway meant the bodies of patients who'd died during trepanations had been transferred from the room in the basement to graves in the woods. I just knew that I better get Leo out of there before he was transferred, too."

"Do you think any of the nurses or orderlies knew what was going on?" Aunt Jane May asked Harry.

"I think a few of them suspected, but who would they tell, and who'd believe them?" he said.

What Harry was leaving out, I thought, was the education level and the skin color of almost all the nurses and orderlies who worked at Broadhurst and the color of renowned, Harvard-educated Dr. Cruikshank's skin. Like Jimbo had told me when I asked him why nobody from Mud Town would go to town meetings, "Us givin' our opinions to those in charge is 'bout as useful as throwin' a T-bone to a toothless dog."

Harry shook his head. "Honestly, I can't blame the hospital staff. It's still hard for me to believe that Cruikshank was doing what he was." He took a quick swallow of the lemonade Aunt Jane May had brought him and a nibble of one the shortcakes. "All I knew for sure at that point was that patients were mysteriously disappearing in the middle of the night, and I spent most of my time sneaking around the hospital, trying to figure out a way to the third floor to free Leo. After I discovered the back staircase off the kitchen led up there, I crept up it a couple of times when Dolores wasn't around, but I couldn't open the door to the locked ward."

When Bigger told us that Harry had been "skulkin' 'round my kitchen," we all thought he was trying to steal aluminum foil, but he'd been looking for a way to break into the door on the third floor and rescue his brother.

Harry said, "So when I heard Albie complaining to Jimbo in the yard that they'd have to watch the Fourth of July fireworks from the third floor because Clark Kent was getting transferred that night—"

"That was on the day Albie thought you were escaping, right? The day you gave me the note," I said.

After Harry nodded, Frankie stuck her into Viv's shorts' pocket pulled out the piece of paper he'd pressed into my hand, and set it down on the table in front of him. "But if you just found out that afternoon that Leo was gonna get transferred, and you thought that meant his life was in danger, how come you had this note all printed up and ready to give to Biz?"

Harry smiled and ripped a piece of paper off the pad his journalist brother had in front of him and wrote: *Tell Audrey Cavanaugh they're going to kill Leo.*

I wasn't a handwriting expert, but any fool could see that his scrawl didn't bear any resemblance to the beautifully written note he'd passed me through the wrought-iron fence that afternoon. If I'd given me the one he'd just written, I would've thought he was referring to the Mondurians and had gone off the deep end.

"So, if you didn't write the note you gave me, who did?" I asked him.

"Florence."

Well, I didn't see that coming, and neither did Frankie and Viv.

"She came into my room the night before," Harry said, "handed me the note, told me to put it in my pants' pocket, and made me swear on my mother's life that I would. After I read it, I tried to get her to explain, but all she'd say was, "You'll need to give it to little Elizabeth tomorrow." I didn't believe her, of course, but I wasn't taking any chances."

The last time I'd seen my favorite patient was the afternoon Albie had pulled the point-of-no-return siren and all hell broke loose. Florence was standing in the middle of the yard and trying to tell me something. When I read her lips, I thought she'd been saying *Help . . . hurry*, like she wanted me to quick do something to save her from the chaos. But what she must've been mouthing was *Help . . . Harry*.

"Who's Florence?" Aunt Jane May asked.

"She's a patient who's gifted like you," I explained, and—" I almost added "and me," because I was certain by then that I *had* inherited the "little voice" from her. But I didn't feel right bringing it up just then. That seemed like something I needed to talk to her about when we were alone. "But instead of plucking things out of thin air like you do, Florence can predict the future."

In an attempt to discard the mantel of guilt she'd been wearing, Viv asked Harry, "So *were* you tryin' to escape that day? Is it my fault that Albie give you that shot?"

"No, I was unnerved by Florence's note, and when I heard Albie tell Jimbo that Leo was going to be transferred the night of the Fourth on my way to look for the Mondurian you told me was hiding behind the hospital—"

"I'm sorry," Viv said. "I shouldn't have said that."

"No need to apologize. It wasn't your fault that I panicked, and Albie thought I was trying to escape when I ran to tell my mother that Leo's life was in danger," Harry reassured her.

Audrey Cavanaugh said, "I saw the terror in Harry's face when he came racing toward the fence that day. He's always been cool under fire, and I knew he wouldn't have reacted that way unless the situation was dire. But the orderly was practically on top of him by then, and I couldn't afford to be seen and questioned, perhaps even charged with trespassing, so I stepped back into the bushes. That's when he came running to you girls."

Harry turned to me. "I should've trusted Florence and given you the note as soon as you showed up for your visit that day. I'm sorry for hurting you, Biz."

"It's all right, Harry." I showed him my wrist. "See? Good as new."

Audrey Cavanaugh, who looked enormously relieved to have gotten through the reliving of that ordeal, leaned back in her chair and said, "You know what happened next."

Not only did we, but the whole country knew.

During their visits together, Harry had shared the layout of the hospital with his mom, so she knew where she was going the night of the Fourth. After she removed a fuse from the box in the basement, she snuck up on the new nurse, took her keys, and shoved her into the supply closet. She let Harry out of his room first. He insisted that she free Ernie Fontaine as well before he ran up to the third floor. Harry was the one, not his mom, who gave Jimbo a love tap on the head with a fire extinguisher. After he used the new nurse's keys to free Leo from his cell, they must've fallen out of Harry's pocket when he and Leo ran down the hall. Or maybe Eddie King dropped his keys when he went up to the third floor to watch the fireworks. We'd never know for sure how the mayor got a hold of the keys that he used to free Hopper, but only the girls and I knew that he had, and our lips were sealed. After Mrs. Cavanaugh, Harry, Leo, and Ernie ran out of the hospital, they cut through the Withers' to the back road where Mrs. Cavanaugh had left her car. By the time the sheriff and his deputies got to the farm, they were already speeding back to Chicago via I-94.

Ernie Fontaine, who had been listening so quietly during the visit that I almost forgot he was there, laid his stuffed bunny down on the pine table and said, "You were so brave, Mom."

Viv jumped up and said, "He's your boy, too? For criss—" Her eyes darted toward Aunt Jane May and then came back to Audrey Cavanaugh. "For Christopher Columbus's sake, how many boys do you have that ended up in a mental institution?"

Audrey Cavanaugh smiled at Leo and Harry and said, "As of now, just these two lugs, but I'm in the process of adopting Ernie. When it's final, we'll be moving back to Summit. I grew up in a town very much like this one, and I'd like to raise him here."

"And I'm gettin' a puppy!" Ernie turned to Viv and winked—just once. "So maybe you can come to my house and pet it, or we could go to the movies or dancing sometime."

"Or knit," Frankie said under her breath.

Viv batted her eyelashes at soon-to-be Ernie Cavanaugh, who seemed to like the opposite sex after all, and said, "Count on it, buster."

Rehashing the story that'd changed all our lives had been cathartic, and after we spent some time talking about things of a more pleasant nature, Harry asked the girls and me to meet him on the front porch of the house.

"Thank you," he told us when we got out there.

"For what? We didn't do anything," I said. "We never even gave your mom the note."

"If it weren't for your shining faces and those shortbread cookies to look forward to, I'm not sure I would've made it all those months in Broadhurst, Biz, and I wanted to repay your kindness," Harry said. "Your aunt told us that you've been very worried about Florence, so Leo did some digging, and you'll be happy to know that he tracked her down to a wonderful hospital in Lake Geneva. Before her family committed her, Florence was a schoolteacher, like my mom, so she suggested that Leo arrange for us to pay her a visit on our way up here today." He smiled and how good it was to see him do that. "Florence told us she knew we were coming and asked me to pass on some messages to the three of you." He looked directly into Viv's green eyes that were so close in color to his own. "You're on your way to becoming a famous actress," he said, then turned to Frankie. "Your smarts and willingness to do battle are going to pay off in a courtroom," Lastly, he came to me. "Florence said that you need to keep writing stories because someday your books will touch peoples' lives."

Not sure if Frankie and Viv believed those predictions, but they grinned and I did, too, because who doesn't like to hear that their dreams might come true?

I would've liked to spend more time visiting with Harry, and I wanted to ask Leo how he made his writing feel so real, and Viv could've spent all day mooning over Ernie, but Audrey Cavanaugh stuck her head out the front door and reminded Harry that they needed to get back to Chicago, and they left soon after.

As their car pulled out of the cobblestone driveway, Ernie was waving his fool head off at Viv, who waved back and said, "Yum-yum." When I groaned, she called me a dumb chump, and then Frankie called her boy crazy, and they got into one of their tiffs that didn't stop until Aunt Jane May came out onto the front porch.

She was wearing cherry-red lipstick and a peach shirtwaist dress, white kitten pumps, and her hair was down in loose waves. If I didn't know that she was headed to the 4-H building at the fairgrounds, as impossible as it seemed, I would've thought she was going out on a date.

"See ya up there. Wish me luck," she said.

As the girls and I watched her walking down Honeywell Street, there was more sway in her hips than I'd ever seen, and when Viv said, *"Oo là là,"* I couldn't disagree with her.

Chapter
Twenty-Six

The girls and I played a mostly peaceful game of jacks on the front porch until Bigger showed up and called to us from the sidewalk, "C'mon, now. We got a lot to see and do today."

She and Jimbo had been tied at the hip, but he wasn't with her that afternoon. After Broadhurst closed down, Jimbo was given Lance Howard's town maintenance job at the insistence of the Buchanan family, and we passed him fiddling with the mower on the town hall's lawn on our way to the fairgrounds.

When Bigger leaned over and kissed him, Viv began to sing, "Love and marriage, love and marriage . . ." until Frankie told her to shut up.

First thing we did after we passed through the fairground gates was hurry, as fast as the heat would allow, to the building where the yearly Bake-Off was held. We held our breaths when the judges did the pinning, but every single one of Aunt Jane May's pies and her shortbread were given a blue ribbon, and every single one of Evelyn Mulrooney's entries got a second place. Viv cheered and hooted louder than anyone in the crowd when she saw the look on that so-and-so's face.

After that, the girls and I stood in lines for rides that wouldn't hurt Frankie's leg. Viv tortured us until we agreed to check out the Tunnel of Love, because we'd not been to Whitcomb's in a while and she was dying to know who was making out with whom. It was dark inside the tunnel, so Aunt Jane May and Uncle Walt didn't know we were in the swan behind them, but when they passed under the emergency exit sign, we saw them kissing. I had to slap my hand over Viv's mouth so they wouldn't hear her yell, "Hot damn! Told you so!"

Of course, we skipped the Camelot Ferris wheel that "Sir Lancelot" had once buckled us into, but we did negotiate the House of Mirrors, and let the toothless carnies coax us into playing a couple of games. Frankie won a teddy bear for landing rings on Coke bottles and she gave it to Viv. We ate like hogs, too.

We had front row seats to the Magic and Mystery Show, and boy, that was something. Bigger enjoyed it, too, but when we exited the tent, she gave us more of the worldly, womanly advice she'd been giving us that wasn't anything like Aunt Jane May's "mark my words" warnings.

"I enjoyed the fire-eater and that cow with two heads," Bigger told us as we strolled down the midway, "but a word to the wise, girls: you can't trust a magician named Randy who pulls somethin' outta his pants. And when you're up here the next few days without me, I want you to avoid Giggles the Clown, too. No man in his right mind would enjoy making balloon animals that much."

We caught another glimpse of Uncle Walt and Aunt Jane May as we were preparing to call it a night, but this time they were standing in front of the cotton candy booth and acting like they barely knew each other.

When Viv sighed and repeated something she must've read in one of the ladies' magazines, "Secret love is so romantic," Frankie, who I thought knew more about that kind of love than Viv might ever realize, threw up the two corn dogs she'd eaten earlier.

My father was sitting on the front porch swing when we got home, and after the girls and I thanked Bigger for taking us to the fair, he took his watch out of his pocket, thumbed it open, and said, "Gettin' late, Dolores. May I give you a ride home?"

"No, thank you, Doc. I need to walk off some of what I ate tonight if I'm gonna fit into the dress I bought for the wedding. See y'all tomorrow, with bells on."

I told the girls that I needed to talk to my father and to go out to the hideout without me. When I sat down beside him, I could smell his Old Spice aftershave, and he looked dapper in a white shirt and vest, because no matter how hot it got, he felt it was important for a doctor to project an air of professionalism. His pocket watch was still open and I caught a glimpse of my mother before he snapped it shut.

"Did you and your friends enjoy yourselves this evening?" he asked me.

"Yes, sir. Aunt Jane May did, too. She won four blue ribbons for her pies and cookies."

"You don't say."

I sat there with the man of so few words for a while longer listening to the night sounds before I got up enough nerve to ask him what had been on my mind. "Mister Wilkes wrote in the newspaper that you knew what Doctor Cruikshank was doing at the hospital. Is that true?"

I'd taken him by surprise, and it took a bit before he said, "I felt the procedures were arcane, and I didn't consider what he was trying to cure to be an illness, but I'm just a small-town doctor." The permanent furrow in his forehead deepened. "I was impressed by Doctor Cruikshank's explanations and bowed to his greater knowledge, but I should have fought harder for my patients. Let my mistake be a lesson to you, Elizabeth. *'To thine own self be true.'*"

I could see how much it pained him to tell me that and I wanted to tell him that nothing he could do would make me love him any less, but I'd had so little practice talking to him that I didn't know how to get what was in my heart into words. All I could do was put my head down in his lap and let him rock us on that swing and hope that he knew.

Chapter
Twenty-Seven

⁓

Dell's and Sally's backyard second wedding ceremony the following afternoon was just close friends and family. After Reverend Archie prompted them to say their "I do's" beneath the boughs of the hideout tree, we cried and dug into the sumptuous supper Sophia Maniachi provided. Afterward we danced into the night to Sinatra songs—turned out that Frankie had been named after him because he was Sally's favorite singer— and the rhythm and blues records playing on the hi-fi that Doc had moved to the back porch.

Dell was radiant in a pink dress trimmed with lace, and Uncle Sally—he told us that it was just fine if we kept calling him that—looked like he'd stepped out of the pages of *Gentleman's Quarterly*—or a gangster movie—in a pin-striped gray suit when he spun his bride around on the grass. Aunt Jane May and Uncle Walt tripped the light fantastic barefoot, too, alongside Jimbo and Bigger, who were doing a more interesting dance called "The Jack." So Doc didn't feel left out, I asked him to waltz with me and was surprised by what a fine dancer he was.

When the festivities began to wind down and the fireflies showed up, the girls and I wished everyone a good night and climbed the steps up to the hideout. School would start the following morning, so we would sleep together for the last time that night in our summer home away from home, our inner sanctum, and our repository of secrets of all kinds.

After we shucked off our party dresses and got down to our underwear, Viv summed up how all three of us were feeling when she said, "We're gonna remember this summer for as long as we live."

And we have.

We'd been exposed to unspeakable evil and it had taken something from us that we'd never get back. Frankie limps when it rains, Viv has nightmares, I cannot wear anything around my neck, and our memories of that long ago summer haunt us. For time does not heal all wounds and you cannot always let bygones be bygones, and maybe that's all right. Could be that all any of us can hope for is that when we look back on our lives, we'll find the good outshone the bad, and we had the strength we needed to endure the unendurable. And I like to think that has held true over the years for the girls and me.

The once-bulls-eye-red hideout has faded to a baby-blanket pink, and the ancient oak that cradles it has lost some of its bulk, but here I am, almost sixty years after the summer that changed our lives forever, smelling the lingering scent of peonies, listening to the crickets call to one another as Grand Creek tumbles over the stepping stones, and wishing that my arthritic hips could get me out of this back porch glider and up those ten wooden steps. There's just about nothing I'd rather do more than go back into the house and wake up the girls so we could light the train lantern, lie on our feathered cotton mats, and tell tales of how it used to be and in many ways still is.

Of course, at some point Viv would suggest we grab the rolls of Charmin we keep stocked on a shelf in the garage, toss them into the back of our yellow pickup truck, and drive over to the toothachingly adorable gingerbread house owned by Mayor Brenda Mulrooney—or, as Viv likes to call her, "BM." We've had a lot of practice toilet-papering her place over the years, so we'd be long gone by the time Brenda woke up to a yard that looked less like it belonged in Victorian England and more like something from ancient Egypt. (Mummification is a lost art.)

After we returned to the hideout, shiny with victory, Frankie would goad Viv into arm wrestling, just so she could hold her hand. To outsiders, Viv's and her relationship has always appeared to be built on a shared enjoyment of torturing one another, but I've witnessed the yearning in Frankie's eyes for many years. And how tenderly she still looks at Viv when she's sleeping and how gently she presses her cheek against hers to inhale her exhales, and how happy she is when the two of them go at each other and I make them hug it out. Frankie and I have not once had a conversation about her feelings because there's no need to. She knows that I know and that her secret is safe with me. What she doesn't know is that Viv came to me many years ago and confessed with more than a few tears that she knew "Frankenstein" was in love with her and she loved her, too, just "not that way."

And after our wrinkled lids grew heavy, the girls would set their gnarled hands atop mine and we'd no longer feel our parchment skin or the crooked bends to our fingers. When we whispered to one another, "All for one and one for all," the border between now and then would crumble, and for that sweet moment in time, it would be as it always had been, and always will be, for love knows no bounds.

Epilogue

⁓

I've visited hundreds of book clubs and attended events at bookstores countless times over the years and, according to Frankie, who keeps track of these sorts of things, the most often asked question is, "What happened to the characters after the story ended?"

As previously mentioned, thanks to Wally Hopper, my voice can give out if I talk too long, so Viv, who has experience in this area, suggested that I share in these pages some of what the girls and I got ourselves into after the summer of '60 in case you invite me to one of your gatherings to speak and I run out of steam.

Eight years to the day after the emergency meeting to discuss Wally Hopper's transfer to Broadhurst, Frankie delivered her valedictorian speech on the town hall stage and surprised no one when she was voted Most Likely to Succeed; Viv claimed the Best Smile and Most Talented accolades; and under my picture in the 1967 Summit High yearbook it said: "Winner of the Willa Cather Award for Excellence in Writing and President of Key Club."

Frankie departed for Yale to study law on a full scholarship and Viv took off to New York City to fulfill her acting dreams. Not nearly as adventurous or as certain what fate had in store for me as the girls were, I applied to the school where my father met my mother—the University of Chicago.

I was still passionate about getting my stories down on paper, but my experiences at Broadhurst had stoked my already profound interest in the workings of the human mind, so when I was instructed to choose one or the other in my junior year of college it felt like I was being asked to pick who I loved the most—Viv or Frankie, Doc or Aunt Jane May. But thanks to the good Lord, my "little voice," and my father's reminder—"To thine own self be true"—I managed to double-major in both English *and* psychology, went on to achieve graduate degrees in both, and ended up writing books that I've been told touch peoples' lives, just the way Florence had predicted.

> *"Another remarkably insightful coming-of-age story by Elizabeth Buchanan."*
> —*New York Times Book Review*

> *"An outstanding character-driven blend of historical fiction, mystery, and commentary of the times. Ms. Buchanan is a wonderful storyteller. Perfect for book clubs!"*
> —*Jill Miner, Saturn Booksellers*

> *"Nostalgic and poignant with the author's trademark humor and astute observations sprinkled throughout, Elizabeth Buchanan's newest novel might be her best."*
> —*American Booksellers Association*

Thanks to dedicated booksellers, librarians, and faithful readers, most of my novels have garnered good reviews and sold surprisingly well over the years. As a result of the royalties I receive and the hefty inheritance left to me by my father and uncle; Viv's success as an actress—her heyday has long past, but our four-time Emmy winner and Academy Award nominee still flies to New York and Los Angeles to guest star in a TV show or movie as a feisty, foul-mouthed granny; and Frankie's outstanding legal career—no longer one of the busiest civil rights litigators in the country, she now does outstanding work with *The Innocence Project*—the Tree Musketeers are sitting on, forgive the pun, quite the nest egg.

Our beloved Aunt Jane May remained full of piss and vinegar into her eighties. She and Uncle Walt did eventually tie the knot and move into his bungalow, but after he died from a heart attack, she moved back in with us. When she failed to come barging out of her bedroom one morning to holler, "Up and at 'em, girls. *Tempus fugit,*" we buried her a few days later next to her sister and her husband. Still, to this day, her presence remains a guiding light. No exaggeration, we could almost see her giving us the thumbs-up when we'd do something that we knew she'd be proud of. And Viv swears that she heard Aunt Jane May say, "What took you so long?" the night we had a powwow and voted unanimously to share some of our enormous wealth.

We got the ball rolling by contributing to architectural restorations and other worthy causes throughout town. When the volunteer fire department needed a new engine we rose to the occasion. We funded an addition to the library that we named the *Edith Dirk's Children's Museum* and filled it with those touchy, feely activities. But our most important contribution has been our purchase of Broadhurst. It was left abandoned after the summer of '60 and the girls and I are working diligently to restore its crumbling structure so that someday it might provide hope and help to those among us who are battling with inner demons.

But as rewarding as all that was, and remains so, Frankie, Viv, and I found ourselves growing tired of the accolades and attending tribute dinners. What we really wanted to do was to lighten the load of the good people of our town who worked their tail feathers off from dawn to dusk and still came up short every month—without all the attendant hoopla.

Of course, it was Viv's idea to don dark clothing and sneak around town after the sidewalks had been rolled up to slip a cashier's check with a lot of zeros in the mailbox of Bill Ellis, who'd lost his job at Camp's Dairy because of cutbacks. The following night, we stuck an envelope bulging with bills under the flower pot on Meghan Harris's front porch so she could replace that beater car she drives with a new Subaru. If heavy lifting was called for, say, if boxes of state of the art lap top computers needed to be delivered to the entrances of Mud Town Elementary and St. Thomas Aquinas School in the middle of the night, the girls and I relied on our *aide-de-camp* Ray-Ray Martin—Jimbo and Bigger's gigantic fifteen-year-old grandson—to lend a helping hand.

I cannot tell you what a charge we got out of secretly throwing our money around and watching folks spend it, and we hated to think that it'd come to an end. But other than occasionally finding a book in the refrigerator, or forgetting which letter of the alphabet we parked under at the new shopping mall on Route 4, the girls and I have managed to retain most of our wits. We knew in a town the size of ours that it'd be hard to keep what we were doing under wraps for long. Especially after *Summit Courier* editor-in-chief and great admirer of Woodward and Bernstein, Norman "Norma" Wilkes offered a substantial reward for any information about the "Summit Santa Clause" in a series of articles he'd entitled—"Giftgate."

Sure enough, our fun came crashing to an end the night we tried to covertly thank our longtime gardener and maintenance man, Scotty Jorgenson. He'd always tell us, "Just doin' my job," and refuse bonuses for the outstanding work he's put into the grounds and our home, so we went behind his back. We crept into his yard and pinned a hefty gift certificate to Hanson's Hardware on the door of his tool shed, which went smoothly enough, but our getaway was straight out of a Three Stooges movie.

Viv, who was breaking in a new pair of high top sneakers at the time, took a bad step and landed on her derrière in Scotty's fish pond, which was, unfortunately, situated within hearing distance of his next door neighbor's open window. I hoped the obscenities she yelled would get lost in the sound of machine gun fire in the old war movie Norman "Norma" Wilkes was watching on the TV in his den, but Viv used her booming theatrical voice when she screamed, "Fuck . . . fuck . . . fuck!"

Seconds later, Norman popped up from his recliner, switched the flood lights on in his yard, stuck his head out his back door, and called out, "Halt or I'll shoot!"

We were pretty sure he meant a picture, but he did have that deer head hanging over his fireplace. And Frankie had saddled him with that nickname after she threatened to punch him in the throat if he told anyone that Viv kissed him during *The Incredible Shrinking Man,* so he'd been nursing a grudge against us for many years.

After Norman came hobbling out of his house, he quickly put two and two together and told us, "Well, if it isn't the Summit Santa and a couple of her elves."

"And if it isn't *Tiny Tim,*" Viv muttered because he'd been in such a hurry to catch us that he hadn't slipped on his special shoe that corrected his shorter by two inches leg.

"Knew it was you three!" Norman gloated.

He had not been an attractive child and things hadn't improved as he aged, but Viv sighed and gamely muttered, "The show must go on." If he'd forget he'd seen us at Scotty's place, she told him she'd go on a date with him.

Frankie went legal beagle and mentioned filing an injunction.

My attempt to buy Norman's silence came in the form of an introduction to my literary agent. I knew that publishing a book about what'd transpired in Summit during the summer of '60 was something he'd always aspired to, and he couldn't agree fast enough.

I'm not a monster so, of course, I felt bad about making him that offer when I knew darn well that the book you're holding in your hands would be released before he even came close to finishing his. But, you know, I just couldn't bear him ruining our fun and listening to some vengeance plan Viv would come up with on the walk home that might include a meeting of Norman's normal-sized leg and the chainsaw she bought last week at Hanson's Hardware.

And then she and Frankie would start bickering and I'd end up spending the rest of the night referring an arm-wrestling contest at the pine table in the kitchen instead of quietly sitting on the back porch of the house reading and putting a dent in a bottle of wine, and after all . . . it wasn't his story to tell, was it.

Acknowledgments

Massive thanks to my editor, Chelsey Emmelhainz. Her guidance helped me to see the story in a different light, and I'm so very grateful. My hat goes off to the rest of the talented team at Crooked Lane as well, especially publisher, Matt Martz and Melissa Rechter and Madeline Rathle.

When I submitted the manuscript to my agent, Mark Gottlieb, he got back to me in record time to tell me that he loved it and was sure he could find a good home for it. He has proven to be a man of his word and I'm very grateful for his belief in me. Many thanks as well to the rest of the stellar team at Trident Media Group, especially Nicole Robson.

To my friends who bit the bullet and read early drafts of the story—Megan, Fran, Susie, Nancy, and a legion of others who took time out of their busy lives to give me feedback—thank you. And to the authors who offered such kind words about the story—hugs and a million thanks.

You'd think writing a novel would get easier over time, but during the three years it took me to get the story down, I wanted to throw in the towel many times, and if my dear friend and writer extraordinaire—Beth Hoffman—didn't call me the most hilarious names and encourage me to stick to it, I suspect I would have. I deeply value her wisdom, grace, and patience. (Thank you, my little lilac bud.)

Acknowledgments

I'd also like to give a shout-out to my small Wisconsin town that bears an uncanny resemblance to Summit. We have an old-fashioned theater that has been known to show movies to kids for free and shop owners set out bowls of water for dogs on strolls. The creek that runs through town gives us a place to think and fish, and you will almost always find an artist painting a watercolor on its banks. Great food, too!

The first graders at Thorson Elementary School make me feel like I'm the best thing next to sliced bread, and our newly formed Comedy Club comprised of fourth graders makes me laugh my head off. They give me hope for the future.

I will remain forever grateful to the indie booksellers who gave me my first break. A special tip of my hat to the wonderful Jill Miner from Saturn Booksellers, and Daniel Goldin from Boswell Books.

My daughter, Casey, is my inspiration, best friend, first reader, and I can always count on her to give it to me straight. My boy, Riley, who I miss and love with my every breath still makes us laugh and always will. And my g-babies, Charlie and Hadley, who are so full of love and kindness and empathy that I reckon they were sent to us from the stars.

And lastly, thank you, dear reader. Without your support throughout the years, I wouldn't be sitting here this morning as the sun comes up over the barn, drinking tea in my pajamas with my little dog, Gracie, trying to come up with words that won't begin to express my appreciation. Your kind emails and posts on social media, showing up to listen to me rattle on at bookstore and library events, and always giving me the fancy chair at your book club meetings has led me to believe that at least a couple of you like my stories, and I'd be grateful as hell if you'd continue to do so.